Evolution

Jim Reilly

Sayville Books
www.sayvillebooks.com

EVOLUTION

by Jim Reilly

Sayville Books
www.sayvillebooks.com

This work is dedicated to my loving family.

Prologue

"Welcome back from the break, viewers," the moderator said. "So we are going to continue our conversation here on CNN about religion and science with our guests Reverend Harry Goodwin, author of *History Starts with Eden*, and Dr. Simon Jorgenson, president of the True History League. Goodwin is an evangelical Christian with strong beliefs that the Bible is a word-for-word written history of the world. Jorgenson does not believe that there is a god or deity that created all things and only believes in scientific fact."

The two men were polar opposites in appearance as well as beliefs. Jorgenson, in disheveled clothes and uncombed, longish mane, created a sloppy contrast to Goodwin, who had donned a well-kept suit and sported a neatly trimmed haircut. Both glared at each other, ready for battle.

"We will start with you, Dr. Jorgenson. So what is the danger if some of our leaders believe in a higher power? Does this help or hurt them as leaders?"

Jorgenson, a PhD in anthropology, was a steadfast skeptic on the topic of supernatural claims by religion. He said, "Bill, there are examples throughout history where religion has impeded scientific learning and human advancement because its view is stymied by misguided dogma and superstition. Leaders in the past and even today have used it as justification for conflict, terror, and control. The Crusades, the Inquisition, witch burning, the Holocaust, and the conflict in Northern Ireland come to mind. The Religious Right believe that they have cornered morality, but the fact is that many of the most heinous crimes ever committed have been approved and encouraged by leaders who were influenced by crazy religious beliefs. If our leaders were free from religious dogma and governed using reason and critical thinking, then we could see the human race evolve to unlimited heights. Throughout history, religion has impeded human development with a narrow view of how things work in the world."

The moderator interrupted, "Reverend Goodwin, can you please respond?"

The reverend was a horse chomping at the bit during Dr. Jorgenson's remarks and appeared relieved to finally have an opportunity to answer. "Of course, Bill. So, Dr. Jorgenson, do you expect the viewers here today to believe that science is the place from which we get our morality? Scientists have given us the atom bomb, germ warfare, and mustard gas, to name a few. It is our belief that leaders with a good Christian base would lead as examples and fight the forces of evil. God has taught us from Adam and Eve to today that those who work as a force for good and follow His words will be led to paradise."

Jorgenson cut in, "Oh, please. Adam and Eve. It's a fairytale. Science has uncovered the truth of our origin. We have evolved as a species through natural selection."

Goodwin glared with derision. "Maybe you believe in evolution, which sounds to me like a fairytale, but the Bible is a historical fact written by the hand of God through our earliest ancestors. And it states that man was formed from the dust of the ground and had life breathed into him by God. Eve was formed from Adam's rib."

Jorgenson responded, "Reverend Goodwin, you think the Bible is historical fact? At most, the Bible goes back five thousand years, and our ancestors have been on this planet for millions of years. How on earth could the people of that time possibly know how creation came to be millions of years in the past? It is preposterous to think that an 'Adam and Eve,' created by a god, were the first people to walk on this planet. Personally, what scares me the most is how the Religious Right have combined all of Earth's history to the point that there are so-called museums showing the fictitious Adam and Eve walking the planet with dinosaurs and other prehistoric creatures long extinct before man ever walked the Earth. It's a complete distortion of history, and I, quite frankly, would be more inclined to believe that little green men from outer space are the reason we are here."

Goodwin said, "That is your point of view, Doctor, but if you had faith, then it would be clear to you that there is not just science in this universe, but also an existence of a higher spiritual level, and that level is where we need to aspire to evolve."

"Until you and the Religious Right, as well as all promoters of religious superstition, stop infecting the population with these lies, I see it as a barrier for our evolution to continue," said Jorgenson.

Goodwin countered, "That is your point of view. My faith helps me and all Christians grow as followers of the Lord."

Jorgenson said, "If by 'grow' you mean bring to a standstill."

"Science is not the only source of knowledge."

"It's more in line with truth and --"

"You haven't convinced me!" Goodwin shouted.

Jorgenson shouted, "You are too infected by your dogma!"

"You're too --" Goodwin began.

"Gentlemen," the moderator said, "I want to thank you for this spirited debate that I think will go on as long as we have polar opposite views of the science and religion communities. It would be nice someday if the two opposing communities could see eye-to-eye. I hope to have you both on the show sometime in the future to continue our conversation and look for that elusive middle ground."

The moderator turned to the camera and said, "Now, let's go to the streets of New York City to our reporter on the scene, Laura Morseman, who is asking New Yorkers whether they side with the scientific or religious version of creation. So, Laura, who do you have with you today?"

"The first person we have is Darlene, an administrative assistant working for a law office in midtown. I pose the question to you: Do you believe in Scripture's version of how we were created with the story about Adam and Eve, or do you believe that we are a product of evolution, like scientists believe?"

Darlene, a pretty, blond-haired woman, said, "I believe what I have been taught my whole life, that God created us, and we are His chosen people. If we follow what the Lord has taught us, we will be rewarded with eternal life."

"Thank you, Darlene," said the reporter. "And now we have Gordon, an investment banker working down on Wall Street. So, Gordon, what do you believe?"

Gordon, a finely dressed businessman, smiled into the camera and said, "I tend to lean toward evolution. There is too much evidence that our species came into existence through survival of the fittest."

"Thank you, Gordon," said the reporter, moving to her final person. "And now we are asking Gabriel, a tourist from out of town. So, Gabriel, what do you believe?"

The plainly dressed, nondescript man replied. "I believe that any and all is possible in this universe. It could be that science and religion both happen to be right."

The reporter said, "Thank you, Gabriel." She turned to the camera. "And there you have it from the people on the street. This is Laura Morseman, reporting."

"Thank you," said the moderator. "It looks like we have one vote for religion, one vote for science, and one tie. It looks like people are just as divided as our guest panel."

After a pause, he continued, "Now, to our next segment…"

Chapter 1

Looking down at his watch, he was disappointed that time had not been moving faster, but James Connor, an anthropology doctoral student at Stony Brook University, took solace that this long journey of flight connections, lengthy holdovers, and time-consuming bus rides to a remote location at the Kibish rock formations in southwest Ethiopia would be over in a few hours. As he looked out the dusty windows at the mostly barren landscape of the Ethiopian grasslands, he began to wonder how on earth his father could dig in these godforsaken places, spread out across the globe. He remembered him from his youth, going away for weeks or months, looking for bone and tool fragments of long-dead peoples. But there were the trips to France, to search for Neanderthal bones, on which his dad had brought James and his mother. These excursions gave the young James a taste of his dad's life, a taste that took a long time for him even to think was the least bit appetizing.

Though early on in his education he would rather have been a literature major, growing up in a house where artifacts and books on anthropology were in every corner, he developed, over time, a vast knowledge that helped him breeze through school and follow in his father's footsteps. His career goals were clearly not digging holes and searching for fossils, but rather a career in teaching where he could keep his hands clean and someday become a tenured academic.

James was an attractive man with boyish features and a good heart, which usually were drowned out by his craving for recognition and a lofty opinion of himself.

"Hey, I didn't see you get off the bus at the last stop," said David Cho, another anthropology doctoral student at Stony Brook who had volunteered to assist in this dig, a project sponsored by the university and the Museum of Natural History with the hope of finding artifacts the museum could add to its Early Man collection. He was of Asian and Caucasian descent; however, what was most noticeable about David was not his appearance but his well thought-out curiosity. "Didn't you want to eat the local cuisine?"

James looked at David, whose excitement reminded him of his father's enthusiasm for anthropology and anticipation of what could be discovered, and replied, "No, thank you. I don't want to set foot in this desolate place any more than I have to." James looked out the bus window in disgust. Then he confessed, "I can't believe I actually came here to sift through old dirty rocks all day long. Maybe I should have sifted through the rocks in my head first."

As he started to laugh, David asked, "Then what the hell are you doing out here? I can't believe a student with your perfect grades in the anthropology program would not be overjoyed at this chance to discover evidence of our ancestors buried for some 200,000 years."

The dig, led by esteemed Stony Brook University anthropologists Ronald Gibbs and Roberto Sanchez, was looking for bones and artifacts of the earliest Homo sapiens, or modern man. Famed fossil hunter Richard Leakey and his team of anthropologists discovered the earliest known specimen of modern man in 1967 at the Kibish Formation along the Omo River in Ethiopia, near the town of Kibish. They found part of the skull and a partial skeleton, which they named Omo I. He was believed to have lived about 195,000 years ago. Drs. Gibbs and Sanchez hoped to dig down another 25-50,000 years earlier in the rock formation, where they believed were even earlier samples of modern man.

"Studying anthropology in school was a piece of cake for me because of all the conversations that took place in my house as I grew up, being raised by educators. So the school work didn't seem so hard, and it helped me get on track for a career in academia," James said. "I am more comfortable experiencing it in books and in a nice clean lab where I don't need to spend all night washing all the dust and dirt from my body just to feel clean. If it were my choice, I would be fine just examining and researching the discoveries of others."

"I'm confused," said a puzzled David. "Aren't you the son of Patrick Connor? He is one of the most famous and respected anthropologists in the world. His work with the discovery and documentation of early man is remarkable. I have been to a couple of his presentations, and although you can tell he is uncomfortable speaking in public, he has the ability to describe the most mundane topic and make you feel you are on the adventure of a lifetime. His writings on early man are on every anthropologist's laptop without question, and every anthropology student has cited his thoughts at least once in almost every paper they've written. I can tell you that I learned more about the evolution of early man in one sitting of reading his work than all of --"

"Yeah, yeah," James said, seeming annoyed by David's insistence to speak about his father. "Please don't. I…I have to hear this from every student, professor, and museum curator that I happen to meet. His accomplishments are well documented, and let's leave it at that."

But David looked even more puzzled. "I thought that it would be an advantage for you to be his son, yet you seem angry about it. Why?"

James answered, "Let's just say it is a large shadow to get out from under. Is it an advantage? I don't know, maybe, maybe not. All right, maybe there are some positives. I have access to professors, museum personnel, and university events that many don't have. I am easily progressing through the doctorate program because of all the knowledge I accumulated from all the conversations I heard from my dad through the years whether I wanted to or not.

"But it is a large shadow he casts, and it consumes my identity. Case in point, when I was a high school junior I won the prestigious National Science Foundation Award of Excellence without too much effort. A chosen few students from around the country are nominated and to win it as a senior is an honor but as a junior, it is a tremendous honor. You would think that such an award would have set me apart from his legacy, but no. It was spoken about as 'Patrick Connor's son won an award,' not James Connor won it. Even at the awards banquet, most of the congratulations went to him from the scientists, students, and the newspaper reporters in the hall. Also, much of the conversations around my banquet table were not about my project that won the award, they were about his exploits and vast knowledge about early man. It was certainly deflating to my self-esteem. You probably think I'm angry with him. No, he has no desire for fame, or fortune, or to overshadow anyone, but people seem to gather around him because he is naturally a people magnet. On the other hand, I don't have that natural magnetism. I have to find ways to seize people's attention before I disappear under his shadow and I'm still waiting for my own time to shine.

"Let me tell you, though, it wasn't all roses having the great Patrick Connor as a dad. He was always traveling, going to digs or being in demand on the lecture circuit. As a kid, I never went to Disneyland. No, I was on a dig in Kenya or in Israel or in France as my dad looked for bone fragments. It was just my mom and I holed up in a dusty tent or rundown local hotel in the middle of nowhere. She was my anti-dad. You wouldn't believe it, but she is just as well respected as a professor of theology. She is also wanted on the lecture tour and has been published for her writings, but she just loves walking the halls of Saint John's University's Theology Department speaking to students and faculty alike about religious topics. She has a strong faith from a strict Roman Catholic upbringing and believes it is her purpose in life to help people strengthen their religious beliefs with knowledge."

James' mother was Ann Marie Connor, renowned for her insightful interpretations of the intent of the writers of biblical texts.

"Wow," David said. "You grew up in a household with a strong background in religion and science. It must have made for some lively discussions around the dinner table. Your dad believes in evolution, and your mom, I assume, believes God had a hand in human development. There must have been a lot of conflict between their beliefs."

As the bus driver let the passengers know that they would be in Kibish in about twenty minutes, James thought back, saying, "They did have some very vigorous discussions early in my childhood, where both passionately defended their sides to the point of walking out of the room as the talks became heated, and then became arguments. They even look like polar opposites. My dad always looks like he just crawled out of an archeological dig site, whereas my mom is always in her meticulous best. I think now there is a detente between the two, though, with each holding firm to their own beliefs and at least showing that they respect the other's position. I guess that mutual respect helps them stay totally devoted to each other, and they don't let their differences get between them."

"Then what about you?" David said. "What do you believe? Obviously, you're studying anthropology, but you must have heard both sides your whole life."

James took a few seconds, then responded, "David, when I am just with my dad, I lean towards evolution, and when I am with my mom, creation sounds like the right thing. I don't know. Maybe I still need to think about it some more to come to any solid conclusion."

A few moments later, the bus pulled up to the town of Kibish, where James saw through the dusty bus windshield fellow doctorate student Jennifer La Mont there to greet them. She was standing next to the Land Rovers that would take them to the rock formations and on to the campsite. "Besides, I have other things on my mind."

An alert David, seeing how James looked at Jennifer, said, "Don't tell me you came thousands of miles to a dig, which, to say the least, you are not enthusiastic about doing, to be at the side of another student you have feelings for? The more we spoke the more I was wondering why you came here, and now I know. But the question is, will she be as happy to see you as you are to see her?"

"I didn't help her get chosen for this assignment, and I didn't endure fifty-six hours of travel hell if I didn't think this would help us get closer," James countered.

Jennifer, slender in silhouette with long, straight, dark brown hair, a hint of freckles on her cheeks, and soft inviting brown eyes, was waiting outside the bus as James and David departed the vehicle and gathered their gear. The rest of the way would be by bumpy dirt roads leading to the established campsite.

David was the first to gather his gear and then approached Jennifer, saying, "Hi. I believe we have seen each other on campus, and we were in a couple of classes I think, but we haven't formally met. I'm David Ch--"

James rudely cut in, "Jennifer you would not believe how awful a trip I had to get here. Long flights, long waits, horrible food, and intolerable people."

David could do nothing but chuckle, as he was not too surprised how rude and self-centered his traveling companion acted. He noticed that Jennifer, with her elegant yet unpretentious appearance, smiled toward him as if to let David know that she was not too surprised either.

On the road in the Land Rover, David turned to Jennifer and asked, "What are the people like?"

Jennifer explained, "They are very accommodating and nice. The Surma people dominate this area. They are renowned for the strange custom of having their women slit their lower lips and insert circular or rectangular clay discs when they reach maturity, and the Surma men are known for a style of stick fighting called Donga. Since they're used to foreigners coming to the area for at least forty years, the people are very friendly and hospitable. When we get a break, I can bring you back so you can experience their culture."

"No thanks," said James. "These people don't seem any more advanced than the people we'll be digging up."

"You don't find it fascinating how the Surma developed their culture?" David shot back. "I'd like to know their reason for the lip insertion, or the stick fighting, or if they migrated here versus having been here forever, or types of food they typically eat. I find it fascinating, to say the least."

James said, "The first thing you'll learn is their bathing habits, or lack thereof."

"Oh, James, will you ever become inquisitive and stop letting your biases come out?" said Jennifer.

James just grunted in disapproval.

It was early evening as they reached the project's campsite, where Gibbs and Sanchez greeted James and David.

Gibbs addressed the group. "Welcome to the Kibish rock formations. I hope your trip wasn't too bad. We have high expectations for this dig to be successful, and we hope it will be rewarding to you as budding anthropologists. Classroom study can take you just so far in your education, and being out in the field will allow you to apply what you have learned in a real-life adventure."

Dr. Sanchez added, "It is getting late, though, and we like to take advantage of as much sunlight as we can. Breakfast is at 5:00 A.M., and we'll be at the dig site by 5:30 to be ready for sunrise at 5:46. Jennifer will now show you where to get some food and where your tent is to bunk for the night. Sleep well, for you will need it because we have a long day tomorrow."

"See you in the morning," David said, and they all headed for their tents.

Jennifer showed James and David to their tent area. "Make sure you check your cot and blanket before you lay down for the night, because we have found little creepy crawlers and snakes looking for a warm place to sleep," she said. "We already had a geologist get bitten, and her whole arm swelled four times its size! Lucky for her, we had the right medicine for that particular bug. Anyway, when you get hungry, the tent with the food is in the center of the camp. You can't miss it; it's the one that has all the coolers and refrigerators. So, if there's not anything else, I'll see you guys in the morning?"

James responded quickly, "But Jennifer, I thought we could talk and…"

Jennifer cut him off as she headed to her tent. "There will be plenty of time tomorrow at the dig site for talking. I'm tired from a long day of digging. Good night!" Then she walked away.

A dejected James just stared into the dimly lit corridor between the tents, then peered behind him to see David diligently checking every corner of the tent. "We will do that later. Let's go find some food first," he said.

Walking back to their tent with a few snacks from the food tent, David said, "I can't believe they have chocolate pudding snacks all the way out here. My favorite."

"Modern conveniences make being in the middle of nowhere a little more bearable," said James as they entered the tent, "but please keep your excitement down for tomorrow's first day at the site, because it's a slow and mundane process. Trust me, it will be long days of chiseling rock and sifting through sand. Then, if you are lucky, you might find a hint of prehistoric life in a fossil of some long-dead plant or ancient bug that was plentiful hundreds of thousands of years ago. But the chance of finding an ancient ancestor is very remote. The actual excavating is slowed by painstakingly removing layers one inch at a time, then mapping out each layer on a diagram. It is tedious."

As David finished the last of his chocolate pudding, he told James, "Don't be a killjoy. I've been looking forward to this for a long time. Now I'll see you in the morning. Good night."

David lay on his cot and told him, "I can't believe I am finally going to dig for ancient man in the morning. I can't believe it."

James just shook his head in disapproval.

"Hey, guys! Wake up or you'll miss breakfast!" Jennifer yelled into James and David's tent as she continued on her way.

"Oh, my God. I'm so tired," David mumbled as he tried to focus in the dark of early morning. "It feels like midnight, not 5:30. OK. Right. Jetlag. OK. I'm up and excited to get started."

"Yeah, I'm thrilled to death, too," James said sarcastically.

David and James were late for breakfast but grabbed as much food as they could hold on their way to meet Gibbs and Sanchez for a quick orientation at the dig site before they got started.

"Good morning, guys," Sanchez said. "As you can see, we have already started excavating the area where we will focus our dig. Oh, and by the way, I want to thank your classmate Jennifer for getting in country with the advance team to help set up our camp. She was a Godsend."

James peered over to Jennifer as if to give her a silent, "Good job."

Gibbs took over for Sanchez. "We found this location to be, due to erosion, not too deep into the ground. Our geologist, Dr. Harris, has located a layer between 200,000 and 250,000 years old, yet not too deep in the earth." Sanchez then yelled over to Harris, "How is the arm feeling?"

"The swelling is going down, but it is starting to itch a little," she said.

"Give it a few more days," Sanchez said, and then continued to David and James, "We figure to be at that level in about three more days of slowly sifting through the ground and diligently recording every item."

David asked, "With all the digs that have gone on here since the Leakey Dig some forty years ago, when they found Ono 1, why do you feel this is a good spot?"

"Good question, David," Sanchez said. "We believe this is a previously overlooked part of the Kibish rock formation because previous digs were looking at a much later time in the rocks' age. We believe most of the digs before us were looking for early modern man in earth that was not as early in history as this layer. Since the sun has now given us enough light to start working, let's not waste another second of precious sunlight and get started."

As they broke up, Dr. Gibbs said to James, "I bet your old man is happy you're here, and I bet he wishes he were here too."

James just nodded his head as to agree, but in reality he was glad that the giant shadow of his father that usually made him feel invisible was not there.

After three days at the dig, James was starting to feel dejected, as Jennifer seemed always to be busy with little to no time for him. Every time he approached her, she was going in a different direction, and even though they were only a few yards away from each other at the dig, it seemed they were worlds apart. Yet every night James prodded David with questions since she had been teamed up with him since the first day. James found David a wealth of information because he told James many things that James did not know about Jennifer. He told James how she got the scar on her leg, what it was like in the part of Indiana where she was from, what her parents did for a living, and her aspirations for her career.

Eventually, David told James he was tired of being his information-gatherer and to talk to her himself. Right after dinner and before she got back to her tent for the night, James planned to do just that.

Later on, James was sitting at his table finishing his dinner and waiting for the chance to get a hold of Jennifer, who was in a conversation with some of the other team members. As he was waiting, David, who had been sitting next to him, got up and grabbed the binoculars hanging on his chair.

"Where are you going?" James asked.

"I am finally not too exhausted to go out on that ridge and gaze at the stars tonight on this clear night. I don't get too many opportunities to see the stars without the lights on Long Island polluting the sky and blocking their view. Too much light on the ground makes it harder to be able to see the heavens. When it is dark here you can see so many more stars as the sky fills with them. They are so bright that you think you could just reach up and touch—"

James cut him off rudely, "Go enjoy yourself," then got up to follow Jennifer as she left the dinner area. "Jennifer, wait up," he called as he ran over to her before she made it to her tent.

James looked at Jennifer and suggested, "I thought we could spend some time together since we will be together here for a few weeks. Back at school you are always so busy and had little time for anything other than the school work."

Jennifer was a brilliant student who had finished high school a year early and her four-year bachelor degree in three years. Her dedication to her schoolwork made her a favorite of the faculty despite James' claims to helping her gain access. She was very inquisitive and talented in understanding how things worked.

She said, "Hey, James. I told you back at the university that I'm concentrating on my work and learning as much as I can so I can excel as an anthropologist. Doing a project like this is a dream of mine. I now have the opportunity to take what I learned and use it out in the field. I am slowly digging through the earth to find remnants of life that lived on this planet hundreds of thousands of years ago. I think that this is so amazing. Most of all, James, this is my dream job, and I feel fortunate for the opportunity to be able to do something I love to do."

She then paused and tried to explain to him, "I sense you want to be more than friends, but I have career aspirations that are a world apart from yours. I also feel we should just remain friends because our goals are not compatible. Your personal wants and needs are different from mine. Don't get me wrong, James. I do appreciate what you did for me back at the university, but it would make me feel better if we could just remain friends."

James had thought that all the time he put in trying to get her attention through the years at school would pay off for him now. He was disappointed, but he couldn't let go and responded to appease her wishes with a little hope for himself when he said, "It would be great to remain friends, and maybe things will change as we become better friends, don't you think?"

Her intentions were not to hurt him, but her answer was ambiguous at best. "Sure," she responded.

She then walked into her tent, but quickly came back out, to James' surprise. At first he thought she was coming back out to talk some more with him, but he noticed that she was holding a pair of binoculars and started to walk away from him.

He asked in confusion, "Where are you headed?"

She barely turned around to make eye contact with him when she said, "David mentioned that he would be on the ridge viewing the stars on this clear night." She took a few more steps and reluctantly said, "You are welcome to join us."

But James, like a wounded animal, decided he would rather go lick his wounds. "No, thank you. It was a long day, and I'm tired. I think I'll go back to the tent."

"OK, then," she said as she kept walking. "Have a good night."

James just nodded his head while she disappeared into the darkness.

On the ridge, she approached David, asking, "Do you mind if I join you?"

David was a bit surprised to see his dig partner. "I thought you would be hanging out with James. He was looking forward to speaking to you."

She replied, "We talked briefly." After a moment or two she confessed, "He has always tried to be more than friends, but he is not really my type. I believe that deep down he is not a bad guy. The biggest stumbling block has been that he knows nothing about me, and he has made no attempt to find out. Yet I know all about him because he is his biggest promoter. As a matter of fact, I could probably write his biography. You traveled with him. What did you two talk about?"

A reluctant David replied, "Ah, him."

Jennifer continued, "He doesn't know where I'm from, anything about how I grew up, or what I want to do with my life. To tell you the truth, you know more about me from the last few days than James knows from the last few years he has tried to date me." This caused a brief awkward stare at each other, then she quickly continued, "He does try to help me, but it is more about what he can get out of it instead of for the sake of helping. With the help of James, I have met his father, I have been to university functions reserved for the dignitaries of the university, I have sat in on meetings about the ongoing partnership the university has with the Museum of Natural History, and through his influence, because of his father's status in the university, I've been given the opportunity to be here. I didn't ask for any of it. But his influence there at the university can also be a little disconcerting. I always happen to be in the same class and have the same lab hours he has. No matter what class it is, he is always in the seat right next to me."

In an attempt to defend James, David said, "Well, he likes you and wants to be near you, I guess."

She replied, "It's a little creepy. But even if I could see past his self-centeredness, his goals don't match mine. I want to learn and explore and then take that knowledge to advance my career in this field. I love the fact I'm an anthropologist and have an opportunity to discover something that lived on this planet so long ago and learn about it. He lacks passion, and without passion for and a love of what you do, you're just going through the motions. But on the other hand, he is brilliant, and it irks me that I work extremely hard just to maintain what comes so easily to him, and he just wastes it."

David agreed, "I know. He is like a lot of people I have met in my life that have all the talent in the world, and you would think they could accomplish anything they set their minds to, but they lack one important ingredient, desire. Without that, they can never reach their potential."

After a few quiet moments, both looking up at the starlit sky, they both looked to change the subject from James to the reason they were out there in the first place.

David began, "I love getting to a location far from city lights so I have the opportunity to see as many stars as possible with the naked eye. Back on Long Island, there are too many streetlights, porch lights, car headlights, and shopping mall lights in the atmosphere that block out our vision of the night sky. But out here on a clear night, you see so many stars that you think you can reach up and touch them. If you look over there, you can see the center of the Milky Way, where there are billions of stars. Some of these stars are so distant from us that it takes hundreds of thousands of years for the light to reach us. We are actually looking at the past when we look at them. The light from that star could have originated so long ago that at this moment the star may not be there anymore, but we will not know about its demise until the light from its massive explosion someday reaches us. I find that amazing because I love looking at the past."

Looking up, Jennifer agreed. "As a young girl I would travel with my family to northern Michigan so my dad could go fishing at some of the fresh water lakes in the state parks. The nighttime was special at the campgrounds we would stay at because I would look up and wonder who might be looking down at me and whether I was looking up at something my ancestors looked at as well. It helped me to become interested in history so much that here I am, ready to find an ancestor who might have looked up at the sky in wonder as I am today. So tell me, what else is up in the sky?"

"Well," David said. "It was pointed out to me recently that the bright one above the moon and to the right is Jupiter, and later this month we will be able to see Venus."

David and Jennifer continued to gaze at the lights in the sky for a little while longer as they relaxed after a long day of digging. It was for only an hour, but it gave them time to talk and get to know each other.

For James, the days got longer with his realization that Jennifer did not think of him in the way he thought of her. He was not especially keen on being out in the field, and it reminded him of the boring trips he had to make with his dad. Now each day he had to work at the dig site and notice the budding relationship between David and Jennifer. The dejected feeling he had took its toll on his already sub-par effort at the dig site. It was now three days after the night Jennifer told him she was not interested in taking their friendship to another level, and his poor work was starting to get noticed by the other members of the team.

He also drew the attention of the project leaders, Gibbs and Sanchez, who decided that for the good of the team James would be sent on a task. They did not want his lack of excitement to affect the good morale the team had exhibited so far. But because he was the son of Patrick Connor, and out of respect for him, they decided against sending him home if his attitude did not improve. So they chose to have him scout the local area outside the dig zone for signs of ancient bones that might be on the surface. The artifacts could be visible due to erosion or from being overlooked by earlier archeological digs. Sometimes these finds led to major discoveries when little fragments of bones instigated more extensive digs on that spot.

As James approached the dig site in the morning, Gibbs met him outside the site.

"Good morning, James."

While still wiping the sleep out of his eyes, James said, "Good morning, Dr. Gibbs. I am sorry I'm late. I guess I overslept a little bit."

Dr. Gibbs responded, "That's OK, James. We could all use some extra sleep. Hey, Dr. Sanchez and I were looking to have someone scout the terrain for another dig site in case we have time after this site is fully excavated or for the trip we'll make to this area next year. We think with your experience with this trip and your experiences with your dad, you would make a great choice. So, could you do that for the team?"

Before Dr. Gibbs even finished speaking, James knew what was happening. He thought, "Let's get the bad egg out of sight so not to infect the other eggs". James knew that there were others more favored on the team with more experience than he, who would have a much better chance than he had. All he could do was put on a good face and say, "Dr. Gibbs, I feel honored that you and Dr. Sanchez would choose me for this assignment. I won't let you or the team down."

A relieved Dr. Gibbs said, "That's great, James. Maybe you can start northeast from here because I think that is an area overlooked by previous teams here at Kibish."

James then nodded his head and grabbed a few tools before he headed in a northeast direction.

As James started walking away from the dig site, he thought that there were definitely many others on the team who could have done the job, but knew it was probably best that he get away for a little while so he could clear his head. Even though he had hoped he would be sent home, it would not look good for him, and he knew it. His standing at the university would be adversely affected. No more would there be invites to university functions or to museum openings of new exhibits where he would rub elbows with dignitaries and the famous. Also, the professors at the university would not favor him as they had in the past for just being the son of Patrick Connor.

He said to himself, "I can't let this setback ruin everything. So Jennifer is not interested and may like someone else, so be it. This is not the end of the world." He started to clear his head and concentrate on what he needed to do.

"I need to think clearly and not let my emotions get the best of me. I can't be mad at her. She has to like what she likes, and my forcing the issue probably did not help my cause. It was stupid, and I'm most likely the reason why she is with David. I'm only kidding myself if I am mad at David because the guy only tried to help, and it is my fault they worked together in the first place and started to know each other."

He continued to walk northeast and started to wonder, "What am I going to do now?"

The morning passed, and since James was not hungry, he continued to walk the landscape holding his small pick and a brush. Then he saw something that caught his eye in a crack on the side of a small hill. It looked familiar, like a fragment of a small bone. He slowly brushed away the loose gravel until the fragment became a little more visible. Then he gently used his small chisel and pick to break away some of the rock until he noticed that the fragment was indeed a small bone, and it had another bone right next to it and another right next to that one. They were small, and he realized that they were the bones of a small finger.

He continued to work for the next five hours, gradually removing the items from the side of the hill in the hot sun. While he kept working, he thought about how excited his father would be when he found something like this. He would be thrilled to remove something out of the ground that had perhaps walked on the earth thousands of years ago and not been seen since. James was never as excited as his dad was, but today he felt pretty good.

When he had the fossil secured in his bag, he grabbed his notebook and quickly noted the location with every detail he could observe. He then marked the site, took his fossils and headed back.

As James approached the main dig site, David and Jennifer came out to meet him. They were concerned about him because they felt responsible and sorry for him that he had been sent away from the dig site so as not to be detrimental to the morale of the project members. But James was happy to see his two friends walk up to him and proudly blurted out, "I got a finger!"

David did not know what he meant, and responded with concern, "Well, if you try to be nicer to people, then maybe that won't happen."

Earlier in the day James might have felt combative about a statement like that, but now it made him laugh. Laughing was something he had not done in weeks leading up to the trip, but right now it was what he needed. For weeks he had prepared for this trip, not to search for fossils, but for his conquest of Jennifer. So he did not prepare to come as an anthropologist, even after the endless speeches from his father about what he needed to do. It felt good to laugh as David and Jennifer look at him in confusion.

Finally James told them, "I found a fossil in the side of a hill. I believe it might be a finger of an ancient human."

They looked into his bag and saw little fragments of ancient bone. "Wow," they said in unison.

Then Jennifer asked, "Where did you find them? They look great."

James replied, "About three quarters of a mile northeast from here. I flagged the spot. I was just walking along, and there it was in front of me. It took me a while to dig them out, and it made me feel good, to tell you the truth."

Jennifer insisted that they bring the fossils over to Drs. Gibbs and Sanchez, where James explained to them where he found them. They dispatched Dr. Harris and a few of the other team members to evaluate the layers of earth in which the fossils had been found before it grew dark. James went to dinner with many of the team members, who saw him in a new light, and his two friends who were relieved that he was able to turn his fortunes around. After dinner, David and Jennifer were surprised to see James join them on that ridge to view the nighttime sky.

"Hey there, it's nice of you to join us, mister superstar," David said to a James, who still had his head in the clouds.

"Well, I couldn't sleep even if I wanted to," said James. "And I thought tonight would be a good time to view the heavens."

David explained, "You found what I have been dreaming of finding, and I have to admit, I'm a little envious. All we have been able to uncover on the dig so far are 175,000–year-old creatures that lived on the bottom of the ancient river bed, and we were able to dig up some ancient plant life."

Jennifer said, "I'm proud of you, James, and I hope this helps you develop into a fine anthropologist."

James just smiled at his two friends and looked up. "Wow, that's a bright one," he said. "Which star is that?"

"That is not a star; it's Jupiter," answered David.

"And that one?" he asked, while pointing to another.

"Hey, I don't know all their names," said a flustered David as they all started to laugh. While enjoying their company, James appreciated that he felt that he was one of them now, unlike in the morning when he felt like an outsider to the whole team. This was a time for him to relax and enjoy.

In the morning, Dr. Sanchez joined James, David, and Jennifer for breakfast. "James," he said, "that was a great discovery yesterday. Your dad would be pleased."

"Thank you," said a proud James.

"I spoke to Dr. Harris, and the layer you discovered the fossil in was from about 75,000 years ago, as far we can figure without a much more detailed examination. You did a great job. Maybe next year you can come back to excavate the area," said Dr. Sanchez.

"But, Dr. Sanchez, we won't be able to get to it on this trip?" asked a disappointed Jennifer.

"Sorry, it doesn't look like it. We want to stay here and continue to dig around the 200,000-year level at this site or lower. The goal of this trip is to find a 200,000- to 250,000-year-old individual. Again, I am sorry, but on the other hand, I'm also happy for the discovery," said Dr. Sanchez.

Jennifer offered, "Then instead of the whole team, can James, David, and I spend a couple of days looking to find some more of this specimen? We will do a quick dig and be back before you know it."

After a long pause, Dr. Sanchez looked at the three and said, "Just seeing the excitement in your eyes about a discovery is making me feel excited." Sanchez paused in consideration, then brightened. "I'll tell you what. Yes. You get three days. I will communicate it to Dr. Gibbs. We'll send over some of our team to check up on you throughout the day. Good luck."

Without finishing their breakfast, the three jumped up to secure the right gear to attempt the dig and some supplies for the long day ahead of them. Then off they went, without looking back at the camp.

James quickly got to the site where he had found the fossilized finger. Once there, David and Jennifer set up the site for excavating the side of this small hill, and then they got started by slowly removing the earth and stone from the area. This was a slow and meticulous process, but the excitement of the three doctoral students grew the further they went into the earth. They knew that they had a finger of an individual, and the rest could be nearby. But the work to uncover this individual would take time, and three days was not a lot of time to do this kind of work. They knew they needed to hurry if they were to make progress.

The days were long, and the sun was hot, but it did not deter them. They ate when they were hungry and took breaks when they needed them, but they knew they had little time to waste and worked at a fast pace.

It was the morning of the third day, and so far they had found nothing, but they were not discouraged. David got up early to take advantage of as much of the lit hours in the day as possible and got to the site hours before dawn to set up for the day. When James and Jennifer arrived, the first thing they did was sort through the removed earth to try to find anything significant. By mid-morning, Jennifer saw something, and it was small. She picked it up and slowly chiseled away some of the excess rock.

"Hey, look here. We found a fossilized tooth," Jennifer yelled over to James and David. "We're on the right track! There's got to be more in there somewhere!"

David added, "It's not like this individual just got up and forgot their finger and tooth; the rest must be around here somewhere."

"Not to put a damper on our enthusiasm, but in the last 70,000 years the landscape could have changed many times over. Rivers have changed direction, wind and rain could have caused much erosion, and earthquakes or other land-moving events could have scattered the bones," said James.

"Yeah, and a carnivore could have mauled the individual and carried away the carcass, leaving nothing but a finger and tooth," said David.

"Let's stay positive and focused with what little time we have left here," said Jennifer.

They all agreed and hurried their dig.

As they took a brief break for lunch Jennifer turned to James to say, "I see for the first time that you are excited about what we do. I hope it develops into a passion. I have to admit that the new revived you surprises me. I would never have expected you not only to enjoy doing it, but also to be very enthusiastic about the whole process. Maybe there is hope for you after all."

James said, "I don't know. Maybe all I needed was to get out in the field and get a good kick in my pants. I didn't spend years studying anthropology and not expect to use it. I mean, yeah, I thought my career path would be as a professor in a prestigious university, so I knew I would use what I learned, but I didn't think I would like the field work."

"Well, a little success sometimes goes a long way. Let's get back to work," said Jennifer as she got up.

A little later in the late afternoon, James was feeling a little fatigued, so he stopped to take a breather and stretch himself for a few minutes. To relax a little, he thought he would walk around the small hill into which they were digging so he could regenerate a little. So while David and Jennifer continued to dig and sift through the dirt, he walked around to the other side of the hill. Along the way, he finally wondered what his father would think if he were here.

Patrick Connor saw a son that was not too much interested in what his father did as James grew up. For a while, he thought James would follow in his mother's footsteps and be a theologian. Yet James did end up following his father, maybe not with the enthusiasm he had for the work, but at least he had an understanding for what he did. James right now wondered how his father felt when he found his first discovery. Did he feel as good as James did? Maybe now, he thought, they might have a little more in common or at least a better understanding. Sure, all they found was a finger and a tooth, not a full skeleton, but it was very rare to find a full specimen. His father was always appreciative of every find he discovered because it gave him a window into the past, to touch something that had not been touched for so many years. Today James was starting to feel the same.

As James walked on the other side of the hill he heard his name being called by David. He climbed the hill straight back to where they were digging.

"What's up, David?" James asked from the top of the hill.

David replied, "It is getting late, and we should start closing down. But Jennifer and I thought that we might come back in the evening every night when we are done digging at Dr. Gibbs and Dr. Sanchez's site. It might be good to dig under the stars with a little help from some flashlights."

James laughed a bit and said, "Sure we can, maybe. Give me a minute, and I'll help you two."

James started down the rocky hill carefully. After all, he didn't want to go home in a cast. As he slowly made his way down, he put his foot down on a weak spot that he felt crumbling under his foot. Before he could adjust his weight, the rocks gave way. Down he went into a cavity in the hill as he yelled, sliding to the bottom about twenty feet down on a decline.

When he regained his senses and the dust in the air started to thin out, he first made sure he was all right with no serious injury. After checking himself, he realized he was OK and looked up to where he had fallen through, only to see David looking down at him.

"James, are you OK?" David yelled down. "Can you move? I will get a rope and come down to get you!"

At that moment Jennifer reached the hole where James fell through. "Is James OK?" she asked.

"He's OK! He's OK," said a relieved David. "We'll get him out of there." David went back to their supplies to find anything that would help get James out of the hole.

As James' eyes started to adjust to the lack of light, he noticed something with the smallest indication of a shiny metallic glow from the light that came in from the hole up above. At first he thought it was something he had dropped, but then his eyes focused a little more and he was looking at something odd. He started to see the outline of what looked like a table embedded partly into the rock.

"Can you throw me your flashlight?" he called to David. "I think I see a table down here."

A confused David asked, "Did you say a table?"

"Yeah, please send down a flashlight," said James.

Quickly finding a rope, Jennifer tied and lowered down the light.

Once he got it, he flashed it on to the metal-like table, but the wide angle of the light made him notice a much larger cavern. Then as he shined the light around the cavern, he noticed instruments on an enclosure about the size of a school bus. He then looked back up to David and Jennifer to tell them, "There is a cavern about thirty feet long down here with a structure that has instrumentation on it."

A confused Jennifer speculated, "Maybe it is some sort of mining equipment? That doesn't make sense, though. First off, there's nothing valuable in the ground that I know of other than ancient fossils, and, secondly, I didn't see any other entrance as I surveyed the hill before we started to dig."

David wondered, "I don't know, maybe some amateur anthropologists thought they could profit by securing as many fossils as possible using mine equipment, then buried the entrance when they failed to do so. Let's figure this out later and get James out of there before some rock falls on his head." So he yelled down to James, "Let's get you out of there."

James replied back, "Hold on, let me get a closer look." He freed himself from the loose small rocks around him, and as he moved toward the instruments, he wondered what odd tools these miners used. Then he must have set off a sensor because lights came on, and they were very bright. Using his hand to block the brightness from his eyes, he then yelled up to his colleagues, "It looks like the place is still operational!"

A small stone, loosened from when James fell into the cavern, gave way from halfway up the cavity, then bounced down off the sides of the wall, then off a large rock and the table, then on to what looked like an instrument panel. The rock hit what looked like a lever, one of many. The lever moved, and for the next seven seconds a loud sound erupted that vibrated the rocks. Some of the rocks cracked and gave way. The whole hill shook as rubble separated from the hill. James was knocked unconscious and buried in much of the rubble. David and Jennifer were thrown in different directions, then collapsed on the ground below.

For the next seven seconds, all wireless communication did not work on the side of the planet holding Kibish at its center. No Wi-Fi, no FM or AM radios, no cellular, wireless, or satellite communication in any frequency functioned. There was nothing but static on radios, phones, and television. Then, all of a sudden, they worked again.

Chapter 2

There was dust and rubble all around him, and James felt a huge weight on his chest and legs. He was in a daze and couldn't hear a thing. Slowly, he looked down and saw his right leg crushed between two large, sharp boulders. His chest was pinned between the table and some small broken rubble from above. He then noticed David, with a cut bleeding on his forehead, standing over him, saying something he couldn't understand while frantically pushing some of the rubble off his chest.

Then James started to hear David say, "James…James…James. I'm going to get you out of here. You will be OK!"

Jennifer then reached them, "James, are you OK?" she asked.

He started to feel a lot of pain in his right side and told Jennifer, "I think my leg is broken."

"Don't worry, we're going to get you out of here," she said.

After he cleared the rubble off James' chest, David pushed one of the boulders a few inches to the side, dislodging James' leg. They both grabbed James and lifted him up to the now large opening. Carrying him a safe distance from the now-collapsed hill, they lay him down carefully and gave him sips of water to clear his throat while Jennifer cleaned some of the dust and dirt from his face.

"Are you guys alright?" asked a tired Dr. Gibbs, who had run all the way from the other dig site after seeing a plume of dust rise in the distance.

A few seconds later, Dr. Sanchez and a few others arrived. "What the hell happened here?" yelled Dr. Sanchez as he viewed the collapsed hill where layers of rock had been for thousands of years. "Was there a gas explosion? Did you hit a methane gas pocket?" He looked into the crater in the hill. "Wait a minute… what is that equipment doing there?"

They all stared in disbelief, trying to comprehend what they were looking at. They all saw what looked like shiny new equipment, but no one had any idea what it was doing there.

"All right," said Dr. Gibbs. "Are we looking at old mining equipment, or could this be an abandoned drug lab or something?"

There was silence, as not a person there had an answer to give because no one knew what he or she was looking at. Dr. Harris broke the silence. "I don't know what that is, but look how the rock formed around the whole structure like it has been here for thousands of years. You would think that the structure would bend and break over time, but why would it still have power for the lights if it were here for a long time? I don't get it."

"Hold on here," said Dr. Sanchez. "Let's not jump to conclusions. All I can say is this obviously could not be built by an ancient people, because it has power. So is this a modern invention? Can this be space debris, like an old satellite? It might explain how it got so deep into the rock if it traveled from orbit at a fast rate of speed."

Dr. Gibbs answered for everyone. "I don't think so; just look at it. It has technology I have never seen before, and if it were a satellite that crashed into the rock, it would not be in such good shape."

They all stood there, except James, who was lying on the ground with his leg wrapped and his head resting on a soft bag, looking at what might have been considered a vehicle or a craft of some sort sticking out of part of the hill that had broken away during the vibrations. It was the size of a school bus with what looked like large engines underneath it and in the back. The surface was smooth with a very high shine and not a scratch on it. The whole left side of the vehicle had been opened upwards like a canopy as if to give shade, and the table was under it. In the exposed interior, there were control panels with instruments unfamiliar to the many team members.

There was no national insignia or any writing or symbols of any kind anywhere to be seen. Anything a space agency would send into space would have some sort of markings.

Dr. Sanchez then surmised, "Maybe this is some secret NASA vehicle that landed here, and the rock caved in around it or melted around it due to the extreme heat from reentry?"

A skeptical Dr. Harris said, "It can't be. The rock didn't melt around it. It formed around it, and that takes a very long time."

Jennifer ran over to Dr. Gibbs. "We need to get James to a hospital. He has a broken leg and possible broken ribs. There are no signs of a head injury, even though he does look dazed, but he is in a lot of pain, and we have to move him."

"All right, let's get him out of here," said Gibbs.

James started to fade in and out as he tried to focus on the structure in the rock he could view from his position. He finally passed out as the pain overcame him.

Dr. Gibbs walked over to Dr. Sanchez. "We need to contact the university, the museum's air and space department, and even NASA and the European Space Agency. Maybe we can get someone in here to help explain what the hell this thing is. This looks like a sophisticated piece of equipment, and someone must be looking for it."

"I agree," said Dr. Sanchez. "But let's try to keep this under wraps for the time being, so wild rumors won't start to fly around until we can get a better idea of what we have here."

The Humvee was brought over, and James was lifted into it. Two of the team members stepped forward. Anthony "AJ" Johnson, a thirty-one-year-old former Stony Brook student, was now a second-year adjunct professor at Suffolk Community College on his second dig. Kevin Jones was a retired insurance agent, volunteering his time for a chance to fulfill a dream of working in an archeological dig to find ancient fossils. Together, they took James on a trip fifty miles north to an Ethiopian military base where they got him on a military transport to the capital and then to a hospital. Once they reached the base, medical personnel stabilized James and got him on a helicopter for the trip.

As per procedure for being on a university project outside of the United States, Johnson contacted the university by satellite phone, and they made all the arrangements for James. Once James was en route, Johnson and Jones used the phone and a computer at the base to let friends and colleagues know what they had seen. Without Gibbs and Sanchez' knowledge, Jones had been able to take a few pictures with his digital camera prior to leaving with James. Before returning to the camp, Johnson and Jones, unable to resist the temptation to show all their contacts what they had seen, shared the information via Facebook and Twitter. Whatever hopes Gibbs and Sanchez had of keeping the find under wraps was dashed as word got out, and it did not take long for each member of the team to be bombarded with calls and emails.

James, meanwhile, was taken by helicopter to another military base with an airport. He was then taken by small plane to Addis Ababa. After a day in a local hospital, he was then transported to Rome to have surgery. He was mostly unconscious for four days, due to the painkillers he received from medical personnel along the way. When he awoke and realized where he was, he then started to remember what had happened back in Ethiopia at the rock formation in Kibish. In time, he turned on the television and found the BBC's twenty-four-hour news channel. One of the stories they spoke about piqued his curiosity because it was about the expedition in Kibish.

"This morning we have some breaking news," said the female anchor as the words Breaking News rolled in red at the bottom of the screen. "In a joint news conference via satellite feed, NASA and the European Space Agency have stated they can find no cause for the seven seconds of interference half the world experienced four days ago. In an interview with NASA Deputy Director Jean Sisco, she said, 'So far, we have no reports that a sun flare caused the interference, but it seems unlikely because the part of the planet affected by the phenomenon was not facing the sun at the time. But we are looking at other possibilities.'

"Another story that is getting worldwide attention is the unknown craft found in an ancient rock formation outside of Kibish, Ethiopia."

James perked up at the anchor's explanation of the mystery of the find while pictures taken by Kevin Jones were shown on the screen. Because James had been injured, he did not see much of the craft after the vibration broke the rock away. He looked at the pictures in amazement.

"We are told that it was discovered by a doctoral student named James Connor on a Stony Brook University anthropology dig led by Doctors Ronald Gibbs and Roberto Sanchez. In his briefing this morning, Dr. Gibbs said, 'We do not have any new information to give you this morning except to say that we are bringing in experts from around the world to get their consultation, and many are arriving daily.'"

James noticed that there were many more people at the site than when he left, but in one of the clips, he did see Jennifer and David in the background. All he thought about was that he needed to get back to the site, but he knew that wouldn't happen for a while because pins had been inserted into his leg during surgery, and he would be immobile for a while. The concussion and broken ribs only compounded his dilemma, and he would need weeks of therapy to be able to walk.

As James lay there in the hospital in pain, he got a phone call from a familiar voice.

"Hi, James. How are you doing? I was so worried."

"Hi, Mom. I'm a little banged up, but I'm OK now," said James.

"Your dad had to change his flight plans a few times during his route to you because we got conflicting reports as to your location. But he will be in Rome sometime tonight. I stayed here because the university said as soon as you can be moved, you'll be transferred to the hospital on campus."

James could hear the emotions in her voice that any mother would have when her child was injured. He let out a deep breath, knowing he had a long rehab ahead, and told her, "I'll be OK. I'm just a little disappointed that I can't be back at Kibish with all the others. It looks like I'm missing out on some big discoveries."

"No, James. You have made a big discovery out there. They are just trying to understand what you found."

James paused a second, feeling weak. "Hey Mom, I'm getting tired. Can I talk to you later?"

"Sure, I'll talk to you in the morning. Your dad and I...well, we are very proud of you. Get some rest."

A few hours later, James woke up to a presence he recognized.

"You know, James," the man said with a concerned laugh, "this Indiana Jones crap only works in the movies with fit movie stars. Bookworms like us end up in a hospital with bandages and casts if we're too adventurous."

"Hey, Dad," James said. "When did you get here?"

"A little while ago. I didn't want to disturb your rest. You need it after what you've been through."

James said, "I've been asleep for days. I'm OK."

Patrick seemed relieved that that James was in good spirits. "I just wanted to come by to see that you are OK, but I can't stay long," Patrick told James.

A disappointed James asked, "Why not?"

Patrick responded, "The University asked me to assist Gibbs and Sanchez with your extraordinary discovery."

A perked-up James quickly asked, "Really? What's going on there? All I've heard is what is on the news."

"Well," he said. "I don't know much, except that they have dug around the craft and found ancient human remains. I am not sure if they believe the remains are relevant to the craft, but I've been asked to assist.

From what I have been told, it's a circus over there. More journalists and photographers are starting to show up every minute. The news organizations want up-to-the-second updates, and they don't understand that we don't work that way. In any find, it usually takes years of study before publishing a paper about it. This is really crazy."

James looked puzzled and asked, "Journalists and photographers? Really?"

He replied, "Oh, yeah. This was not kept a secret, and, as a matter of fact, there are journalists and photographers camped out at this hospital waiting to speak to you. But you will not have to worry about them. The hospital will shield you from them, and when you get back to the university tomorrow, they will have their public relations department communicate for you."

Patrick looked at the time and quickly grabbed his belongings. He headed out the door, but looked back to James to say, "I have to go, but I wanted to tell you that I'm proud of you. Not for stumbling on to that craft, but for the remains you found. Gibbs and Sanchez told me how excited you were. It made me happy."

Then Patrick smiled and left the room. He still had a long journey to go to reach the camp and hoped to reach it by the next afternoon.

The next day, Dr. Gibbs was sitting on a rock outside to supervise the dig around the unknown craft when David called him over to see their progress. David and some of the members of the team were chiseling away rock from an anklebone. They were clearing an area near the table. Right above the location of the original remains there were three large cylinders that had been uncovered two days after the discovery of the craft.

The team believed that they might find a complete specimen judging by how good the ankle looked. David brought Dr. Gibbs to show him that they were ready to lift the cylinder off the spot where they expected to find the rest of the fossil. The cylinder was about six feet long with a diameter of about three feet.

David pointed to the cylinder and said, "We have been able to move it now, and it doesn't seem too heavy. So if you can stand back, we can lift it."

Then David and three others started moving it to the side, but Cameron Steele, a newly arrived anthropologist from the museum, was startled and yelled, "There is some sort of liquid in it!"

However, the uneven ground and the sudden weight redistribution in the cylinder caused Cameron and Rodney Thomas, a respected biologist whom Dr. Sanchez had recommended, to drop their end. The impact caused the other end to be dropped. It lodged on an incline with one end higher than the other. The impact forced what looked like a lid to open. Because of the angle, a blue liquid spilled out on to the ground and began to evaporate in the air.

Doctor Harris then screamed, "Gas!" They all ran about one hundred feet away in case it was toxic. It was about twenty minutes later, as they inched closer to the cylinder, that Jennifer noticed that the lid might have moved.

"Jennifer, back away. We don't know if it's safe," said Dr. Gibbs.

Steele told Dr. Gibbs, "It may be a good idea to stay away from the area outside the craft until the hazmat suits arrive." This safety equipment was to be brought by the arriving teams.

While everyone hung back, Jennifer still had her eyes on the cylinder as the lid slowly opened and out fell a body the size of a young man.

'Look!" she yelled.

The team was shocked when the body started slowly to move. Then it picked itself up and stood. The team saw an individual about five-foot-six without any clothes, but quite hairy on most of his body. What was most intriguing and garnered the most stares was his head, with its small cranium and sloped forehead.

As they were looking at him, he started to gain his balance and realized he was surrounded. The confused being saw a gap in the crowd around him and with cat-like reflexes sprinted through the gap. He ran in a side-to-side stride down what was left of the hill to about one hundred yards away from the craft. He ran into newly arrived members of the team and came to a stop as he tried to get his breath. David and the others caught up to him, and he was surrounded. He continued to breathe heavier and heavier as he looked around at a place he was not familiar with. His eyes started to roll to the back of his head, and then he fell to his knees. As he collapsed to the ground, one of the new team members caught him. With his last breaths, he looked up at an astonished Patrick Connor, who had in his arms a person he had always dreamed he could meet. After a long journey to the site, a very tired Patrick held not a young man or a boy, but a fully-grown man. To Patrick's surprise, he was not a modern man.

Patrick surmised to himself as the others gathered around, "He is…umm…he is not Homo sapiens. The brain case is larger than Homo erectus. It is earlier than Neanderthal. He looks like he is more developed than Homo heidelbergensis and a little less developed than Homo sapiens. In any case, this might be our closest direct ancestor."

He couldn't believe his eyes because this individual was from a species that had not walked on earth for hundreds of thousands of years. All he kept thinking was, "This is not possible!" But according to his extensive knowledge, the characteristics of this man were clearly of an ancestor of modern man as he gazed over this helpless being.

As Patrick put the body down on some plastic sheeting someone had brought over, Jennifer interrupted the group. "You've got to see this, and you are not going to believe it."

Still in disbelief, Dr. Sanchez said, "I just had an ancestor nobody has seen for two hundred and fifty thousand years stand in front of me. What is more unbelievable than that?"

Jennifer just motioned with her hand to say, "Come on." Then they walked over to where they had lifted the cylinder. Pointing to the exposed area, Jennifer explained, "As we had hoped, there is what looks like almost a fully fossilized skeleton of an early woman here, but when you look to the left we found this." Jennifer pointed to a second find, which, unlike any find anyone had ever seen before, did not resemble any human ancestor or any other creature known to walk this planet. In the rock they saw the remains of a creature that were not only its bones. It still had skin and muscles fossilized -- or more like mummified. The head had a round shape with eyes twice the size of a man's, and limbs much longer than those of the fossilized human ancestor right next to it. If it were to stand it would be about six feet, six inches tall.

Even though members of the team had thought it, they had not wanted to say the craft was not from this world until now. They just stood there in quiet disbelief and stared at the odd-looking being.

In Long Island, a semi-recovered James prepared to speak to the press.

"James, it is time to go before the wolves. I hope you are ready," said Hilary Barns, the head of the public relations department for the university. Due to the size of the press and their equipment in attendance, the gymnasium had needed to be organized into a makeshift pressroom. Not only was the press there, but also the stands were filled with all types of people, from scientists to writers to UFO enthusiasts.

It was packed to capacity, and when Hilary came to the podium, she was almost blinded by the many camera flashes in the audience. "Ladies and gentlemen," she said. "James Connor will be out in a moment, but first I wanted to remind you that he is still weak from the injuries he received at the Kibish rock formation, so there will be a limited number of questions for him today. Due to the number of you here, we have selected a few of you to ask a question, and hopefully many of you who were not able to ask a question will get a chance in follow-up news conferences. Now, let me introduce James Connor, a doctoral student studying anthropology."

As Hilary was introducing him, James could hardly believe that he was seeing this large audience waiting to hear what he had to say. It was now about four weeks since he had been injured in Kibish. His ribs and his head had healed, but his leg had needed follow-up surgery. He was wheeled up to the podium because he had a cast on his leg that would be there for weeks, followed by months of therapy to regain his full ability to walk. As he was about to speak, he couldn't help thinking about the dig going on for the discovery he had made. He wished he were there. As a matter of fact, he was jealous that his friends David and Jennifer were still there exploring and he had been sent back home to recover from his injuries.

All he could do was communicate with them by phone and email, but those were slowed by being controlled to keep information from getting out. The museum and university employed a security firm to monitor the flow of information, and the university was using their public relations department to control the information going to the general public. Usually the museum and university were not confronted with this much interest in one of their scientific discoveries. Normally, a significant find would have to go through a lengthy process to validate the discovery before the museum would present the find to the scientific community and the general public. But this was not a normal discovery and there was nothing usual about it, especially with a public that liked its information updated every moment with twenty-four-hour news channels, the Internet, emails, blogs, and social networks.

Hilary finished her introduction and turned the microphone over to James, who sat next to university scientists, professors, and leaders. James at first could not speak as he shielded his eyes from the sea of camera flashes. Finally, when the flashes subsided, he started to explain what had taken place when he made the discovery.

Early in the news conference, as he explained the events that had taken place, he used terms like "the team", "our group", "the project," and "we." As the news conference continued, however, it started to sink in how important his discovery was and his place as the face of the unbelievable find. Sure, he had watched much of the twenty-four-hour news coverage of this story, but it was not until he was in front of this crowd of people that he realized how famous he was and that he was taking part in arguably the most important discovery in human history.

After a reporter asked him, "How does it feel to be the most famous person on the planet?" it was a revelation that he was finally out from under the shadow of his well-respected parents and could make a name for himself. Towards the end of the conference, he began to refer to his own actions, separate from the rest of the team.

When the news conference was over, his mother came to the podium to help safely move him off the stage. James barely acknowledged her, as his mind was elsewhere thinking about all the interviews and talks he would have to do because of his newfound fame.

It took nine months from the time he left the States for Ethiopia to return, and Patrick Connor was relieved to be home. Even though he met his wife for excursions in Cairo and Madrid during breaks, he missed her company most of all, as he was not usually away from her for so long. This discovery was not like the others, and he had been asked to help.

A homecoming was not the reason he came back, however. The university was hosting a conference on the discovery, and they had brought in the key personnel from the project and NASA, as well as respected scientists from around the country. There were physicists, biologists, paleontologists, and anthropologists from many of the best institutions in the country. At the request of NASA and some of the other US government agencies in attendance, there were no foreign scientists, which was odd for such a discovery on foreign soil. Many of the government personnel wanted to keep some of the information secret, at least for the time being.

Patrick walked through the crowd before the meeting began to see the people he had been working with for the last nine months, and also saw colleagues from around the country he had not seen for a while. He imagined that this was going to be a meeting like none he had ever been to before. Things like fossilized remains of ancestors who have been dead for two hundred thousand years, a walking, talking primitive man, and a possible spacecraft with fossilized passengers needed to be discussed. Whatever the outcome of this conference, the way human beings looked at themselves, as well as how they looked to the sky, had changed forever.

As he took his seat, he heard from behind him, "Hi, Dad. How was your trip?"

He turned around to see James standing there in his new expensive suit. "I didn't know there was a dress code," Patrick replied in jest. Patrick was the kind to be more comfortable in his wrinkly clothes with dirt under his nails.

"If you took the time to read the schedule you'd see that I'm speaking later in the afternoon," a proud James told Patrick.

"I thought you'd be all talked out after all the talk shows and lectures you've given," said Patrick.

"Hey, what can I say? I'm in demand," James told Patrick.

But Patrick just smiled back. Patrick was happy that James was making a name for himself, but he was also concerned about where he was taking his career.

"Please take your seats," said Mike Wells, the head of the science department for the university who would be running the conference and who happened to be a good friend of Patrick's. "I want to thank you all for coming and apologize for the non-disclosure agreement you had to sign in order to participate in the conference. So, let's get started. As you know, James Connor stumbled across what may be the find of all time, and we are here to try to make sense of this. James found a craft unlike any made on Earth with technology that will take us years, heck, even generations to understand. Then there were the fossils of the ancient human remains and three individuals. There was one individual, who was encased in a chamber filled with a thick blue liquid and controlled by advanced technology, who happened to get up and run away until the poor soul collapsed and died. The other two chambers have yet to be opened, but we think there are individuals inside them as well.

"And before I forget, there were two passengers of this craft fossilized alongside the ancient human remains. Early indications are that they were living about two hundred and fifteen thousand years ago. So, that is it in a nutshell."

Mike paused for a second to take a drink then asked, "Any questions?"

Without any hesitation, almost all the participants raised their hand to speak, and Mike heard one voice over the others: "How do you suppose the craft got stuck here?"

"Good question," he said. "We believe that there was some sort of catastrophe that buried the individuals, such as a mud slide or volcanic activity."

Another question came up: "What do we know about the creature who came out of the cylinder or chamber?"

Mike took a deep breath and said, "His skeleton and the size of his cranium suggest he was not of the Homo erectus or Homo heidelbergensis species, but his DNA suggests closer to Homo sapiens."

A human anatomy expert from the University of Kansas asked, "Do you suggest this was the species that came before Homo sapiens, and we have discovered a new species?"

"Honestly," Mike said, "it is puzzling, and we have not come up with an answer yet."

The question-and-answer session went on all morning and into the next day. There were a lot of questions and very few answers that most would agree on. It did show that there was a lot of passion in the room with vigorous debate, but it caused much of the schedule to be pushed back.

On the afternoon of the second day, Mike said, "Let's hold off on this spirited questioning because it has put us behind schedule. So let me introduce the head of NASA, Dr. Ronald Mays."

"Thank you for letting me speak to you today," said Dr. Mays. "I first want to update you on the status of who gets the rights to the craft. As you know, our government would prefer that we get it because whoever unlocks the obviously advanced technology could change the balance of power. The Ethiopian government will most likely sell it to the highest bidder. We might have to partner with the European Union's space agency to outbid the Russians and Chinese."

That statement was not received well with the scientists in attendance because they all knew that when governments got involved, with all the politics taking place, it would muck things up.

Dr. Mays continued, "The next thing I want to talk about is the disruption in wireless communication that occurred nine months ago. You might be wondering what this has to do with the discovery of the craft. Well, communication was disrupted for a little over half the planet. We ruled out things like solar flares because part of the area in question was not facing the sun at the time. This is not common knowledge, so please keep it under wraps so we don't scare the public. From what we have calculated, the epicenter of the disturbance was Kibish, Ethiopia, or more precisely, the Kibish rock formation. We have concluded that at the moment James Connor triggered the reaction that freed the craft from the rock, it sent a communication of some sort out to deep space that interfered with all wireless communication on that side of the Earth."

Many in the room were shocked and asked, "For what reason?"

Dr. Mays replied, "Your guess is as good as mine. Since there might have been a catastrophe that rendered the passengers of the craft immobile, maybe it is an automatic SOS or something. All we know is the ship sent a message to someone or something."

This caused uproar in the conference as Dr. Mays was bombarded with questions. This discovery was of an incident that had happened over two hundred thousand years ago, and each person took comfort that the civilization that visited Earth must be long gone or very far out into space. An invitation had been sent out to return, making this find a worry for the present. Everyone wondered, the civilization that returned, what were their intentions going to be? What would they think of humanity? If they were this technologically advanced two hundred thousand years ago with the craft in the discovery, then how were they now? These were questions they would like answers to because they were not only curious, but also a little afraid of what the answers might be.

While everyone in the room wondered about the consequences of the communication, James thought about how this would help the book he started to write. He barely had time to write it, but he felt that with a public that was clamoring for information, it would be an opportune time. Since the discovery, he had been wanted for interviews and lectures that had not only increased his fame, but also made him realize it could line his pockets with the large fees he could command for speaking. He was not the only one taking advantage of his new fame. The university and museum had leveraged his notoriety to improve their donation drives by having James in attendance at lunches and banquets. James' discovery had not only changed the world, but also James.

"Hey, stranger, remember us?"

James recognized that voice and quickly turned to the people standing beside him.

"Jennifer, is that you and David? I haven't seen you guys since they put my broken body on the truck. How have you been? When did you get here?"

Jennifer replied, "We're good, but a little late for the conference."

David added, "It was a nightmare getting out of Ethiopia. Since your discovery the country has swelled with journalists and sightseers. Also the permits for new digs have skyrocketed with interest from around the world. It was great to see so much interest in history and archeology, but it was getting to look like a circus out there. For every legitimate dig site with teams of respected anthropologists and paleontologists meticulously using fine dentist picks and soft brushes to slowly investigate for fossils under the ground, there are three dig sites with nuts dressed in Klingon and Jedi outfits using shovels and backhoes looking for ET and the ship that brought him. Maybe I should be happy that interest in ancient man has increased. Anyway, the Ethiopian government is happy for the increase in foreign currency for their economy, but so far their infrastructure has not caught up to the demand. I hear even Kenya has seen an increase."

A concerned Jennifer said, "James, how are you? I see you still have a slight limp."

After he looked down at his leg, James said, "It's getting better, and if I had time to sit to rest it I would be all better by now. I've been so busy speaking and writing my book."

"Why don't you tell us all about it at dinner?" said a hungry Jennifer.

A curious David asked, "Are you going to mention us in your book? We were with you when you fell in the hole."

"First off, I didn't fall in the hole. I slightly stumbled into it after an exhausting day of investigating, and, of course, there will be a small footnote of your participation."

Jennifer and David just laughed with each other at James' revisionist memory of events.

They both said, "Come on, James. Let's go get something to eat, and you can tell us all about the book."

Chapter 3

The moderator said, "Today on MSNBC, we have Dr. James Connor, who about three and a half years ago discovered an ancient spacecraft buried in a remote part of Ethiopia. Today he is here to promote his new book *Gods and What We Believe*, the follow-up to his record bestselling book, *We Walked with the Gods*. First of all, Dr. Connor, I want to congratulate you on your marriage to socialite Brittany Morgan, the daughter of shipping billionaire Jonathan Morgan and a favorite of the paparazzi."

"Thank you. We are very happy," said James.

"Now, Dr. Connor," the moderator said in a little bit more serious tone. "This is a very fascinating book, but the knock on this book, just as with your first one, is that you have taken what others have written, like *Chariots of the Gods*, by Erich von Däniken, and put your own spin on it. Can you answer to this?"

James looked at the television camera and said, "The difference is that great authors like von Däniken only speculated about what aliens might have done, but I have walked where they walked and have seen their power. My answers to questions about where we came from are answered with scientific truth due to the discovery of the Ancient Visitors in Ethiopia."

Then the moderator followed with, "If that is the case, then why…"

At that very moment, Eva Moran walked into her living room to yell at her husband, "Can you turn that off, Eddie? I am sick of hearing about the Ancient Visitors this or Ancient Visitors that. They have been dead for hundreds of thousands of years, and we are still talking about them. I should be so lucky to be talked about that long after I'm dead and buried. Let them rest in peace, and let's move on." She walked over to the stairs to yell up to her son, "Steven, do you want dessert? I made brownies."

A frustrated Steven said as he walked by his mother toward the front door, "I just got on the scale, and I'm two pounds over. I need to burn some calories, or I am not going to make my weight at the weigh-in tomorrow, and I will not be in the wrestling tournament. I'm going out for a long run tonight so I can sweat it off."

A concerned Eva said, as she always did when Steven went on a run at night, "Be very careful. I hate when you go out in the dark. I worry that you won't come back."

Steven, as always, assured his mother, "Don't worry, it's not too late. It's seven o'clock, and I'll be back before eight." Steven then grabbed his University of Kansas sweatshirt and headed out of the family home.

As Eva started to close the door behind Steven, her two other sons Tommy, who was fifteen, and little Johnny, who was ten, ran up to the door and asked her, "Can we go, too?"

"No way," she said. "You're too young. He is just going out on a quick run and will be back in a bit." She then closed the door and went about her business, tending to the house.

Steven jumped in the pickup truck in the long driveway and quickly headed over to his former high school, knowing that he had to make this fast. He always called his girlfriend, Brenda, at eight-thirty every night so they could talk for a few hours. They had been together throughout high school, and she had enrolled at the University of Kansas so they could be together. He felt that they were already married because she was always bossing him around. His father, Eddie, told him, when his mother was not around to hear it, that he should just get used to it because it was no use fighting it. Both their families expected that they would be married after Steven and Brenda completed their college studies. There was pressure to get married now, but Steven didn't mind because he loved Brenda and he couldn't see himself with anyone other than her.

Steven, who had a lean and finely toned muscular frame to go with his Midwestern rugged farm boy features, had just turned twenty and was a sophomore. He grew up just outside of Topeka, Kansas, where he was a two-time state wrestling champion. Being able to get a scholarship to wrestle at the University of Kansas had been a dream of his since he was a little boy growing up on his parents' small dairy farm. It was also a relief financially for his parents, who just got by with the money they made from the farm. The University of Kansas was just down Interstate 70 in Lawrence, and his family was close enough to be at some of his wrestling matches. The coach of the wrestling team was appreciative that Steven wished to stay close to home and chose his program, because with his talent he could have been a part of any wrestling program in the country, with a full scholarship. All the coaches in the country desired Steven because he had achieved national honors and was an "A" student. Already Steven was the number one-ranked NCAA Division One wrestler in his weight class. Many of the coaches believed Steven was by far the best wrestler, pound for pound, in all of the sport.

After he arrived, Steven walked onto the track at his former high school and stretched for a little bit before starting to jog laps around the oval track. He liked the track at night because it was well lit and the lights didn't automatically turn off until nine o'clock. It was a soft rubber surface, easy on his tired legs after the grueling practices he endured to keep his ranking. He also liked that no one else was on the track, so he could relax and comfortably get his run in. During wrestling practice, the coaches got all over him and his teammates, and they all endured long practices to be on top of their game. This was the time on the track when he enjoyed a period of peace and quiet. It was even more enjoyable tonight because of the nice clear sky with little wind, and unseasonably warm air. Tonight the sky was full of stars with no clouds, except the lights on one aircraft flying high in the sky.

Steven had just finished three laps of the eight he planned to run on the 400-meter track when a bright flash that lasted about a second startled him. He immediately looked up, suspecting that one of the large lights on the light towers around the athletic facility had blown out. Steven continued his run, knowing that his mother would be waiting for him back home and that he needed to finish up. After he took a few more steps, he started to hear a slight humming sound and then noticed a breeze start to pick up. A few moments later, another light, even brighter than before, lit up all around him as he put his hand up to cover his eyes. Ten seconds later, the light was gone. All that was left on the track was a set of keys for the Moran family pick-up truck and a half-filled bottle of water.

Realizing he was lying down, Steven figured that he must have passed out while running. He believed that he must be weak from the constant dieting he did to keep his weight down, and he must have passed out when he overexerted himself. He then picked himself up slowly until he could stand. Even though he was still dizzy, immediately he recognized that he was not on the track at the high school and then noticed that he was not alone, because he started to hear voices in the large, dimly lit room. As he came to his senses, he noticed there were lots of voices, all in a panic, with some yelling and some crying.

One person with Hispanic features grabbed his shoulders and said, "¿Dónde estoy?" (Where am I?) "¿Cómo puedo llegar a casa?" (How do I get home?)

Another man joined them and yelled, "Où nous sommes?" (Where are we?)

He pushed them away and started to turn to run when a woman pulled on his arm to say, "Что является этим местом?" (What is this place?)

Steven pulled his arm away and said, "I don't know what you are talking about! I can't understand you." He tried to run away, but there was nowhere to run because the large room was filled with hundreds of people. Next to him he saw a man of Asian descent wearing a karate outfit with a black belt on it trying to speak to a woman sitting on the floor.

He said, "誰がこれをした？"(Who did this?)

The woman, unable to understand him, just mumbled, "Tanrı lütfen bana yardım etmek.." (God, please help me.)

Then they were joined by another Asian man who said, "我为什么在这里和我什么时候可以回家？" (Why am I here, and when can I go home?)

The only thing Steven knew was that they were all just as confused and scared as he was. Steven wondered where these people came from, how he got there, and where "there" was. He thought that he had to find someone he understood and yelled out, "Does anyone understand me? Does anyone speak English?"

Off in the distance he heard, "I can understand you."

From another direction came, "Where are you? Raise your hand. I will come to you."

As he saw a man and a woman signaling as they moved toward him, he continued to yell out, "Does anyone else speak English? Please? Anyone?"

Others started to respond.

Then Steven turned around at the sound of someone running up to him from behind. "Over here! I'm an American. My name is Mark Roth. Do you know where we are?"

Steven said, "I don't know. One minute I was running at the high school, and the next minute I remember waking up here. I don't understand what is going on because these people are definitely not from Kansas."

A puzzled Mark reacted to Steven, "What do you mean, Kansas? We're not in Phoenix anymore? I was hiking down Camelback Mountain trying to finish before it got dark. How long was I out?"

Steven just looked around the room as he replied, "I just don't know. I just don't know anything."

Soon others gathered with them, including Marcus Latterri, a drill sergeant from Fort McClellan, Alabama; Tim Parks, a construction worker from Chicago with well-defined muscles; Matt Schaeffer, a national-caliber long distance runner and Rhodes Scholar from Portland; Cynthia Moss, a dancer touring with the Philadelphia Dance Troop; and Janet Livingston, an aerobics instructor from Charlotte, North Carolina. Before long, even more people were gathered with them as the room full of people started to congregate into groups of people who were able to communicate with each other at least somewhat. In each group, the people were relieved they could talk to each other, but they looked frightened that they could not figure out why they were there. Many of the people were bilingual and started to communicate with other groups as they tried to get information. One such person, Gabriel Peters, volunteered, "I am multilingual. I can go around the room to gather any information I can get," then walked off quickly to do so.

Many of the groups even divided into subgroups, such the English-speaking group, which held Americans, Canadians, Australians, and people from the United Kingdom. Everyone shoved and pushed their way towards their countrymen. As people made their way, Steven got knocked to the ground, and the person who hit him reached down to help him up.

"I'm sorry. Let me help you up. Can you please tell me if someone is playing a joke on me?"

Steven replied, "Hi, I'm Steven. I hope this is a joke because I have this bad feeling this is no joke."

Then Mark, who also helped Steven up, looked at the man and said, "I am Mark. Aren't you D'Shawn Williams? You play wide receiver for the San Diego Chargers and almost set the single-season reception record last year in your rookie year!"

D'Shawn just shook his head, looking around the room. "I hope this shit doesn't make me miss practice because my coach is a ballbuster."

Mark said, "I hope you make practice, and we all get out of here." Eventually the three just stood there as they looked at other people who passed them by with looks of anger, nervousness, and confusion.

Noticing that the group was totally disorganized, Matt Schaeffer, who had been a natural leader most of his life after being a class president and captain of the track teams through school, spoke up: "Does anyone know how we got here, other than there was a bright light and then you woke up here?"

People shook their heads or said no.

"Does anyone else have motion sickness?"

Many indicated yes.

"Then maybe we're on some kind of boat," he suggested, and some people agreed.

Steven asked, "How many of us are there?"

"Good question," said Matt. "Can anyone make a count?"

Marcus Latterri, a former drill sergeant, volunteered to do it. When he was done, he yelled, "There are 149 people in our English-speaking group."

"Good, that was great," Matt said to Marcus. He asked the group, "Is there anyone who is bilingual so we can communicate with the other groups?" A few hands came up, and Matt sent them off to the other groups to find out what they could.

Three hours later, Marcus called everyone over and said, "Gabriel was good enough to gather some information. He has spoken to the other groups, and this is what we have so far. First, no one has any idea why we are here. Second, there does not seem to be any door to get in or out. But whoever put us here got us in here somehow. Third, after questioning everyone to see what we might have in common, there seems to be no common denominator other than most are in good physical shape. There are athletes, bodybuilders, outdoorsmen, and fitness instructors. No one knows the reason for that. Also, there are 552 people trapped here, with ages that range between 19 and 27. But none of this means anything until someone comes out to tell why they put us here."

Steven asked, "Does anyone know what kind of room this is?"

Matt replied, "As you can see, the floor and the walls are very smooth with a metal I have not seen before. We think this rules out this being an oil tanker. There are what look like animal troughs in each corner, but this does not look like a place to store livestock. The center of the room has an area that looks like a large drain, but when you look into it there is a green liquid about two feet down. The whole room is completely clean, so maybe it is used for transporting animals for medical purposes, but no one is sure. We began having some people tap on the walls to see if we get some sort of a reaction. So stay put, and we will let you know if we hear anything."

D'Shawn sat along one of the walls with Steven, Gabriel, and Mark while the four looked around. D'Shawn shook his head and said, "I don't know what the story is for you guys, but I signed a large, long-term contract for a lot of money. These kidnappers are holding me for my money. This has got to be about money. Right now they are contacting my family and team to secure a large ransom."

"That makes sense for you, but it does not explain why they would want me. I'm not worth anything. My family just barely gets by off our dairy farm," Steven said.

Mark speculated, "Since I'm not anywhere near being wealthy, either, I'm confused, too. Maybe we're being ransomed as a whole, and the United Nations or our country is being forced to pay up?"

As soon as Mark stopped speaking, the wall they were leaning on started very lightly to vibrate.

"Something is happening!" Steven yelled.

Everyone in the room stood up as the vibration intensified, all looking around the room for the source of the vibration. As people pulled back in their groups, Cynthia screamed out, "The room is getting bigger!" She pointed to the ceiling.

Many felt their heartbeats accelerate with fear and anxiety. Some panicked, some tried to hide, and some ran, but there was nowhere to go. The relief that they would find out why they were there was overwhelmed by the fear.

Noticing how frightened everyone was starting to get, Gabriel offered, "Listen, I know that everyone is scared, but we should not let our fear overtake us! My father would always tell me that fear is like a disease, that if you let it, it can devour your whole body and render you hopeless. But if you fight the fear, then you have a better chance to overcome what frightens you. I always trust what my father said."

Very slowly, the ceiling rose, and they were able to see a walkway above the room that resembled a guard's walkway above a prison yard. The walkway had dim silhouettes of people guarding them that went around the whole room even as the ceiling was still rising. When the ceiling with the lighting fixtures embedded in it reached the top, the walkway lit up. The silhouettes were not Somali pirates or Columbian drug lords or any potential kidnapper anyone thought would be standing there. No, they were different.

Steven stood there looking up at beings he would never have expected to see anywhere but a Hollywood science-fiction movie. They were holding what looked like large floodlights. He quickly noticed that very few of them were similar. Some had long necks, while others had short arms. Some had large foreheads with scaly skin, and some had dark curly hair covering most of their exposed body with eyes set deeply in their heads. Many in the room started to scream and frantically searched for a place furthest away from the creatures on the walkway. Bedlam ensued as some people ran and screamed, while others stood there frozen in total disbelief.

As people frantically fought to find a place to hide in this room without any place to hide, in walked beings they all recognized but couldn't believe were standing above them. These were beings they had seen almost every day for the last three and a half years in the newspapers, on television, and the Internet. There had been magazine stories with in-depth descriptions and 3D models. Now, right in front of them, were live Ancient Visitors. They had last been seen alive way back in man's ancient past. The two fossilized beings had been buried over two hundred thousand years ago in Ethiopia. When people thought about them they thought of about dinosaurs and woolly mammoths, something from the distant past. But now there they were standing and peering down at them.

They had large heads, but their eyes looked disproportionably large with sunken ears and noses. The color of their skin was gray with a hint of green. A fabric that looked like suede covered their bodies and long limbs. Each had a different style, unlike in the movies, where all the aliens were naked or wearing the same outfit. Each of them had subtle differences in their physical features and in some cases major differences in how they maneuvered their facial muscles. Their heights and body shapes were each slightly different, while some looked stronger and others looked quicker.

The one that seemed in the lead signaled over to the beings holding the floodlights and guarding the people below as if to begin something. Some of the guards had a strap with some sort of electronics around their necks or a harness, while others had the same type of strap around their torso. The moment they were signaled, some of the electronics started to glow, and then the guards let out a roar as if they were in pain. Many captives screamed while others frantically ran through the sea of people, not knowing what the creatures' intentions were.

Cynthia Moss and Janet Livingston joined Mark, Steven, and D'Shawn, and they tried to form a defensive circle as they looked up the wall at the creatures that surrounded them. Then the guards on the wall manning the large floodlights turned them on, all twenty of them. Out came a light aimed at one of the people on the floor, but the light seemed strange, the light stream denser than a beam from a flashlight.

The first person the light was aimed at started to scream, and her body started to twitch uncontrollably as the people around her ran away in fear. Soon the other guards manning the large lights targeted other people. The first person targeted began to rise off the ground, still twitching, and was lifted high in the air over the guard walk. She was then handed off to two guards with smaller devices hanging over their shoulders. They took her, still floating in the air, into one of the two large openings up above. People on the ground heard her scream as she disappeared into the opening, and multicolored lights shot out in all directions.

As the guards went around the room capturing people, Mark, Steven, D'Shawn, Cynthia, and Janet tightened their circle as the guards moved closer to where their group stood. Mark yelled out, "Maybe if we hook arms they can't pick up all of us at the same time."

The five grabbed hold of each other as tightly as they could. Janet screamed, "What the hell are they doing with us?" as one of the guards took aim at them. The guard grabbed hold of Mark, but they were still holding on to each other. All the guard could do was pull them up about ten feet in the air before he lowered them.

Mark, Steven, D'Shawn, Cynthia, and Janet enjoyed a small victory and briefly felt the elation of a catch for a first down or a wrestler's winning a point or a basketball player's making a basket to tie the game, and it was all just as short-lived as the guard reached into his pocket for what looked like a ball and threw it at Mark. The ball flew through the air, and as it got closer to Mark it started to glow bright orange and emit sparks. It hit Mark directly in the chest, and he went down as if all the life in his body had disappeared. This broke the circle, and a couple of the guards aimed at the rest of the group.

Steven was still locked with D'Shawn's arm as he was pulled in the air, and then another guard captured D'Shawn as he was falling to the floor. Steven tried to reach again for D'Shawn, but he could not reach out. All he could feel was all his muscles twitching uncontrollably. He remembered what it felt like when he hurt his back during a wrestling match and the trainer working on him used an electrical stimulation device. This had the same feeling, except he was experiencing it all over his body.

He was lifted over the guards' walkway where two creatures that looked more like the monsters in a computer game than someone he would come face-to-face with brought him in through the large opening into another room. Inside were containers the size of bathtubs, lined up in rows. Steven saw that there were hundreds of them. Each had tubes and some sort of electronics around the sides. As he was being moved to a tub, he noticed the others being set into theirs.

People were struggling and screaming as the guards and the aliens who had visited Earth before submerged them into a blue gel or some sort of thick liquid. Once they were submerged in the tub, the gel emitted multi-colored lights before the aliens moved onto the next tub. Steven then realized the guards had stopped moving, and he was being placed in a tub fully clothed. He felt a cool sensation with pins and needles throughout his body pulsating harder and harder. He feared this might be some sort of food processor to prepare him for the Ancient Visitors.

As his head was about to be pushed into the blue gel, Steven was terrified, and he thought about his family, his friends, but especially Brenda. He would give anything to see her again, even if it were for only a moment. Steven vainly tried to struggle as the gel slowly entered his nose and mouth. He then felt nothing and slowly drifted into unconsciousness.

As he awoke, he slowly gained awareness that he was still alive and opened his eyes. At first, he could only see blurs. He tried to get up and couldn't because he was dizzy. Soon, someone was kneeling over him asking, "Are you OK? You're Steven, right?"

Steven looked at him and recognized him as one of the first Americans he had met in the strange room. "I remember you. You're Tim. Where are we?"

Tim replied, "It looks like we are back in the room with the guards still looking over us. You are not going to believe this, but by my digital watch, they had us in that goop for six weeks."

Then Steven heard a huffing D'Shawn say, "Oh, good. They didn't eat me."

Then Steven noticed who was not there. "Where is Mark? Mark, where are you?" he yelled out. When there was no answer he got up to look for him, and when he couldn't find him, Steven went to Matt. "Mark Roth is not here," he said.

Matt looked at him with worried eyes. "Yeah, I have not seen Gabriel Peters either. From what I'm hearing, many of our people are still missing. Not only us, but also the other groups as well. Some of them were injured while frantically avoiding that tractor beam or whatever it was. So maybe they are being cared for and are receiving medical help. Well, that's what we hope."

Disappointed and worried about Mark, Steven started walking back when one of the walls started to glow dark green. In the center of the wall, an opening appeared where there had been no door or even a seam in the wall. Out walked one of the Ancient Visitors with two guards behind it. The Ancient Visitor walked through the crowd of people, who were still dizzy and weak from their ordeal in the tubs, then over to one of the troughs in the corner of the room.

The alien was an imposing creature standing about six foot five. Close up, the clothes he was wearing were not too different from what a man would wear. He had on a collarless long-sleeved shirt with a pair of slacks. What was different was the large wristband containing a screen and buttons that he wore on his wrist.

The alien then pushed one of the buttons, and a paste came out of a large faucet that fell into the trough. The alien then spoke, but Steven could not understand what it said. All he noticed was that the alien spoke in a high rate of speed, and Steven thought that even if he could understand its language that he could not keep up with its quick pace. The Ancient Visitor then picked up some of the paste in his long fingers and put it in its mouth as if to show that it was all right to eat. When he was finished, he waved his hand as if to say, "Eat up." Then he walked out the way he had come in, guards following.

Nobody even thought of eating the paste at first, but when a couple of days had gone by, hunger led people from every group to eventually venture over to the trough. In the one near Steven, Janet Livingston could not stand the hunger any longer and picked up the paste-like substance. She smelled it, but it had no good or bad smell to it. Then as if she were downing a harsh shot of whiskey, she swallowed a small piece.

A very hungry D'Shawn quizzed her, "What's it taste like?"

She replied, "For the most part, tasteless." When after a few hours they did not see any adverse reaction Janet might have had to eating this food-like substance, they all grabbed a handful for themselves.

"Even though it doesn't taste like Mom's cooking, it feels good to finally get something in my stomach," said Steven.

"Hopefully it doesn't kill us," said Tim apprehensively.

"Oh, this tastes like shit. I was in Chicago last week for a game, and some of us went out to Morton's Steak House for some fine pieces of beef. This shit is on the opposite side of the universe," said D'Shawn.

Days passed, then weeks, and many of the people were just sitting around bored but happy still to be alive. Today, however, there were more guards than normal on the walkway. Soon, they started manning the large floodlight-like devices that lifted the people out of the room as before. One by one, they were lifting people in the air, then handing them off to be brought to the tubs. Though many were still resistant, the melee that occurred the first time did not happen again. Many were tired and weak or had lost hope of going home.

Steven was brought up to the same cylinder he had been placed in the last time. The last thing he thought was that the Ancient Visitor had smirked at him as he was submerged in the blue gel. It was something he had not noticed before, and he had no idea why he took notice now. It was the last thing he remembered.

Again, Steven felt himself coming to, and he felt the warmth on one side of his face. He then felt a slight breeze move his short hair, and he could smell vegetation and soil. When his eyes began to clear up, he realized he was outside, lying on dirt in a large field. He thought that finally they had been let out, but where? Are we on Earth or some other place?

As others woke up, many started to yell out in joy.

Confused, D'Shawn asked Steven, "Where are we now?"

"I'm not sure, but at least we are outside and not confined in that room," said Steven, elated. The place where they woke up was a somewhat barren, dusty place with scattered vegetation and rocky mountain terrain in the distance. They had to shield their eyes each time the wind kicked up the dust. Then word came through one of the other groups that they were in Africa.

Realizing they couldn't stay there because they did not have food or water, they all got up, all four hundred and six of them, and started heading east, led by Matt. Soon they came across a small village to ask for help. The first person they met was a local villager who looked at them strangely and directed them to a Red Cross jeep where some medical personnel were doing checkups on the locals.

Matt ran up to the two individuals to ask, "Do any of you understand me?"

"I do," said one of them, a woman with an English accent.

Matt said, "Good. That's great. We all were kidnapped, then tested on, and then left here. Can you help us?"

The woman pulled out a device the size of a cell phone and placed it on the hood of the all-terrain vehicle. Up came a projected screen above the phone where the woman moved objects on her virtual desktop and clicked an icon that brought up a visual of an operator.

While she was contacting the authorities to get them help, Steven said to Tim, "That's weird. I don't remember technology like that on a phone."

Tim was just standing there looking shocked.

Steven said, "I know; it's amazing."

Tim was just shaking his head. "I don't care about the phone. I just looked at my digital watch, and I thought we were imprisoned almost eight weeks, but my watch says it is almost two years later. I can't believe it. How long did they keep us in those tubs?"

As the two locals went to get help, Tim and Steven were confused about how long they had been gone. Later, they would learn that it had been even longer than Tim's watch said. The two years' time frame was relevant to them, but not to the people they had left back on Earth.

Steven said, "That can't be. It felt like we were gone for just a few weeks."

Steven and the four hundred and four other people who had been with him on the ship would have to get accustomed to the fact that they had not been gone six weeks or two years, but seven years. They were subject to relativity, whereby objects traveling near light speed in low gravity move slower in time. While they had been traveling, they had aged at a slower pace than the people on Earth.

Three weeks after his return from Africa, Steven was being driven home. He could see the long driveway to his parents' dairy farm. He still couldn't believe he had been gone so long. He kept saying to himself, "Gone seven years, but it felt like weeks."

The government had kept him in a hospital for three weeks testing him, though for what, he didn't know. He had spoken briefly to his dad two days before to let him know that he was fine and that it was really he. Driving up to the house, Steven could only think how happy he was to be home with his family and friends because he had thought he would never see them again. He was especially interested in seeing Brenda, but when he mentioned it, Dad kind of changed the subject.

When the government car reached the house, he saw all his family and friends rush out from the house, which had banners hanging to welcome him home. Even though psychiatrists at the hospital had explained that the people he knew would be older, it didn't really hit him until he saw them in person. He did recognize his mother as she pushed her way through the crowd of people to get to him, but when he looked, he didn't see Brenda anywhere.

Eva saw the government vehicle drive up to the house, and she could not control herself and rushed the car to open the door. Steven was barely able to stand when she hugged him and sobbed uncontrollably. She bawled, "I've got my boy back. I really got him back."

His father then grabbed him. "Welcome home, Steven." His father then turned to show Steven two young men who had been fifteen and ten when he was taken, but were now twenty-two and seventeen. "Do you remember these guys?" he asked.

"Tommy? And is that you, Johnny?" Steven asked, as he couldn't believe his eyes. In his mind, he had only left them weeks ago, and now it turned out to be seven years, a fact that he couldn't seem to comprehend. In any event, standing in front of him were his brothers. He was very happy to see them, and he couldn't believe that he had missed so much of their growing up.

Throughout the rest of the day, people who from his point of view he had just seen looked older and spoke to him as if they had not seen him in a long time.

He also noticed that they and his family were looking at him a little strangely. He thought that it was because he had been gone for so long from their point of view. In fact, everyone there was looking at him differently because he was different from how they remembered, and they thought it was odd.

Through all the commotion, there was still one person he wanted to see the most, and when everyone who had come to see him went home, Steven asked his mother, "Mom, when can I see Brenda? How come she is not here?"

With tears in her eyes she said, "I just spoke to her, and she will be here in a few minutes. Um, I want to say that she -- we all thought you were gone." Tears rolled down her face when she said, "Some moved on," because she knew the pain her son was about to have. When the car arrived, she did not have the strength to witness Steven's seeing Brenda, and she scuttled into her house.

As he waited the few minutes, he wondered what she meant by "moved on."

Steven saw the car pull up, and in his excitement to see Brenda at last, he ran down the driveway to meet the car halfway. His heart was pounding as he recognized her parents, who got out to open a back passenger door. The whole time they did not pick their heads up to have eye contact with him. They helped a woman out of the car and brought her over to him.

Steven was expecting to see the girl he remembered growing up through high school and college. He remembered she had long blond hair and hazel eyes that he could gaze into all day. All the time they were dating, she was very skinny, and her parents were worried she was too thin. The last time he saw her, they were heading to class on campus and planning to go to a dorm party over the weekend.

But to Steven's surprise, Brenda's parents were holding a woman who was about eight months pregnant with short hair and wearing engagement and wedding rings on her left hand. Inside the car were two small children and a silhouette of a man. Even though her face was different, he knew it was she because as he looked at her eyes he just knew.

"Oh, Steven," she said as she put her arms around him. "I am so, so sorry. I thought you were dead. I thought I was never going to see you again," she said as tears streamed down her face. "I didn't want to give up, but years passed by, and I thought waiting any longer would be fruitless. So, I moved on."

"Oh, Brenda," said a bewildered Steven. "I feel this is a nightmare I can't get out of. One moment I thought my life was set and I knew what my future held, and now I don't know. I'm so confused."

"I know you are," she said, trying to console Steven. She had always been there for him, and he for her, but these were extraordinary circumstances. She knew he was hurting, and she felt powerless to help. All she could do was to say, "Steven, I am so sorry. I'm sorry. I'm so, so sorry."

Sensing that Brenda's legs were weakening, her father worried for the baby, grabbed her, and took her back to the car as she started to cry hysterically.

Her mother said, "We are so sorry. You take care."

Steven just stood there as they helped Brenda into the backseat, and then seated themselves and drove away.

Her father backed the car out of the driveway with Brenda's husband and children in the back of the car, consoling her. Her mother looked intently at Steven as he put his hand over his face to hide his sadness.

She wondered, "What the hell did they do to that poor boy? I feel so heartbroken and --"

Her father cut in, "I don't know why the government let these people out so soon to see their families. How can they be really sure it is really them or copies of them or an alien in a Steven costume?"

With Brenda crying uncontrollably in the back seat, he asked, "Did you see him? He was different. He was taller than I remember, and did you see his head? It was definitely much bigger than I remember. And did you hear how fast he was speaking? This is wrong, honey. I say we keep Brenda away, far away."

What Brenda's parents noticed was what Steven's family and friends would notice as well. Steven had changed physically. But what he changed into and why still remained a mystery.

Chapter 4

"Hey dear, it's time to get up. You don't want to be late, do you?" his wife of nineteen years said. "Why do we have to do this every Sunday morning? You know there'll be no service if you're not there!"

He reluctantly picked his head off his pillow. "I'm getting up, dear. Just give me a few minutes," he said, putting his head back on the pillow. After being nudged by her again, he slowly raised his stiff body out of bed and headed for the shower. As he entered the bathroom, the light automatically came on as it should, but this morning an electronic voice said, "Lighting fixture down to 5%."

He thought, Oh, great. I have to change the bulb or whatever they call that now. Once in the bathroom, he said, "Shower on to 95 degrees," and the water came on. He added, "Sink on to 105 degrees." As he began shaving, the five-inch television screen in the right hand corner of the mirror turned on. "CNN," he directed it.

The CNN anchor said, "Our top story, as it has been for the last few weeks, is the Ancient Visitors' return of the abducted. Dr. Beth Summers is here today to discuss what many are saying is proof of alien intervention in our evolutionary development. Good morning, Dr. Summers."

"Good morning to you too," she said. " James Connor's discovery over ten years ago and now the releasing of these altered captives give credence to what some in the scientific community have said since the alien craft discovery: that there may have been an extraterrestrial hand in our evolution. The Ancient Visitors have clearly done what we thought God had done to us. There was no Adam, nor was there an Eve. There were just Ancient Visitors, tinkering with our development."

"MSNBC," he said.

"Today the Ethiopian government has announced that bidding on more of the alien technology will start, beginning at one hundred billion dollars for each item. Some of the technology being licensed includes the anti-gravity landing system and the video system that can view items millions of miles away. So far, only one-third of the ship has been procured by some of the richest corporations and countries. Much of the craft is still being studied by teams of scientists to find out exactly what some of the functions are. Rumor has it that when it is all said and done, the total net worth of the craft will be ten trillion dollars. This has been a revenue gold mine for the Ethiopian government, at one time one of the poorest nations on the planet, now among the richest."

"Let's try Fox News," he said, starting to get irritated.

"We've just gotten word that the Syrian-Iranian Alliance has now deemed the returned captives an abomination of God's work, and any former alien captives in their territory will be arrested and put on trial. Their borders have been sealed, and anyone with features like the returned captives will be held. They plan to --"

"Ah, TV off," he said.

When his shower was done, he got dressed and came down the stairs of his modest home to the breakfast his wife had made for him. He sat down to eat it while his kids were in the living room playing their virtual reality games.

Before he got to take his first bite, he heard his neighbor's child knock on the door and ask, "Reverend Robinson, can I come in and play with Susie?"

He turned and said nonchalantly, "Sure, but only for a little while, because we have services today." He let the child in and thought how strange it was being called a reverend now. Things had changed for him and his congregation. Because donations were so low at his church, he had stopped taking a salary. So for the past five years, he worked at a local print shop. There at the shop he was just known as Charles, and he was just one of the guys. At church, though, he liked to be called Pastor

Charles.

He went about his business like any other person in the neighborhood who needed to provide for his family. At one time he was a pillar of the community, and the community appreciated what he did for it. He remembered coming to his church for the first time as a young minister looking to do his part to help grow the congregation. They loved his fire and brimstone approach to preaching so much that when the pastor retired he was quickly promoted to the position.

But times had changed, and he didn't fill the church as much as he had before the discovery of alien intervention to the dominant life on this world.

"Will you stop feeling sorry for yourself and finish eating? I know that look on your face," said his wife, who had noticed over time that he was disappointed in how things turned out. She remembered how passionate he used to be when he gave his sermons. The first time she saw him up at the podium, she fell in love with him because his sermons inspired her to be passionate as well. She had felt as if he had lit a fire in her soul that ignited a passion for God's love. Now she saw the pain he was feeling in his heart, and it was crushing her. She tried to be strong and encouraged him to get to up to lead the service as he had for so many years before, though she did this in her own way.

"Do I have to kick you in your big reverend butt to get you moving?"

"You scared the devil out of me, woman," he said sarcastically as he finished up and decided he had better head off to church before she actually did kick him.

Pastor Charles walked out his doors and said, "Lock, and we are all out."

The computer's voice acknowledged, "Locked," and the house went into unoccupied mode. The car opened the doors as soon as the car recognized the family members' approach.

Once the whole family was in, the doors shut, and a voice prompted, "Destination, please?"

His wife cut off Pastor Charles before he was able to speak. "It's Sunday, you dumb old car. Take us to the First Congregation Church."

It replied, "Destination the First Congregation Church; estimated time to destination fourteen minutes." Then without Pastor Charles' even touching any instrument in the car, it pulled out from his driveway and drove to the church.

As the vehicle made its way, Pastor Charles looked at the car and thought that if the Ancient Visitors had given them advanced technology like what was powering this car, it would have been just fine. He appreciated the fact that now all the automobiles on the planet ran on power engineered from the Ancient Visitors' ships and that this had done wonders for the environment. Not only cars, but also homes and factories had been environmentally transformed to help make the air people breathed much more pleasing to all life on the planet. The fact that they had come to Earth and perhaps influenced human development, however, had made people rethink their belief in God. It had made people doubt, and Pastor Charles, like many in religious communities, was not prepared to answer their questions adequately.

As he was pulling into the parking lot, Pastor Charles remembered the first time he had come to the First Congregation Church. He was from Tampa, Florida, and had not been up to Charlotte before. He was so happy the church's elders picked him out of the many who applied to be the assistant pastor. When he pulled up to the church he had to wait in line and was barely able to get a parking spot, but what really surprised him was that he was very early. When he got out of his car he could hear the choir warming up and could see some of the ladies setting up the table outside for a pie sale. He remembered smelling the many pies as he walked by. That Sunday, like every Sunday back then, everyone was in their best Sunday outfits, and mothers were yelling at their kids playing on the grass not to stain their clothes.

When someone noticed he was the new assistant pastor, he was rushed by the crowd and given the warmest welcome he had ever received. When the esteemed Reverend Duford opened the large, brightly stained doors of the finely manicured building and grounds, a sea of people poured into the tall white church.

When he went inside next to Reverend Duford, he heard someone yell out, "Halleluiah," when the Reverend said, "Let's begin." It was a celebration like he'd never seen, and what amazed him was that this was not a special day; it was just an ordinary Sunday. This was long before evidence of the Alien Visitors and what they might have done.

Now, he arrived a few minutes before the service to see that the parking lot was as empty as it had been for a while. He had his choice of spots in the lot that now featured many potholes. The grounds got mowed every few weeks when Pastor Charles had the time to get up there, but he hadn't made it up in a while. The bushes around the building were overgrown, and some were dying or had long died off. The church was still somewhat white, except for some black mold along the top. The Sunday school out back had cracks in some of the windows and a lock and metal chain on the doors. When he climbed the three steps to the large, dull doors, he did not have to push through a big crowd to get to the pulpit. There were only about the same ten people he had seen for months now, and three of them were his family members. This morning was a little different, as Mrs. Barnwell had brought along her granddaughter.

The little girl said, "Good morning, Reverend."

He responded with his best face, "Good morning to you too, and what is your name?"

The girl answered, "My name is Sha'nay Barnwell, and Grandma said we came here to be with God our Father."

He looked down at her and said, "Because you are here, I am sure

He will be among us today."

Inside, he walked over to the podium to see, not standing room only, but a few elderly people still holding on to their faith. There was no choir next to him to praise Halleluiah during his speeches. No, there was none of that. The fire had burned to embers and there was no brimstone to be seen. There was no need to turn on the microphone for this crowd of ten plus the young girl gathered near him. His sermon was low key, as it had been for the longest time now. Gone was his passion, and he knew it.

His wife knew it too, but she had hope that he would find his way again. She couldn't bear to see the man who inspired her love because of his enthusiasm for God's work just disappear into the abyss. She put on a strong face, but she was scared of what this was doing to him. Seeing him walk to the podium, she saw a man who was lost and broken. She remembered a man who had been good at helping other people who were lost to find their way.

When he was done with the service she told him, "Why don't you go around back and sit on one of the benches so you can enjoy this beautiful Sunday? It's sunny with not a cloud in the sky, so you go enjoy. Don't you worry about a thing; the children and I will clean up here. You go relax."

Off he went, moping like a child who had missed the ice cream truck.

Out in the back of the church, Pastor Charles sat on the only bench still intact. The other benches had been broken by neighborhood kids, who used them to do tricks with their electronic skateboards. The one he was sitting on was not much better, for it needed a good sanding to get rid of the splinters and a nice coat of paint to cover the graffiti all over it. While sitting there, he remembered how many of the women after the service used to sit here all dressed up while their children played on the green and lush lawn. They would speak about their work, their children, their men, what was going on in their neighborhood, or even what they wore to church that Sunday. The small children would be running around playing tag, or someone might have brought a ball to kick around. The older children would be in Sunday school, which was filled with teachers and children. The fathers would be on one of the softball fields getting their trousers dirty or hanging out underneath one of the trees talking about sports, politics, or their women. Church elders would be in the church hall talking budgets and church activities. After the school let out, many of the families would stay and have a picnic.

It was an all-day affair, and Pastor Charles thought, "We were a community."

That was before the discovery ten years ago of visitors from another world, who came here and somehow influenced humanity's ancestors. How much? Pastor Charles didn't know, but he had been called on to answer a lot of questions. He was asked, "Did aliens make us? Was God the father an Ancient Visitor? Was the Christmas star a spaceship? Do we need a strong radio to speak to God in space? Was Jesus an illegal alien?"

These were questions he had never anticipated getting, questions he believed now he was poorly equipped to answer. It was bad enough that he had had to answer questions about evolution prior to the discovery or about how the stories in the Bible did not match up to scientific discoveries made about ancient man. He never imagined that he would need to explain how extraterrestrials would fit in the Bible.

Over time, the congregation shrank because many felt that their questions were not getting answered. Doubt crept into the community like a virus, and it slowly choked the atmosphere of trust this congregation had enjoyed for so long. Pastor Charles fought a losing battle because the flow of information from twenty-four-hour news, the Discovery Channel, the Internet, books, and online social networks was too much for him to combat.

One day there was a revelation regarding alien technology, and the next day James Connor's new book explained that the alien discovery was evidence that aliens were responsible for many events in the Bible. It was a tidal wave of information and misinformation that confused the masses and made them question and rethink many of their beliefs. Most people stopped going to church, and Pastor Charles saw his congregation slowly disappear.

When it was learned that the aliens had returned some of the people they had captured, the congregation almost vanished when it was learned that they were physically altered. People stayed home waiting to see if the Ancient Visitors were coming to take them, while others just simply lost their faith. Pastor Charles was not just sitting idly by during this time. He diligently went to church conferences, read all the recent Christian books and Christian articles for their take on the visitors. He also joined social networks on the Internet whose members were other Christian clergy of many denominations, and he even approached preachers of other religions to hear their views. What he realized the most was that he was not the only one confused and unprepared for these extraordinary times. The belief in God had almost become as extinct as the ancient species of man buried for so long.

One of the effects of the low turnout of worshippers was that many of the charities the church had supported over the years had suffered. No more were collection baskets passed among the crowds to be filled with money for the poor. Pastor Charles felt bad when he had to tell his charities that money would not be coming. He was upset because the charities did such good work helping the needy. It pained him to think that the children his charities had fed would now go hungry.

Now there were only small pockets of worshipers around the world. Word had it that they were trying to organize, but Pastor Charles had resisted joining them because many of them were what he called the fringe element of religion. Their call for drastic means to win back the worshipers was not his cup of tea. He knew their group's name was the Followers of Divinity. Charles did not agree with the methods suggested and just avoided contact with them on the social blogs. He figured that this crazy group, like all crazy groups, would just fade away as people learned more about them.

Now he felt helpless sitting on this old bench looking out where there had been a community celebrating every Sunday. All he saw was empty benches and picnic tables, no one standing under the trees or playing on the ball fields. There were no groups of children getting their Sunday best dirty or anxious Sunday school children chomping at the bit to join the fun. Not now because the school and the church were empty, the grass that was still alive was a mess, and the area for the softball field had been sold off a few years back to help pay the bills.

Even more discouraged than before, Pastor Charles put his head down into his hands and prayed, "Lord, please help me. I don't know what to do. I am sorry I have failed you and let my flock go away. Please show me the way out of this darkness. Can you please give me a sign, any sign?"

He then broke down, crying into his hands as he had every Sunday for the last few years now.

Moments later he felt a presence next to him on the bench. It was Sha'nay, Mrs. Barnwell's granddaughter, and she asked in a concerned tone as he pulled out his handkerchief to wipe his eyes, "Why are you upset, Reverend? It is such a beautiful day. You should be happy."

He took a deep breath, and though reluctant, looked at her to say, "Well, Sha'nay, I'm sad that my church at one time was full of people praising the Lord, but today we only have a few. I feel like the shepherd who lost his sheep, and I don't know how to get them back." So he gave her a sad smile while asking her, "So, Sha'nay, what would you do if you were me?"

She thought for a few seconds with her eyes squinting and said,

"Well, if I lost something, I would go out to look for it." She thought some more and asked, "What would God do when He had nobody at His church? Whenever I have a question about what I should do and I ask Grandma, she always tells me to do what the Lord would do."

Speaking to her brought out a little happiness to counteract his mood.

She continued, "Grandma said that you're not a fisherman if you don't put your line in the water."

He thought about how Jesus started his ministry by going out to the people and said to Sha'nay, "You are a wise little child. How old are you, young lady?

She was quick to reply, "I am eight years old, and I am in third grade."

As he heard her name being called, he said, "I am glad we spoke, and I thank you for your advice. I think your Grandmother is calling you, so you better get along now. I will be all right." Then off she went, but before she was too far away he yelled to her, "Thank you, Sha'nay."

She turned to smile at him and yelled, "You should trust God. Good-bye, Reverend," and then continued to run to her grandmother.

Pastor Charles helped his wife finish shutting down the building, and they left for home. All the way home and through dinner that night he could not get his conversation with that little girl out of his mind. It made him consider that when he got to his church he already had a big congregation, and when membership started to decrease he acted in a defensive mode to keep his flock intact. He had thought about what he was losing and not what he could gain. Could taking his message out to the local people like Jesus did be the way for him to spread the good word? He realized he had gotten lazy just preaching on the church grounds and waiting for people to walk into the church doors. Maybe looking at how the Lord's ministry got started in the first place would help him rebuild the one he was losing.

When he finished his dinner, he muttered under his breath, "Out of the mouths of babes."

His wife asked, "What was that, dear?"

He answered her, "No wonder the Lord said, 'The kingdom of God is for these' when he spoke to his Apostles about the young. They are the innocents."

His confused wife said, "I don't understand what you're getting at."

He got up from the table to help clean up and told her, "I am going to take some good advice, and I'm going to be a better shepherd and trust God's plan."

The next day after work at the print shop, he walked the streets of his community speaking to anyone who would listen to him. He hung out at the barbershops, the tattoo parlors, the coffee houses, the Internet cafés, and any other place he saw people congregating. He did not bring any books or pamphlets or sermons on memory chips, or 3D videos of his sermons on his PDA; he just brought the words from his heart and the clothes on his back. When he met people, he didn't bring his fire and brimstone. He came down from his high horse. He walked with the common people and spoke to them as one of them.

What he most wanted to improve about himself was his ability to really listen. So he let the people he met do all the talking. He heard their concerns, heartaches, pains, and hopes for the future. He was not going to be like the salesman who did all the talking without taking the time to hear his customer's thoughts then wonder why he did not get the sale. He was going to be more like the bartender who quietly listened to the people sitting in front of her. Even though the bartender might not have answers to give, she knew a person's opening up to her sometimes made all the difference. Instead of pushing his values onto the people around him, he started to learn their values and the things that were important to them. He then used that as a foundation upon which to rebuild his church.

He realized that it did not matter that bones of ancient man were uncovered to cast doubts on creation, or that there might be alien intervention in mankind's history, or anything else that could trouble a person's beliefs. Religion was not about that. It was about faith, and faith was not about science. It was about what people believed in their hearts. The girl he met at his church showed him that he was too worried about the faith of his flock when he should have worried about his own and the kind of shepherd he should be. So he continued every night that week talking to as many people as he could talk to, and he listened to them. Each night he walked among the people learning to become a better shepherd for his flock.

The next Sunday, his wife saw a difference in him. He got up early that morning without her urging. He got dressed quickly in his best Sunday service attire. He ate a hearty breakfast and went back for seconds, and got his family up to the church early so he could finish the final preparations for the service. He greeted everyone who walked in the door of the church as if they were a long-lost favorite relative or friend. When he got up to the pulpit he looked down and saw three new faces to the Sunday service. On this Sunday he had a little more fire to his fire and a little more brimstone to his brimstone than he had in a long time, but most of all he had a little more compassion and appreciation for the people who came to hear him preach. When he looked out at the flock he saw a child with an innocent face who taught him that problems don't always need complicated remedies, and sometimes it was the simple remedy that cured the problem.

When the service was over, his wife saw new life in her pastor husband and said to him proudly, "That was an excellent sermon, Pastor Charles. Now, why don't you go sit on your bench, and we will clean up? Go now."

Off he went to the bench he sat on every Sunday, except this Sunday was a little different. The grounds of the church were trimmed a little better than usual because Charles had made an effort to come up the day before to do a little work around the church. He fixed some of those windowpanes that had been broken for so long, and for the next week he purchased some lumber to fix the other two benches along with some paint and stain to make the somewhat white church a little whiter and the front door as nice as it had been in the past. The biggest change there was not the cut grass or the trimmed bushes or the plans to put a little love into the church; it was in Pastor Charles, and he could feel the change. So this morning, instead of putting his face into his hands and crying, he put his face in his hands to give thanks.

As he was giving thanks, he smelled something he had not smelled there at the church for a long time. It smelled like pecan pie, and when he looked up he noticed a little girl sitting next to him saying, "Good morning, Pastor. It is a wonderful day, don't you think?"

As he pulled his hands from his face there were no tears this time, only a smile. He said to her, "Good morning to you, Sha'nay, and yes, it is a wonderful day."

Sitting next to him in her best Sunday attire, she was holding two small plates with slices of pecan pie and said to him, "Grandma got up early to bake this pie. Would you like some?"

With his smile growing larger, he took what was offered to him and said, "I most certainly will take your offer. Pecan pie is my favorite, and I thank you."

The two of them sat there eating the pie, and a few moments later she asked him, "Did you find what you were looking for? Last week you said you lost something."

He then looked at her with appreciation and said, "I most certainly did, and I want to thank you for your insightful wisdom. I hope you come back here to visit us some more."

After finishing the last of her pie she said, "You don't have to worry. Grandma said I could come with her every Sunday for services. You are going to see a lot of me." A teary-eyed and happy Pastor Charles looked down at his slice of pecan pie and thanked God, not for the pie, but for the little girl seated next to him.

The next week and every week after that he went back out among the community to talk and listen to the people.

Chapter 5

This time of the year, it was still pretty cold in Boston, Jennifer thought while she was sitting on a bench outside of the Harvard Science Center. It was late March. There was still snow on the ground, and the people walking by were bundled up. She was waiting for David and James to finally bring over her decaf coffee from Starbucks. Jennifer would have gone with them, but she was not as mobile as she used to be, being eight months pregnant. This was an important meeting, and she didn't want to miss it no matter how much David protested. David thought that he would update Jennifer later, but she wanted to see for herself. Jennifer thought that because she was on the President's Panel for the Study of Alien Influence that it would be important for her at least to make an appearance.

"Sorry for the wait. We stood in line for a while," said David as James trailed him.

"It is hard to imagine with a Starbucks on every corner that we had to stand in line for most of our break," complained James.

"Ah, this will warm me up," said a relieved Jennifer. As she was drinking the coffee she considered that it would have been warmer inside, but the fresh air felt good since they had been locked up now for two days inside the science center. The meeting would be over in the evening, and then she could head back home to Long Island and begin analyzing the results of all the tests and scientific data put forth by the meeting members. Then she could make out her report for the panel.

"So when do you guys find the time to have kids? You spend most of your time on two different continents, for God's sake. How many kids you have now, about a dozen?" asked a playful James to his married friends.

"When we are together, we make sure our time is quality time. And this will only be our second," responded David.

"Well then, that wild little Andy just seems like a lot of kids," joked James.

David said, "If you could stay married long enough, then you might see some of these things for yourself." He was referring to James' recent second marriage to Hollywood sci-fi vixen Janice Shaw. It was a marriage that had lasted about three weeks and was a great source of stories for the tabloid news sites as paparazzi traced their every move.

"We couldn't do a thing without a picture being taken. If we had had a kid, the moment of conception would have been seen on every news site in the world! We did find ten minutes to be alone together, but that was when we realized our quickie marriage was going to be a quickie divorce. Only in Hollywood, right?"

A sympathetic Jennifer said, "You'll find the right person someday when you finally decide to look beyond the surface."

David's screen on his headset popped on to remind him the meeting would start again in ten minutes and they needed to head back into the building. Jennifer then turned to James to say, "I hope this meeting was helpful to you for your new book."

James knew that his two friends had to use their influence to get him access to this important meeting. Some in the scientific community looked upon his books and lectures with disdain for making statements without validating his theories with research. His conclusions as to the influence of the Ancient Visitors were also condemned by the religious establishments for undermining their traditional beliefs by using his vast popularity to promote his view of why people believed in God and how James believed people were really created.

"Yes, and I appreciate all you guys have done for me. I don't get much access anymore. At least, not like I used to," he said. "Whatever goodwill I had being Patrick Connor's son has now dried up."

David interjected, "Well, if you had just looked at the discovery a little more like a scientist and not made statements that were not well researched, and then you could have still been well received. Maybe in the end your ideas will be right, but to get acceptance of your conclusions, you'll need to be published in science journals and have your ideas backed up with solid evidence. Today they look at you as someone who wants to sell books."

James responded, "What are you talking about? We were all in the spacecraft, and you saw what they did to our ancestors."

Then David replied, "I'm not saying you're not right. I am saying you should do it the right way. You should have acted like the scientist you trained to be, by collecting data through observation and experimentation, and then formulated and tested your hypotheses."

Jennifer then injected, "Remember when you found the fossilized finger and tooth? You carefully extracted them from the rock and recorded them. Then back at the camp we prepared them for study. What we are saying is to slow down and make sure your conclusions are right. Sometimes things are not as they first seem."

At that moment an aide to one of the scientists summoned David on his headgear. They walked to the meeting hall that was usually filled with students having a class. Today, the hall was filled with scientists studying the research done on the Ancient Visitors' influence on the human body and what it might mean going forward. Even though much had been debated in the news media on an almost daily basis and experts injected their opinions in a multitude of documentaries on the matter, the scientific community was still trying to understand all the data. They tried to schedule meetings in private so as to avoid the press. The meetings were filled with conjecture from all parts of the scientific community, but they had yet to come to a consensus.

"All right, please settle down so we can finish up and conclude the meeting. So, to recap the last few days --" said the lead scientist.

But James immediately interrupted him as an embarrassed David looked on: "Can I ask a question?"

"Sure," said the reluctant scientist as he looked over at his peers.

James stood to address the room, "How come there is so little research done on alien involvement into our culture? We have thousands of examples of possible contact by these aliens that have touched almost every culture on earth. There are ancient writings describing incredible innovations by our primitive ancestors. They have done things that we today would have a hard time accomplishing or explaining. When will this get attention?"

David sunk down in his seat as the debate turned into a shouting match. While James was disrupting the meeting, David thought of some of the revelations that had come out. There was the revelation that the two remaining cylinders produced two ancient human beings very much alive. There was a female and a male. This new species was given the name Homo kibishensis, or Kibish Man.

The whole thing was a dream come true for an anthropologist like David who had always wondered what he would say if he ever had a chance to meet an ancient individual such as one he hoped to find on a dig. He would now get that chance as he planned to forgo his research at the Kibish site and head to the UCLA Science Institute to begin research on the two subjects with a newly formed research team.

Another revelation came about because the abducted people had been marrying and producing children since their return. The early tests showed that two thirds of their offspring had retained the characteristics their parent had acquired from their enhancement by the Ancient Visitors. One third of them showed no influence.

So the Ancient Visitors had what seemed like a success rate of 66%. It was debated during the meeting that this could explain why there were so many different branches to the human family tree that did not evolve as far as other branches. Also argued was the idea that those branches would eventually die out and become obsolete, as the people enhanced by the aliens would come to dominate the landscape.

David thought about how he was now a member of that part of the family tree that would become obsolete with the emergence of these enhanced people. These people would now look at him like he was going to look at the two Homo Kibishensis individuals he would study at UCLA.

The revelation that sparked James to be so passionate at this meeting was a discovery in central Ethiopia near the Awash River that unearthed a small metallic instrument next to the fossilized remains of an Ardipithecus ramidus, or one of humanity's possible earliest known ancestors. These beings lived four million years earlier than the fossilized individuals of the James' Kibish find. The metallic instrument was made of compounds exactly like the metallic table found with the craft. This attracted James' attention because it supported his opinion that that Ancient Visitors had repeatedly visited Earth and influenced human culture.

As the heated debate went on and James continued to prod the scientists, the lead scientist gave all the people in the room a break to cool down. Outside back at the bench, Jennifer tried to calm down a red-faced James.

"Listen, you are not going to just make them go along with your findings. If your findings do end up being proven correct, then they will of course have no choice but to listen, but there are too many things still unanswered before we in the scientific community can come to an agreement."

"I agree," said David. "More discoveries and more research are needed. The human family tree goes back for seven million years, and we have barely touched the tip of the iceberg. There are seven million years of secrets buried out there, and we have a long way to go to find them to unlock the mysteries of our existence."

A disappointed James took a deep breath and said, "Hey, I know that I don't have all the answers, but there are a lot of unanswered questions our discovery has uncovered. We were there, and I have to say that the experience has been an eye-opener for me. I see the world and the universe in a whole different light now, and I think I have to voice my opinion."

Jennifer then said, "That is the point, James. It is your opinion, and you need to substantiate your thoughts, or you will not be taken seriously by the scientific community."

Then David jumped in, "If you think James is frowned upon by the scientific community, you should see how well received he is by the religious community. He has tried to debunk every aspect of the foundation of almost every religion on Earth. Using the discovery of the spacecraft as proof that God doesn't exist and man has only been manipulated by beings from other worlds, he has made simple folk question their faith. Your conclusions go against everything the religious community believes. It has caused chaos as people try to understand the meaning of God's place in the universe or if there were ever a god in the first place. I think this is dangerous ground on which to pick a fight. There are many scientists who through their own reasoning reject the notion of a supreme being who is responsible for making everything, but they respect the beliefs of others and don't attack their way of life. It is fine if you don't believe, but to make an effort to disprove long-held beliefs can cause a lot of hurt to those strong in their faith."

"All I can say is that the truth will set us free," said James.

"But what is the truth?" asked David.

"You saw it in the ground at Kibish," argued James.

"But I doubt all the answers to our questions about our existence and our place in the universe will be found there," countered David.

"I just got the call to go back inside," said Jennifer, standing heavily on her legs. She continued sarcastically, "You guys can restart this fascinating and never-ending debate at dinner."

"No dinner for me," said James. "I have to catch a flight to make my way to Kibish to speak at a convention there. It will be my first time back at Kibish since the discovery, and I'm looking forward to it."

"Oh, no," said a disappointed Jennifer.

David told James, "You won't recognize the place when you get there, but at least you won't have to sleep in a tent or on an uncomfortable cot."

James said goodbye to them and headed to the airport.

After hours of travel, his plane descended for a landing at the Kibish airport. As the plane got closer to the land, James glanced out the window to see a transformed and expanding city of Kibish. This once dusty and small Ethiopian village was now a bustling city built to cater to the swell of people coming to see the spacecraft and to venture into the hills to find their own discovery. Replacing the small huts were large hotels and casinos with names like Marriott, Hilton, Trump, and Wynn. Right before the landing, he noticed that there were large cranes on the outskirts of the city putting up additional building projects. During the ride to the hotel, he noticed many restaurants and retail stores that lined the paved streets while tourists with shopping bags walked along the sidewalks next to the convention center where he would be giving his speech at the World UFO Society's annual convention.

James thought about how things had changed since he was there over sixteen years ago. Even though he was not interested at the time, he remembered Jennifer's telling David about the strange local customs of the Surma people.

When he looked at the monitor in the auto-piloted electric limo, he saw that one of the hotels was advertising a dinner show of the Surma culture, but these were just actors with fake clay disks, not the actual Surma people. James surmised that the Suma who did not assimilate to the big city environment must have ventured further into the wilderness.

At the hotel, a large crowd of fans seeking autographs greeted James as he stepped out of the limo. It was not as though he could have walked through the lobby unnoticed; his likeness was all over the city, and his speech was widely anticipated. Fans were rushing up to him to have their 3D picture taken with him. He was starting to feel uncomfortable, and he had nowhere to move. Security pushed through the crowd to bring him to his secured suite where a finely dressed woman was waiting for him.

"Hello, Dr. Connor," she said in greeting. "I'm Mackenzie Davis, the event coordinator for the World UFO Society. First off, I want to apologize for our late security detail, and I promise that that will not happen again. We were not prepared for this great a reaction to your first time back to the site of your discovery. The reaction was so intense that you would have thought Elvis or the Beatles had shown up. Anyway, we are glad, Dr. Connor, that you finally made an appearance to one of our conventions here in Kibish, or what we like to call the Las Vegas of Ethiopia."

"I am glad to be here, and I appreciate the invite, but please excuse me. I'm tired from the trip," he said.

She excused herself and left the room, leaving security to guard the door.

After she left, James just laughed to himself as he thought about the reason he had actually come here. It was the cash. The World UFO Society had finally come up with an acceptable speaking fee and made sure he was afforded the best room in the best hotel. These days, James earned some of the largest speaking fees in the world. He had now out-earned celebrities, sports heroes, corporate CEOs, and even former Presidents in making a living speaking to crowds of people. His managers were busy filling in a schedule that was booked for the next four years. Every new revelation added to his discovery increased his fee. He was earning so much now that he had to take a sabbatical from his teaching position at the university because the speaking fees beat the salary he got from the school by a mile. The earnings from speaking circuit improved

James' life style to that of movie stars and the very wealthy. It kept him busy traveling to Europe, Russia, and to Asia for large engagements viewed in person and via 3D video conferencing for the smaller scale settings.

The fame and the wealth he received, he relished. Being a university professor was small by comparison to his much larger life as a well-paid celebrity. He stayed at all the best hotels and vacation spots. He partied with many of the elite, whether they were movies stars or government leaders. He had women at his beck and call if he so chose, and as a matter of fact, they sought him out. It was a good life, he thought as he took a glass of fine brandy over to the balcony.

He looked out in the distance across the Omo River at the rock formations of Omo National Park and the discovery that had changed his life. After his morning lecture, he was going to visit the site for the first time since he had been carried away due to his injuries. It was there that he arrived as the son of a noted anthropologist and left a worldwide celebrity in a changed world, a world he had a large hand in changing.

The next morning, James was standing offstage at the Kibish Convention and Sports Complex waiting to be introduced to the crowd of fifty thousand who wanted to hear him speak about his discovery. Most of the people he would be talking to were UFO enthusiasts, who before the discovery of the spacecraft had been thought of as kooks or nuts. Now that a spacecraft had been found, they were regarded in a better light. Instead of amateur writers, UFO hunters, and unlicensed radio show hosts, there were doctoral students doing dissertations, astronomers with PhDs, and members of the mainstream media. Things had changed in the world's view of UFOs in the last sixteen years, and when people looked to the sky, they wondered who might be looking back and whether the lights or streaks in the sky might be alien spacecraft.

He heard his name introduced and walked out on to the stage to the roar of the crowd. It was a standing ovation from fifty thousand faces jam-packed into the arena. The event was also simulcast throughout the world. He was their most respected emissary and the one who brought the existence of extraterrestrial life to the forefront of mainstream science, whether scientists wanted it or not, and he was the biggest promoter of alien influence on human society. To them he was a rock star, and James savored being adored by them.

This morning they had come to the place of his discovery to hear his description of the events of his finding of the spacecraft. The story he spoke about featured him exclusively, and it was quite different from actual events. Barely mentioned were David and Jennifer or Doctors Ronald Gibbs and Roberto Sanchez, or anyone else on the dig team. He said his reason for being on the trip was not to be near the doctoral student to whom he was attracted, but for the thrill of adventure of unearthing a piece of history. His version of why he was sent to look for other possible dig sites was that the project team leaders utilized his extensive knowledge to hunt for unbelievable finds and not because he was sent away so he wouldn't infect the rest of the team with his bad attitude.

He had done this originally to enhance his brand as the world-renowned alien spacecraft discoverer and improve his earnings potential. Over time, however, he believed in his version more and more as the real account faded from his memory. His popularity was great, and his ego was greater.

This morning's speech was only a prelude to the long week of speeches he would make to his large following. In two days he would make his most anticipated talk, entitled "Alien Influence on Religion." He had new Revelation and conclusions, drawn from the scientific research others did, about the Ancient Visitors and the returned captives. Many of the people who followed him believed he had proved that God did not exist and that humans were a product of an evolution designed by the Ancient Visitors. They thought what he would reveal would help end once and for all, religion's version of history that they believed had been fictional all along.

After a lunch with some of the board members of the World UFO Society and members of the city council, James headed with some of them to the rock formation. The security personnel had to push through the crowd in the hotel lobby to get James and his party into the limousines parked out front. Once they were in the limos, the security police vehicles escorted them out of the city to the Ethiopian National Science Facility built over and next to the craft.

During the ride, James spoke with the Mayor of Kibish. "I have to tell you, this place has changed since the last time I was here. I remember this being a bumpy gravel road in our all-terrain vehicle, and now it is a paved highway."

Mayor Alemu Asfar added, "There was virtually no tourist infrastructure within the park, and there was very little support for travelers to the area, due to the influx of people traveling here. But with projections of the tourist revenue that could be earned, the government invested the funds to improve the infrastructure with the royalties from selling the Ancient Visitors' technologies. We were able to create recreation centers, pave roads throughout the area, and improve communications while investment from major corporations has funded the building of hotels, restaurants, and entertainment facilities. In villages throughout the area, there are Holiday Inns popping up where in the past you needed to bring your own tent and sleeping bag. All of this has been done to increase our capacity to accommodate the deluge of tourists."

Looking out the window, James said, "I am very impressed. You've done wonders and made Kibish into a fine metropolis."

As the limos and security vehicles approached their destination, crowds of people were lining the road to witness James' triumphant return to his discovery that changed the world. Some of his most avid supporters even laid palm leaves across the road as a symbol of another whose return to Jerusalem was enthusiastically anticipated over two thousand years earlier. The symbolism did not get past James and his ego as he departed the limo with his hands raised high and headed slowly into the science center with his large entourage trailing behind him. The extra security at the science center pushed back the crowds as they entered the building.

Once inside, a familiar face approached. "It's good to see you again, James," said the old friend.

James turned to him. "Dr. Sanchez, it is great to see you too. It looks like the place has changed a bit since I was here last."

Dr. Sanchez agreed, "Yes, the Ethiopian National Science Agency has built this large complex around the spacecraft from all the royalties it receives on an annual basis. It was set on pilings to disturb as little of the ground as possible. This facility allows us to study the site and provides a viewing platform for the craft and the fossilized remains we still have here. It is a very popular attraction, and virtually every visitor to Kibish makes the trip over here. While we get our fair share of UFO enthusiasts, many universities from around the world send research teams of their best people to study the site and see what was found."

An impressed James, always cognizant of his place in the scientific community, asked, "So you see some of the best minds come through here?"

"Oh, yeah," replied Dr. Sanchez. "And there is a long waiting list to schedule any research time. The Ethiopian National Science Agency does its best to let in the academia, but they have to share the time with foreign government agencies and large wealthy corporations looking to learn the alien technology. It is through them that they receive large royalties for access to the Ancient Visitor technology."

Dr. Sanchez brought James and his entourage into the site observatory. It was a massive structure covering the location of James' dig site and the spacecraft. "The craft has been completely excavated out of the rock," said James.

"Being it was such an extraordinary find, it took years of painstakingly hard work and research to try to comprehend the extent of the find. We've learned so much, and there is so much still we don't understand," said Dr. Sanchez as James and his party walked around the rotunda surrounding the site. The viewing platform encircled the site with thick protective glass. The rotunda was large enough to house sightseeing visitors and scientific researchers. At the top of the dome was a large window for light during the day and seeing the stars at night. James thought it was an impressive structure and a perfect place for an impromptu news conference.

Following James into the rotunda were selected members of the major news organizations and social network blogs. He called them over to begin his news conference as those organizations came on live to hear what James had to say. With his worldwide audience waiting to listen to him, the many reporters began their introduction.

The CNN news anchor reported, "We are told the James Connor news conference is about to begin, so let's go to our reporter at the site, Megan Armes."

"Good morning," said the reporter. "We are here to witness Dr. James Connor's return to the site of what many consider the greatest archeological finds of all time, proof that the Earth and its people were visited by extraterrestrial beings commonly called the Ancient Visitors. These beings not only visited our ancestors, but also came back to abduct some of our people and make changes to them. Many in the scientific community believe that these visitors from space influenced the development of our species for some unknown reason. So today, Dr. James Connor came back to --"

She was alerted through her earpiece to an incident in Kibish. "Umm…my producer is telling me that there are reports of an explosion

98

in Kibish City." She then moved to a window in the lobby to have the cameraman view the city in the distance. "I can see a plume of smoke...and wait...I see two more. I am wondering if the city is under attack, or maybe this is some kind of natural disaster. I can't tell at this point."

Outside the window of the glass-enclosed lobby were the city in the distance and the highway linking the city to the science center. Coming through the security station was only the usual UPS truck and its usual driver, but it did not turn down the road to the shipping dock at the back of the complex. Instead it headed to the lobby.

The frantic reporter yelled, "Oh my God! It's speeding up, and it's going to hit us!"

Then there was silence on CNN. The hosting anchor called her name, "Megan...Megan...Are you still there?" There was more silence, and then the anchor continued, "It looks like we lost the connection, and I hope she's all right. We will try to reconnect with her. Hold on...now we are getting word that there are reports of other explosions in other cities around the world in what I suspect is a coordinated attack. We will go first to London where we will hear from Dorothy Hines. Dorothy?"

The reporter still looking at her screen on her headset jumped right in. "This is Dorothy Hines reporting. I'm outside the Science Museum in South Kensington, London, where what looks like a bomb has exploded. It has completely destroyed the front of the building, and people are being evacuated through the emergency exits. There are no reports yet of fatalities, but officials are expecting them due to the extent of the blast damage. Fire trucks and emergency vehicles have been fighting the fire and administering to the injured. Also --"

The anchor cut in: "Sorry for the interruption, Dorothy. We will get back to you in a moment. We want to go now to New York, where it is reported that there were multiple explosions at the Museum of Natural History. Our reporter on the scene is Andrea Givens. What can you tell us, Andrea?"

The reporter was standing near the entrance as people rushed out with black smudges on their faces and clothes while first responders raced in behind her. "Many of the people escaping the smoke-filled New York landmark have told us that the floor with the early man exhibit has been virtually destroyed, and fire has spread to the adjacent floors. The other two explosions were in the Hayden planetarium section of the grounds, and fire officials have said the damage was total."

The anchor then asked, "Are there any reported casualties that you know of?"

She replied, "I have heard estimates of fifty dead and hundreds injured, but unfortunately the New York Fire Department officials expect those numbers to grow."

The anchor then said, "Hold on for a second, Andrea. We are now getting video footage of an explosion on Long Island at Stony Brook University. I'm told that the building on fire in the video is of the science department. Well, ladies and gentlemen, it looks like this has been a coordinated, worldwide attack as reports come in from around the world. Now we are told that the President with the National Security Advisor will hold a news conference momentarily to discuss what they know about the events we are now witnessing."

Waiting outside the hallway where the President would pass on the way to the podium and standing with the other scientific advisors, Jennifer frantically tried to call and email David to make sure he was OK. There were reports that the UCLA Science Institute had been hit, and David might have been there when the blast went off. Each moment she was getting more and more anxious to hear from him that he was fine and unhurt. If word had leaked out that the two ancient ancestors were there, the UCLA Science Institute might have become a target. A major concern she had was that the people behind these terrorist activities were not only targeting any science center, but also targeting scientists. David was prominent in the discovery and research of the dig site around the alien spacecraft. He might be on a list of individuals they planned to target, and she was hoping that David was smart enough to hide until these attacks were over.

As the President and the National Security Advisor passed her, her phone rang. "Hey, Jen," she heard the voice on the other end whisper.

She quickly responded to the familiar voice. "Are you OK? I was so worried with all the scientists' being targeted." After a few deep breaths, she continued, "You scared me. I was so afraid for the kids, too."

"I am fine," he said, but he was concerned as well. "Are you and Andy safe?"

A relieved and pregnant Jennifer said, "I am fine. Andy and my mom were secured by the FBI and taken to a secret location."

Also relieved, David said, "That's great." After a few moments of silence to reflect on being grateful his family was all right, he asked, "Who the hell did this? And why would scientists be the reason they would do such a horrendous act?"

She explained, "A group called the Followers of Divinity who believe they are the hand of God has taken responsibility for the attacks. These are not your everyday religious fanatics because this seems to be a multi-religion terrorist group. The White House is releasing to the news organizations the list of demands they sent to all the world's governments as we speak. The group consists of religious zealots made up of Christians, Jews, Muslims, and members of many other religions throughout the world. They are not connected by any one race or political view.

"They blame the intrusion of science for what they believe is their religions' lost memberships. They think that people of science are responsible for the loss of faith of the people in their churches, temples, and mosques. By eliminating scientists and their organizations, they want to eliminate any ideas that conflict with their fundamentalist teachings. They would prefer that we go back to the Stone Age where religion ruled the day. I don't know. It sounds crazy. The worst part is that they worked together, whereas in the past they have fought each other tooth and nail. It makes for a very dangerous situation if the world is engaged in a religious war with an enemy that could be anywhere and willing to die for their beliefs."

"Jen," said David. "I have to get going now. We are bringing the two Homo Kibishensis subjects to a secure location now that they have been sedated for the long travel ahead. The FBI and the local police are going to take us away. I will contact you when I am settled. I love you."

Jennifer replied, "I love you too. Be safe."

As she was turning off her headset, another call came in. "Hi, Jennifer. It's Ann Marie Connor. I'm worried about James. Can you tell me anything? All I know from the news reports is that the city was hit and they got to the facility housing the spacecraft. It looks like the place is in total chaos."

Jennifer was also concerned as she tried to relieve James' anxious mother. "The Ethiopian army went in and declared martial law. Their mayor was killed in the attack on the spacecraft complex, and total anarchy erupted. The state department tracking the Americans there has James as listed as injured but alive. I was told that he has already been stabilized and evacuated from Kibish. The hospitals in Kibish were well over their capacity with the injured, and we were able to help get many of the victims who could be moved out of the city using military transports. It was the only way to get medical treatment for some of them. Once I hear where he was sent to, I will forward that information to you as soon as I can. Sorry that I don't have more to tell you, and now I have to go to the presidential news conference."

James' mother was relieved to hear that her son was alive and grateful to hear any news. "You have done more than enough. Patrick and I are very appreciative. How is your family?"

A rushed Jennifer quickly said, "Thank you for asking. We are fine. I must go, and I will let you know about James soon."

As the week went on, reports from the various news organizations continued: "Welcome back to Fox News International. I'm Phil Jenson. You have heard the President speak about the worldwide coordinated attack less than a day ago by a religious group called the Followers of Divinity. This group is unlike any other religious terror organization the world has ever seen because it is made up of a multitude of religious faiths. They are of different denominations of Jews, Muslims, Hindus, Buddhists, and Christians. A renegade Coptic bishop who was disowned by the Coptic Church leads them. His name is Bishop Terapion. Their apparent mission is to bring the people of the world back to a time when religion ruled our lives. The targets of their terrorist activities were the scientific communities, for what it says are crimes against the foundation of the world's religious groups.

"They are not a peaceful group and have acted with extreme deadly force. Their terrorist attacks yesterday resulted in the deaths of ten thousand people and counting worldwide. The President outlined a worldwide course of action in bringing these people to justice. The United States government, in coordination with other world leaders, has condemned this terrorist act and promised to bring the full weight of justice to bear on the individuals responsible."

The news anchor then turned to the panel assembled in the studio. "We have with us Rabbi Corry Levy, Imam Muhammad Hakam, and the Reverend Erin Smith. We will go first to you, Rabbi Levy. Why do you think these Followers of Divinity have organized so many different faiths?"

"Phil, fanaticism is not owned by just religious idealists," said the orthodox rabbi. "It is anywhere there are a few who believe their ideas supersede the ideas of the majority and feel that if they eliminate the thoughts, ideas, rights and beliefs of others who oppose them, they can take power and force the people to do what these fanatics believe is the right thing to do."

"Thank you, Rabbi Levy," cut in the news anchor. "Now, we are joined by Imam Hakam, who leads a mosque in Southern California, said to be the largest in the western United States. Imam, why do you believe this group is turning to violence to get their point across?"

"Well," said the Imam, "They believe they can't get their message across any other way than by this misguided path. Phil, violence will only lead to despair, and my other two colleagues here will attest that in the past our religions have used violence on not only other religions, but also on our own people. None of our religions advocate violence, and yet our histories are filled with it. I guess that where some will read scriptures and see enlightenment, others see it as a call to fight with permission given directly from God. Sometimes misguided individuals with a strong faith bring passion, and sometimes that passion leads to violence."

"And now on to you, Reverend Smith," said the news anchor. "How can we stop these religious zealots?"

The New Hampshire Lutheran pastor replied, "Some will say fight fire with fire. But I don't. I think the only way to get them is to speak to their concerns. I believe the root of their concerns is that they are scared. Scared of the future. They are scared because a population in this world that is more educated than ever before challenges their beliefs. Technology and knowledge of our world have outpaced our religious establishments. For the longest time we were the rock or pillar of our communities because our ways and messages did not change much. But today, religious leadership is challenged with an ever-more educated following that has asked questions we are slow to answer. With that said, we as leaders need to come forward and relieve their concerns. We will need to evolve in light of the alien discovery and its implications."

Chapter 6

"It looks like he's coming to," James heard one nurse say to another out of his sight. He thought, "A hospital, I'm in a hospital. But where am I?" He could barely see and realized he was looking out of one eye with a bandage around his head. He could also feel bandages around his body, braces on his legs, and a cast on his arm. He tried to move but was unable because he felt very weak.

The nurse said, "Welcome back. Do you understand me?"

James slowly nodded his head and, with a raspy voice due to his dry throat and mouth, he asked, "Where am I?"

The nurse, attractive with dark hair and a few freckles, looked right down at him. "You are at Stony Brook University Hospital on Long Island, New York. You have had some injuries from an attack and have been recovering here for some time now."

Unable to remember what had happened, he felt dazed. "I don't understand. What happened to me, and how did I get here?"

As she checked his vital signs, she told him, "You have been through a very dramatic experience and it may take a little time to remember due to some head trauma."

Minutes later, another nurse brought in someone he recognized, and she said, "James."

"Mom," he replied. Ann Marie, her eyes watery, leaned over the hospital bed to hold his head in her gentle hands. He blurted out, "What happened to me?"

Reluctantly, she told him, "You were a victim of a terrorist act and were injured in the rubble of the spacecraft complex. Many were hurt, some badly, but you were taken out of there and ended up here where you have been taken care of. Your injuries were pretty extensive, and many surgeries were done."

Still confused and starting to look very weak, he asked, "Why did it happen?"

He dozed off, and in a way, Ann Marie was relieved that she did not have to tell him that the reason for his injuries and the ensuing chaos that had engulfed the world was directly linked to his discovery and its aftermath. She just sat there holding his hand and waiting until he regained consciousness, dreading having to tell him that the world was in chaos, and he was in the center of it.

A little while later, the nurse was checking his vital signs and James woke up. He was a little more aware of his surroundings. He tried to move, but he was feeble and his injuries were painful when he moved. He looked around the room and saw that he was the only patient. Then he noticed that there was a university security guard outside his room while military personnel passed by in the hallway. It seemed a little odd, but James figured that due to his growing popularity the hospital must have arranged to have the extra security to keep his many fans from hindering his recovery. Then he remembered his mother had mentioned a terrorist attack. He wondered what the reason was for the attack, and who was responsible.

Ann Marie entered the room with a hot coffee and said, "Oh, you're awake. How are you feeling?"

He responded, "I feel like a house fell on my head."

Then Patrick walked into the room. "It did, and you're lucky to be alive. You should avoid Kibish. Every time you go there, you end up coming home on a hospital stretcher."

James then curiously asked them, "What happened to me?"

Ann Marie countered with, "What do you remember?"

James tried to recall. "All I remember is that I was at the spacecraft complex making an appearance, and the last thing I remember is that I heard people start to scream. That's until I woke up here."

Patrick took a deep breath and said with no facial expression, "There was a terrorist attack by a group called the Followers of Divinity. They are a fringe group, made up of various denominations, that blames science for the growing loss of members to their sects. In essence, they are the fanatics and zealots of almost all the religious faiths. It is a dangerous group that is hard for the authorities to put down because they vary so much. Seven weeks ago, they hit fifty cities worldwide with car and truck bombs. Their targets were scientific facilities and the scientists inside them. They hit universities, museums, and science centers. After the first day, over ten thousand people died and two hundred thousand people were injured. It was a huge loss, but in the last seven weeks --"

James interrupted, "I've been unconscious for seven weeks?"

Ann Marie answered, "Because of your injuries, the doctors induced you into a coma so that you could heal properly."

Then Patrick continued, "During that time, additional attacks have left another 25,000 dead and 150,000 injured. After virtually all the universities and museums were hit, they started to target individual scientists. We lost many good people, and many of the rest went into hiding. One of the places they hit was Kibish and the complex surrounding the spacecraft and the dig site. Many lost their lives that day. The city's hotels and convention center were hit hard, and the complex around the craft was destroyed. You were one of the few lucky enough to get out.

"Many, like Dr. Sanchez, were not so lucky. I lost many talented friends from the University of Ethiopia who worked in the complex studying the remains there. But it didn't end there. We lost Mike Wells and many others here when the university was hit. This is a huge mess. The world has almost come to a standstill. Many of the large cities are in lockdown. In many countries, the governments have instituted martial law. Schools around the world are closed because teachers fear for their lives and their students' lives. This is just what the terrorists hoped for."

James asked in concern, "Jennifer and David…are they all right?"

Ann Marie put her hand on James' shoulder and said, "They are OK and have been secured by the FBI along with their families."

Patrick added, "They were a target due to their part in the spacecraft's discovery."

James then realized, "If they're a target, then what am I?"

Ann Marie, showing motherly concern to protect her son, replied, "Maybe we should talk about that later, and you should get some rest."

Patrick was reluctant to speak, but knew it must be said. "James, you are their number one target. You are the one who discovered the spacecraft that led to realization that the Ancient Visitors had been an influence in the development of the human race. To make matters worse, you then took this information as a basis to disprove the existence of God and explained many of the mysteries of many religions as alien intervention into the activities of man. The fame of the discovery and your own popularity helped promote your conclusions throughout the world. Even though it made you famous and wealthy, it has made many people very angry. They are angry enough to stage an uprising and today scores are dead with many more hurt. You have been moved from hospital to hospital under assumed names so not to give away your location because if Followers of Divinity had a line on you they would make a move. You were brought back here to the university's hospital for a procedure, and soon you will be moved again. We have been in constant fear that, at any time, they would attack you."

Patrick then walked behind where Ann Marie was sitting on a chair and put his hands on her shoulders to comfort her. They waited for James' reaction.

James asked, "Then what is being done?"

Patrick answered, "Except for some already religious countries who lean towards the beliefs of the fanatics, many governments have used the military and law enforcement to track down these criminals and bring them to justice. Many have been arrested and killed, but their organization seems to be large and it will take time. When you add up all the religious fanatics in the world, it is not a great number, but the damage they can do could be enormous. That is because they believe that God will reward them here in this life and in the afterlife. Their devotion to their beliefs blinds them to their ability to reason. What is even more scary is that we are hearing that their numbers are growing and more parts of the world are joining their cause. Even people with less fanatical beliefs are joining them, mostly because they feel isolated from the rest of the world that has moved away from some of their religious beliefs."

"Let's give him a break for a while. This is a lot for him to digest," said Ann Marie, noticing James was looking exhausted. She continued, "We'll be back in the morning to see how you are doing, and don't worry. The security is tight, and no one outside the staff knows you're here."

After they left, James couldn't sleep and stayed up just thinking about the enormity of the events that had taken place. Many people had lost their lives and many of them were colleagues. They were people in the pursuit of knowledge and were not in the business of harming others, yet they had been cut down. Many innocent people who were caught in the line of fire were killed or were badly hurt. He angrily thought the reason for it was that some people couldn't accept a history devoid of what they had been taught by their religions. They felt people of science were out to disprove their long-held beliefs, and now they deemed the scientists as enemies.

They were not the first to use violence. History was riddled with groups large and small who persecuted and killed people who didn't believe as they did. Even if they did believe in the same deity, but had an alternate view of those beliefs, they were often at risk. James could only think that it was crazy.

A few days later, James was able to have the bed raised so he could view the 3D television screen. He spent hours switching back and forth while the news channels sized up the magnitude of the terrorist attack. While watching, he thought, "They hit the Smithsonian Air and Space Museum. I can't believe it. They have got to be stopped." On the interactive screen, James was able to pull up the names of the people in the scientific community who had lost their lives. Many of the names he recognized, and it made him angry and frustrated. His temper erupted, and he screamed out, "Those crazy lunatics! How could they do this?"

No sooner than he said that when David walked into the room and replied, "Because they are scared and afraid."

"Hey, David. It is good to see you are OK," said James.

"And you look better than your mom described to me," said David with a smirk.

Laughing a little, James responded, "She always felt my pain more than I did, but I have to tell you, I feel pretty bad. To your point that they are scared and afraid, the people they are terrorizing are scared and afraid."

"That is true," explained David. "But when your whole world revolves around a strong belief in God and others come in and discredit your beliefs, you feel lost and afraid, and some become angry. Many hold their religious beliefs as a standard for which they lead their lives, and if it gets taken away there is a huge hole in their lives. Some people see other viewpoints as a desecration of their religion. They have such a strong belief and feel they must strike back at the nonbelievers. Many of them turn to fanatical approaches, and people get hurt.

"I believe that sometimes we as scientists help fuel the fire of these extremists. Yes, we look for the truth of our existence in this world and universe. We have come up with evidence and theories from the beginning of time with the Big Bang to our own evolutionary timeline, and our knowledge is expanding every day. Many in the religious community have a hard time reconciling the new discoveries with their

110

beliefs and reject them as heresy. We as scientists need to be conscious of religious beliefs and not make bold statements that hurt."

"You mean me," James said.

"Yes," David said to his friend with unveiled certainty. "Your conclusions have offended some, and you were the terrorists' main target. You are lucky to be alive. The heavy Ethiopian military security force held off the terrorist foot soldiers coming in to finish you off after the craft complex blew up."

After thinking about his actions prior to the attack, James countered, "You can't blame me for that."

"Yeah, I know, but you are involved. We all are. I believe communication and understanding is needed between the scientific and religious communities. There is too much tension between the two sides, and it needs to stop. The terrorist attack was just tension boiling over. A tension you ignited with your campaign to discredit religious writing, customs, and long-held beliefs. You certainly did set off a powder keg."

As David finished, a breaking news headline appeared on the television screen: "Abducted Missing."

The news anchor said, "We have received reports that the returned abducted are missing once again. They were reported to be in hiding with their families since the attack, but now we are hearing from around the world that they have been taken. At this point, it is unclear if they were taken by the terrorists or were abducted again by the Ancient Visitors."

David's headset phone registered an incoming call, and he answered it. "Hey, Jennifer. What's up?"

As David spoke to Jennifer, James watched as the faces of the abducted were shown on the screen. Many of them were people he had interviewed, and it made him feel uneasy as to their eventual fates. If the terrorists took them, then those religious extremists would most likely have killed them, and if the Ancient Visitors did, no one knew what they might have in mind for them. Not everyone had returned from the last mass abduction.

When David disconnected the call, he relayed what Jennifer had told him. "She said that through the night the abducted, under government protection, disappeared while nearby family members and security personnel were rendered unconscious by some mysterious means. All security footage was made useless, and NORAD showed no unusual activity in its normal scans of the skies. The consensus is that the terrorists didn't do it, and the Ancients Visitors may have come back to reclaim them. These people just vanished."

James surmised, "We may see increased activity from the Ancient Visitors now that they know we are here, and who knows what they have planned for us."

David took a deep breath as he looked out the window of the hospital and concluded, "This news is going to plunge the world deeper into chaos. After the terrorist attacks, the financial markets collapsed into disarray, and most of the governments of the world instituted martial law. I had hoped that the world would turn back to normal after some time had passed after the initial discovery, but now I feel things will never go back. I fear for the future, a future my children will now have to grow up in. God help them."

A few moments later, David said good-bye and left, but what he had said lingered in James' mind. The world was in absolute chaos, and the root cause was easily seen. Since the moment he had stepped on the loose rock and fallen into that crack in Kibish, the world had not been the same. The news of his discovery sixteen years ago had sent ripples through human understanding of how man evolved and put into doubt many long-held religious and evolutionary beliefs. It had caused people to be confused and angry, and that anger led to violence. Many thousands of people were hurt or dead, and bedlam reigned through the rest of the world.

To make matters worse, he may have triggered a signal from the spacecraft that would spur the Ancient Visitors to continue their plan for mankind, a plan that was still not known. Fear, anger, chaos, and a loss of faith could be attributed to James' discovery and his actions since that moment. As he lay there he couldn't shake the fact that he had a big responsibility in what had transpired. He thought about the many friends and colleagues he knew who had lost their lives, and the thousands of innocent people who might have been in the wrong place at that horribly bad time of attack.

It now started to overwhelm James, as he felt more and more responsible, not only for what he had discovered, but also for his actions and his words. The discovery would have eventually been found, but his conclusions about how mankind developed and, to be more precise, how he tried to demystify long-held beliefs, had caused much anxiety to people strong in their beliefs. As James lay there with the television showing recorded 3D video of the devastation of the attacks, people lost, and the ongoing war to combat the terrorists, he muttered in despair, "What have I done? Oh, God what have I done?"

After a sleepless night staring out the window of his private room, James heard footsteps entering. Still unable to move very well, he tilted his head to see his mother walking up toward his bed.

"Good morning, James. How are you today?" she asked with motherly concern. James just looked at her with a halfhearted smile.

She continued, "Later today we will move you to another location to continue your rehabilitation. Due to the security concerns, you have been moved from one hospital to another, and we are trying to stay one step ahead of the terrorists while keeping the healthcare personnel around you safe. At the moment you are registered under a different name, and only a few select people know who you are, but sometimes secrets do manage to get out. Some of the caregivers have been hired from the beginning of your care to accompany you from location to location so you could receive consistent treatment. Those people are working under false identities for their protection. We only get a few hours' notice from the security firm we hired when they decide to move you. But they say…"

As Ann Marie continued, she noticed that James was not that interested, and as mothers do, that something was bothering him.

"James, what's the matter, honey? You seem down today. Are you feeling OK?" she asked him. He didn't respond to her right away. She persisted, "Come on, James. What's bothering you?"

Knowing that she always seemed to be able to tell what he was feeling and was perhaps the one person he could confide in, he blurted out, "Is it my fault? Did I cause all of this turmoil?"

His mother, not wanting to blame him but wanting to help him resolve his question, said, "Who's to tell? If you hadn't discovered the spacecraft then someone else would have eventually, and you were not the first to speculate about alien influence in mankind's development. I don't know. Maybe it was the way you went about it. Maybe you could have used a little more understanding before you promoted your ideas and thought about the reaction some might have to them, as well as the consequences."

Shaking his head from side to side, he said, "I was so sure my theories were right."

Patrick then walked in the room and jumped into the conversation. "Your analysis of the facts is your perception, and showing someone else the facts could lead them to a different conclusion. All we can do is keep learning more. In the study of ancient man, we believe we have a handle on how we have developed, and much of the proof seems undeniable, but our beliefs are still theories. The fossilized remains we find buried in the ground are just a fraction of what walked and grew on this planet. Most lived, died, and perished without any trace they existed in history.

"Do I believe we evolved from a primitive primate, and it took millions of years for us to evolve into the species we are today? Yes, but we still have a long way to go to understand fully not only our existence

114

here on Earth, but all the mysteries of the universe we inhabit."

Ann Marie jumped in, "In the religious world, perception is a critical element in understanding God and what He has asked us to do. The terrorists perceive themselves as fighting for the sake of God without breaking God's laws. We as children of God have a lot to learn. Do you think God ordered the Crusades or the Inquisition? No, it was man's perception of what needed to be done. Think back to Moses' coming down from Mount Sinai with the Ten Commandments and finding the people losing their faith. He slew the people who were weak in their convictions. Maybe that was his perception of God's intent even though the Commandments forbade killing. What we are saying is that people perceive things and situations differently. Some will agree with you, and some will not."

James was dismayed, and there was not much he could do. The weight of his part in instigating the response from the attackers weighed down on him heavily. Thinking about all his interviews and lectures, and how his mother had always remained steadfast, he asked her, "With all your religious convictions and your strong beliefs, did my conclusions ever upset you?"

With a caring smile she told him, "Not at all. My faith is as strong as ever."

"But there is proof that the human race has been influenced by an alien people, and science has uncovered evidence that contradicts the Bible," he added. "Evolution is not a myth. There is factual evidence, but you still believe. Why?"

"Well," she said, looking at her confused son. "I saw nothing that refutes the existence of God. Look, James, scientists cannot prove that God does not exist. There will never be any mathematical equation or lab experiment that will prove without doubt that a divine hand did not make the universe and all that is in it. It is not possible. On the other hand, religious people can't prove that God does exist. What it comes down to is that it is up to each person to decide for him or herself to have faith or not in God. I personally believe and continue to grow spiritually. Do I believe that everything in the Bible is a factual event? No. I believe that much of what was written was the perception of those who wrote it. But I do believe that the essence of what is written is a message from God as to how we should live.

"If you look at not just Christian faith, but all faiths, what God gave us was how we should ethically behave. Most of the Ten Commandments were rules on ethics, and if you look at most faiths, ethics are much of their message. Imagine what history would be like without the ethical hand of religion helping along the way. Sure, people have used religion to do horrific things, but that might have been their interpretation of God's intent, or they just maliciously used the people's belief in God to get them to do those horrible things."

She walked over to the window and continued, "James, I believe that science and religion have the same goal: finding out the truth. Religious people should not be afraid of scientists because God is a scientist, the greatest scientist, I believe. If He made all of this, He has to be. From the smallest molecule to the farthest galaxies, His imagination dwarfs our greatest minds."

Patrick added, "Just the invention of gravity is amazing. It holds the universe together."

Ann Marie continued, "You have not killed religion, and don't count it out. It has been with man since the beginning and will continue to be with him until the end of time."

Then she remembered, "You went to church with me every Sunday and listened to the gospels. Do you believe with all your heart that God was not listening to your prayers?"

He thought about it for a little while and said, "I guess I stopped thinking about it."

She said, "Maybe you should look at it again. Not all the answers we seek can be found in the physical world." Then she handed him the Bible she carried with her.

At that moment the security guard signaled to Patrick that it was time to leave, and he said to James and Ann Marie, "It's time to go. They will be here in a few seconds. Remember, the faster we move the less likely we will be discovered."

James was quickly moved from his room and taken to a transport vehicle for the trip to a secure location for his rehabilitation. Everyone moved in haste, and they prepared James for the trip. It was into the transport vehicle, then to an airport. He estimated that they were in the air for a good four hours, and when he was put in the transport vehicle at the next airport he noticed how warm it was.

Peering out the window, he saw mountains and asked the attendant, "Where are we?"

He responded, "You are in Phoenix, Arizona, and your rehabilitation will be at a small place in Scottsdale that is a little north of here."

James then looked out the window of the vehicle and braced himself for the long recuperation, which he knew would not only be for his body. This rehab would be for his mind as well.

Two weeks later, James' ability to move was improving significantly. The nurse he had in the university hospital was still his primary care nurse. James' family, through the security service they had employed for his safety, had hired Lauren Ritter. She put him through a strenuous physical therapy program. Along the way they got to know each other, as they were together for many hours a day. She was very focused on her job all the time, while politics and world events were of little interest to her. She hardly knew who James was or why he was famous or infamous to some. Her focus was on helping other people. James felt calm and comfortable around her and could drop his persona as this "great discoverer."

At the end of a long day of rehab he asked her, "Would you mind sitting with me at dinner and eating with me?" He had been eating in his room now for weeks and longed for some normal conversation. She was very down to earth, and this intrigued him.

James welcomed it when she said, "Sure."

They talked through dinner that night and every night for the next few weeks as his rehab progressed, and they became friends. Developing friendships was not something James did well; typically he was looking at what he got out of it and not at the value of having a friend.

She noticed his mood change as he watched the news one morning, and asked him not as a healthcare provider but a person who cared about him, "What's the matter, James?"

He flung his hands in the air. "I can't understand why we can't combat these religious fanatics."

Without giving much thought, she said, "Maybe we should learn to understand what they are like. You know, understand their hopes and desires and what bothers them. The proverbial 'walk a mile in their shoes' in order to get to know them. Any conflict I have ever been in usually started because of a misunderstanding."

James thought about what Lauren said about understanding and his mother said about perception. He looked over on his nightstand and saw the Bible his mother had given him and thought that maybe it was time to be reacquainted with it and try to get a feel for the people he had angered. He thought, ah, what the heck. I have a lot of time on my hands now.

So he picked up the book and tried to put any preconceived convictions out of his mind. He turned to the first page of the book that he had spent years trying to discredit and started reading the Old Testament. He not only started reading the words, he also began to research their place in history for a better understanding of the different passages and their context. What started that day would continue to be a learning experience for James, a onetime believer.

Chapter 7

Steven Moran opened his eyes to a bright sun, and a warm breeze blew across his face. Even though he did not know where he was, he was happy he was not still on the massive alien ship. All he could think about was that he wished he had never been returned to that cold, impersonal place. Around him he saw vegetation similar to the last time he was in Africa, and as his eyes focused he recalled the same mountain range in the distance he had seen the last time the Ancient Visitors returned them. He sat up and said, "This is Ethiopia again."

Then D'Shawn Williams sat up near him, "Thank God. I love Ethiopia. Oh, I love Ethiopia." They got up, looking around to see who made it back in a group of people that was definitely smaller than the one on the ship.

"I count about 280 people," said Steven as he looked around.

"Two hundred and eighty-three, to be exact," said D'Shawn.

"Oh, my," moaned Steven. "Then a total of 122 people didn't make it back with us. God help them. I'm so glad we did." After a moment of thinking about the people left behind, they thought about their fate, and both felt colder.

Marcus Latterri, now fully awake, noticed a craft of some kind heading to their location, followed by two more.

Matt Schaeffer looked over to Marcus, "Do you recognize it? Is it friend or foe?"

Marcus replied, "I don't recall that kind of ship. It must be a new design since we left. My guess is someone utilized the Ancient Visitor's technology. How long do you think we were gone this time?"

Matt shook his head. "I'm not sure." Then the lead craft hovered over the group.

Marcus pointed out to Matt, "There's a United Nations decal on the side of the craft, but I'm not sure if that means they are friendly. Much could have changed since we were taken."

As they looked at it, a voice was amplified over the returnees, "Welcome home." Then the crafts landed and out walked UN security and medical personnel. They brought out food and water to all the returned people.

Slowly, the leader of the craft spoke: "Hello, I am Captain Luis Contreras of the UN's Global Security agency. We are happy you have returned safely. We've got a lot of questions for you when you settle in, but I'm sure you have plenty for us right now."

Matt stepped up. "I guess for starters, how long were we gone?"

Luis slowly replied, "Six years and about two months." This left the returning captives speechless for a few seconds as they realized what they had missed.

Steven then asked, "When we were taken there was an attack? Is my family OK?"

Luis raised his hands. "All your families are fine and secured, but the world has been through a war that has taken its toll on us all. It was a religious conflict that pitted brother against brother. Many were lost. Fortunately, we are slowly coming out of it. The UN controls and has secured about 70% of the world so far. There are still areas of conflict that need to be resolved, and we hope the tide is with us. The world political environment has changed, with more UN authority and less with the former superpower nations."

Matt cut Luis off anxiously, "When can we return to our families?"

With a smile for the returning captives, Luis said, "It will probably be a few hours, after the medical examination and return interview."

An impressed Matt said, "That's pretty fast considering many of us are from around the world."

As another transport landed, Luis proudly said, "You weren't the only people getting faster. While you were gone, the religious conflict that did so much damage did, in fact, have a silver lining. We have seen more cooperation as we fought off the terrorists known as the Followers of Divinity. That cooperation extended into the world political arena and in innovation and technology as never before. Even though a portion of the world is still in their hands, you have fortunately landed in the safe zone. We have come a long way, but so have you, so let's get you on board and back home as quickly as we can." He and the other security personnel escorted them onto the transports and back to their families.

A few weeks later, back in Washington DC, a meeting was called with the President's Alien Affairs Council and the United Nation's Global Security Commission to discuss the interviews of the returned abductees and get the perspective of a leading member of the captives. Heading up the meeting was Dr. Jennifer La Mont, leader of the President's council and a member of the UN's Board on Alien Intervention.

"Good afternoon, all," said Jennifer, both to the few in the audience there and to many more over the 3D teleconference system seen throughout the world. "Today we will hear firsthand from one of the captives about his experience on the alien craft while deep in space, and will find out what he was told regarding the fate of mankind. He partook in advanced educational studies between the two abductions, like many of the captives. Some got their PhDs or other advanced degrees in record time. Their grasp of linguistic skills is extraordinary. They could speak to someone in another culture and quickly understand their language. With that said, our guest will announce what he learned from conversations with the Ancient Visitors. Please welcome Matt Schaeffer, who has a story to tell us."

The present council members and cameras from every news organization on earth focused in on him. Worldwide, almost every person able to view a PDA, headset television, or giant projection virtual reality link listened in. Making sure he was speaking slowly and clearly to the world, he began: "Thank you for having me today, and I hope to fill you in on what I know about the plans the Ancient Visitors have for the human race."

After an uncomfortable pause, Jennifer asked, "Matt, could you please tell us in detail about your experiences and what you learned so that we can understand?"

Standing there with the weight of the world on his shoulders, Matt was relieved to answer what would be hard for all to hear: "I will be thorough in my description." He then took a deep breath and began to explain, "This time when we woke up on the ship, we were not as confused as we had been the first time. Fortunately, there were no language barriers between us, and the confusion of the first time we were taken did not occur. We gathered ourselves and began to organize. Not only could we understand our world's different languages, we were starting to understand the different alien races language as well…"

On the ship, Marcus walked over to Matt. "I think we have been here for a week now, and I'm starting to understand these creatures along the walls. As a matter of fact, I think they have a very simple set of languages and don't appear too intelligent. It probably explains why the Ancient Visitors use them as minions. They use them for their brute strength, and the restraint collars keep these creatures from fighting back. At first they appeared to be in league with the Ancient Visitors, but from what little I can gather, they seem to be in the same boat we are, taken from their home worlds and made to serve the Ancient Visitors. While being taken back and forth between the examinations the Ancient Visitors are putting us through, I have had some time to converse with some of them. One creature took the time to explain that these Ancient Visitors have throughout their history repeatedly returned to abduct some of their people. He said his people considered them gods. I think the creature's name was Uloog, and he said he has been here for a long time and claimed the Ancient Visitors have been training them for a battle."

Matt interrupted him and asked, "Battle, what battle? What are we in the middle of?"

Marcus continued, "Uloog said he has no idea when or where the battle will take place. All he knows is that the Ancient Visitors have millions upon millions training on planets they rule. These creatures are from those planets, and all have been abducted from their home worlds. All they do is train for this inevitable battle. Uloog and the rest of the wall guards are the so-called cream of the crop and get assigned to the ship. It is not all roses being assigned to the ship because the Ancient Visitors treat them like we treat a herd of cattle and prod them with the electronic dog collars they have to wear."

Matt informed Marcus, "I've been speaking to one of the Ancient Visitors. His language seems very complicated, and I would say that I might understand no better than 30%, but two of the Ancient Visitors have been making an effort to communicate with me. They seem to take an interest in teaching me their language. I get the feeling they see it as training a pet to do tricks. But I will try to find out more..."

Matt told the assembly, "A few weeks later, I understood them well enough to have a conversation with them. The two Ancient Visitors were called Lango and Sintdon. They were medical scientists who examined the alien races they captured. They were especially surprised at how intelligent we were..."

With a deep raspy voice, Lango said to Matt, "I am so impressed at how well you are picking up our way of speaking. Many of the other races sometimes pick up a few words here and there, but your people are more intelligent than we were expecting. As a matter of fact, it was totally unexpected and has made us curious as to how it happened. Sintdon believes the lack of oversight must have been the reason."

Matt said, "What do you mean 'oversight'?"

Sintdon explained, "We send out scouts looking for life throughout this existence, and they manipulate that life to grow to our specifications. Occasionally, we don't hear from some of these scout ships for a long time. One that was visiting your world never came back, and we did not know that you were falling out of line with the specifications we wanted. In later visits, it was determined that more handling was needed."

Matt questioned, "What do you mean 'specifications'?"

Lango quickly responded, "We need you for a task."

"What task?"

"We have a problem we need you to help us with," said Lango.

Sintdon cut him off. "That is all for now. We must get Matt back to the others..."

"Over time, they trusted me to the point that they took me out of the confinement room, and I toured the ship. It wasn't like a museum tour on a school trip, though. Lango and Sintdon had me collared like a pet dog and yanked on my electronic chain to make sure I walked where they wanted me to walk and touched what they allowed me to touch. What I saw was amazing by our standards. Their living and social areas dwarfed every science fiction movie ever made. I saw things like a transportation system where tubes filled with a liquid substance would send a passenger anywhere on the ship they wanted to go in seconds and then release them, without a trace of moisture.

"Their libraries are filled with knowledge acquired from races throughout the universe, some long dead. They told me that with the science and math knowledge they have, there are equations that explain everything in the universe. Stephen Hawking would be in Heaven. Due to technology embedded in their bodies, they can communicate telepathically, store memories, manage their metabolism, and interface with the living ship. Their every need is taken care of by it. There were parts of the ship that had unbelievable technology, but it was starting to move from my focus. I couldn't help but notice the alien races that weren't Ancient Visitors. They seemed to be subservient , so I questioned Lango and Sintdon..."

Matt asked, "I noticed that your race dominates the other races. Why is that?"

Sintdon looked and answered Matt like a parent answering the silly question of a child, "Isn't it obvious? We are perfect beings, while all the other races are inferior to us. We are their creators and gods. Everything they have, we let them have. They were bred to serve us."

A confused Matt asked, "You are their creators?"

Lango replied, "We did not create the matter they are made of. We direct life forms into what we want them to be. None of these races would be anywhere near as developed if it were not for us."

A startled Matt looked around at the many subservient races and asked, "So you are telling me that you have made all these races by using the life forms on a world and engineering them to your specifications?"

Sintdon looked over at him and said, "Yes, it is all part of the plan."

Matt had one more question for him, and he was afraid of what the answer was going to be, but he asked anyway. "Did you do any engineering on my world?"

Sintdon responded, "Yes," to Matt and then spoke to Lango. "You see, Lango, we did not engineer them enough, and they came out too intelligent. It alters the plan, but we can find other ways to utilize their people. It is getting late, and he has to get back for the training to begin."

Then Matt was brought back to the others...

Jennifer then asked the obvious, "So Matt, you believe that they engineered us to be what they designed? This just clarifies what we have assumed since there was evidence that they visited us in our past at times when we made leaps in our development. The fact that you and the others abducted were transformed only validates those conclusions."

Matt answered, "Yes, they did, but there were problems with our development. It seems that the aliens in the craft found here on Earth did not finish their work, and I believe that we developed not quite as designed. There was also an outside influence, but I will get to that later. But it was clear that we were far more intelligent than all the other races, and the Ancient Visitors took notice of it and tried to subdue us with force. So the training began..."

"Marcus, the pain subsides after a few minutes," Matt told him as Marcus lay on the floor in a fetal position screaming in pain.

Then as the pain dissipated, Marcus looked up to see Steven, D'Shawn, Cynthia Moss, and Janet Livingston standing with others and wearing the same collar harnesses that the wall guards wore.

Steven helped Marcus up. "Getting it on is very painful, and I bet it is even more painful if we don't perform like they want us to."

At that moment, the guards herded them into another part of the ship with a large room that resembled a laser tag or paintball competition facility. Each wore a harness, but they had differently colored lights on them. The guards gathered people into those groups that shared colors. Then they were brought to different sections of the facility where odd-looking weapons were stacked. The guards indicated that they should pick up the weapons and then point them toward the other groups.

D'Shawn looked over at Marcus to say, "What the hell do they want us to do?"

"It looks like war games to me," said Marcus.

D'Shawn put up his arms and said, "This is stupid. Why do they want us to do this?"

At that moment the guard again pointed to the other groups, but nobody moved. In a quick motion, the guard picked up a familiar glowing energy ball and threw it directly into D'Shawn's chest. He was thrown backwards, his body shaking as if he were having a seizure. A few seconds later, the pain went away, and D'Shawn let out a loud moan of relief. The guard then pointed to the other groups.

Marcus picked up D'Shawn. "It looks like they want us to fight the others, and thanks to you we know the weapons are not lethal."

D'Shawn, still shaking and with sweat dripping down his face, said, "Yeah, anything I can do to help." Some of the other groups did not fare as well. The group Steven was in had their harnesses activated, and they fell to the floor in pain as energy was transferred from the collar down a strip along their spine. When it was over, they all got up and started to attack the other groups.

Jennifer asked, "Were they training you for some kind of battle? How grueling was it?"

Matt then took a deep breath and said, "Yes, and they trained us constantly. We were taught to use a large cache of weapons, and as time went on the non-lethal weapons became dangerous. Janet got hurt as she jumped from one level to a lower level during one particular fight. Another American, Tim Parks, came out from behind cover to assist her, and because he was out in the open, he was hit many times by the non-lethal weapons and was doubled over in so much pain that the guards pulled him out of play. Then the guards took them both away, and we never saw them again."

Jennifer interrupted him, "So did you find out where our people went after they were separated from the rest of you? So far they have not returned to Earth, and their families would like to know if they are still on the ship."

Matt then looked down at his feet, his eyes starting to water as he tried to explain what happened to those people who had friends and relatives watching right now…

After the training, they were all brought back to the giant holding room.

"This war games shit is making me very hungry," D'Shawn said to Steven as they came up to the trough in the corner of the room.

Steven asked, "Is it me, or is this stuff starting to taste not so bad? It's not Mom's supper, but at least we are not starving to death, and I think it is making me feel stronger. Each day I seem to throw faster, run faster, and jump higher. They must put vitamins or steroids in it."

Now up at the trough, D'Shawn and Steven began to grab their share of the food provided by the Ancient Visitors and then walked over to where Matt, Marcus, and Cynthia were sitting. As they ate, Marcus noticed Uloog standing guard nearby. Steven and Cynthia asked Marcus to inquire about Tim and Janet to see if they were OK and ask where they had been taken. Marcus then called Uloog over, but he was hesitant to give them an answer.

Lango came over to answer for Uloog, "Nothing is wasted."

Matt, with his eyes now very wide open, asked Lango, "What do you mean 'wasted'?"

Lango then said, "This is a ship with limited resources for the alien population living on this ship. We waste nothing."

D'Shawn then looked down at his food.

Steven and Cynthia both said Tim's and Janet's names at the same time as Marcus and Matt put their head in their hands.

Lango continued, "Even your waste you deposit in the drain in the center of this area is not wasted," and then walked away.

D'Shawn again looked at his meal. "Oh…shit…"

"So the people that did not make it back are not coming back?" asked Jennifer, looking for closure for the families still waiting for loved ones that had been taken during the two abductions.

Matt, obviously shaken and not wanting to say it out loud, pushed out his answer, "No, they are not."

Jennifer then blurted out, "To the families of Janet Livingston and Tim Parks, as well as all the others not returning, you have our sympathies."

After a few deep breaths, Matt explained, "I was told that every resource on that ship was utilized to the max. Everything had a value and could be used somewhere else. In this case, many of our people did not meet the expectations for being reengineered. While most of us transformed from the human we were to what the Ancient Visitors believe is an improvement in our evolutionary stage, the ones not meeting the improvement goals or those who got injured were made into nourishment. They took their remains, bodily waste, and any other organic material and added a type of bacteria found on one of their worlds they rule. These bacteria eat the waste and secrete a protein that they engineer into a food gel."

Jennifer injected, "Our scientists have worked on ways to recycle our bodily waste, but nowhere near the extent the aliens have done to our people. Matt, why do you think they have such little respect for our lives to be able to do this?"

"Well," he said. "I think they believe they are intellectually light years ahead of us, and that our lives are not as valuable as theirs."

Jennifer shook her head and deducted, "To think about it, we are no better than they are. In our past we have enslaved people we thought were inferior. Life forms that gather socially and take care of their young we have barbequed or covered with gravy."

Moving away from that subject, Jennifer asked, "So, Matt, who are they, and where did they come from?"

"Over time," Matt explained, "Lango took an interest in me. He thought that I might have developed into one of the leaders of the humans, and he wanted to study me. Being that we were more intelligent than their usual species, Lango was intrigued by us as a people. So he asked me questions about our existence, and I asked him about theirs…"

"Lango, can you tell me where you came from?" Matt asked him.

"I'm not sure if you will understand" he said, "but I'll try to say it as simply as possible. We have been here since long before this existence began."

Matt asked, "What do you mean 'existence'? I heard you mention it before."

"Well…everything. Like planets, stars, and galaxies," he said to Matt. "We were here at the beginning of matter and time. You are a species who measure things by time. By your perspective of time, we have been around long before this universe existed."

Matt tried to understand. "Our scientists theorize that that the universe came into existence and expanded from a primordial super spot in the center of the universe. They call it the Big Bang and speculate that all matter originated from that one spot. Before that there was no matter or time."

Longo said, "Very good. I am surprised by your people's knowledge, but you only know part of it. To explain I will have to tell you about us. We are from another existence, and there we were not in this physical form. We only came to be like this when we came through the portal that started this all."

Matt asked, "What was before the universe was created? What was it like?"

Thinking back, Lango described, "It was an amazing place. It was a non-physical reality of ultimate wonder and joy. A place you feel ultimate happiness and never hunger. It was the center of all universes and a place where you feel whole."

"Other universes?" asked Matt. "Some of our scientists believe there are alternate universes and other dimensions."

"You are a logical race that is full of surprises. I am impressed. But to answer your question, there is a universe of universes. Some are large and some could fit on your finger. There are more than even we can count because all of existence is immense."

"So," Matt inquired. "Why did you leave such a wonderful place to come here?"

For the first time, Lango showed some emotion as he looked strained to explain, "We were created to serve all of creation and did so for all of existence, but one of us rebelled. Many took sides, and we went with the one that rebelled. Due to our rebellion, we were cast from the center into this universe at the moment of the beginning of this reality. And here we stay..."

An astounded Jennifer asked Matt to verify what she just heard. "So they claim to be here at the beginning of time and are the cause of the Big Bang? Is that what you are saying?"

Without doubt, Matt looked at her and answered, "Yes. They have extremely long life spans compared to us, and they are not as limited by time. The exceptions are a few that were lost, like the ones that came and perished here on Earth, but for the most part, they live forever. One of the reasons that they need us is because they are asexual, and they don't reproduce. Since they don't multiply, they need other life forms to do their tasks."

"Do you have additional information on the one who rebelled and the others who followed?" questioned Jennifer.

Matt answered, "It is hard to say because of my limited understanding of his language. I think the closest translation is 'Prince.' Supposedly, some entity created them. I don't know. I think it translated to 'Ruler of the Realm.' This ruler of some kind ruled the center of creation. The Prince had some kind of disagreement with the Ruler, and the Prince and his followers were banished to this universe. Here they plan on their return."

Jennifer asked, "A plan?"

"Yes," he said. "They plan on some sort of battle to get them back there..."

Lango was still trying to educate Matt when he explained their purpose for being there. "For us to return, we need to force our way through our original entry point into this universe at its weakest point. It is the place of your so-called Big Bang. It will be a collision that will end time and bring us back to fight for our dominance over all of the Ruler's existence. Throughout our time in this universe we have been assembling an army to combat him in a final battle. The Prince and his generals, led by Belial, will conquer the Ruler and place the Prince as the all-powerful leader of all that is. That battle will be the battle to end all battles, and your people will help in our victory. Our Prince will reward you with more riches and power than you can imagine..."

Matt said, "We found out later, from some of the other races, that the Ancient Visitors will soon have the army they need for battle and the fuel they need to generate the energy to penetrate through to the other existence. Apparently, there are four of these large ships scattered throughout the universe looking for life forms and fuel. Once they are satisfied with our training and reengineering, they will return us to populate the Earth with this new DNA strain to spread our seed. We will be tested one more time and get additional training in about five and a half years. The time between intervals of abductions is smaller because their main ship is getting closer to Earth. Then when we get back to Earth, we are to train the generations after us to be ready for the fight when the battle is brought here, about a thousand years from now."

"But," asked Jennifer, "what if we don't want to go fight? What will happen then?"

Matt now took a deep breath and sipped a little water before saying, "For those whose DNA was accepted as in line with their specification, they will be taken to serve in their army. About 60% of the population should have the right genetic makeup."

"OK, then what happens to the people not taken?" asked Jennifer.

Matt replied with a somber look on his face, "As you heard, nothing will be wasted."

This made the people in both the audience and those watching the live broadcast gasp at the thought of their descendants being taken for food.

Over the audience's dismay, Jennifer asked, "Matt, do you think that with this knowledge our descendants might be able to prepare to defend themselves? The technological innovations at that time might give our people a fighting chance."

Looking as if he wanted to say yes and couldn't, Matt said what he was thinking. "I don't know. Maybe. But the Ancient Visitors' technology is billions of years ahead of ours. We have only had the use of computing for less than one hundred years, while they have been traveling the universe for billions of years on ships with technology we would never have dreamed of. So we have our work to do, and maybe we can use our intellects to find a way to stop them. They were surprised to find out how intelligent we were, so maybe we can do something to surprise them even more."

Jennifer then looked toward the audience and said, "Then like Matt said, we have our work to do, and we will have to plan a strategy that may take generations to perfect."

As Jennifer started an attempt to organize the scientists in the audience, Matt hesitated, but blurted out. "There is one more thing. When the four ships combine their power and energy as they speed toward the center of the universe to break through to the other plane of existence, this universe will come to an end."

Jennifer responded, "Then we need to do something so we can save the future!"

Shaking his head, Matt said, "You don't understand. When this universe comes to an end, not only will the future end, so will the present and the past. All of time will end. So it is imperative that we stop them!"

Jennifer and the audience were eerily quiet as they tried to comprehend what that meant. Would this create a paradox? Was the end of time predestined, or were the laws of nature too enormous for man to understand? The possibilities were endless.

After a break, during which Jennifer consulted with some of the renowned scientists in the audience, she walked back over to Matt. "Matt, we appreciate that you have come here to speak with us today, but we have a few more questions. I want to ask you about this ruler whom the Ancient Visitors have this war with. So what do you know about the ruler? Should we worry about him?"

"Well," he said. "As far as they are concerned, the Ruler of the Realm is in the way of their ultimate goal of gaining control of all of existence. They did not tell me much about him or her, other than to say that the entity does not have a solid form like we have, and he or she has been screwing with the Ancient Visitors' plan for the human race. Also, the entity does not have a linear existence, meaning that it can slip through time. I suppose it is as if time was a book, and this entity can easily move between pages at will. Just like the Ancient Visitors, this entity has influenced human development and interfered with their designs for our development. Lango said that it was like a tug-of-war between them. The Ancient Visitors are on one side, developing us to be aggressive in order to be better fighters, and the Ruler of the Realm thwarts those efforts joined with those who remained loyal. Lango believes that this interference might be the reason we turned out to be more intelligent than the other races they are developing for the battle."

Jennifer looked down at some notes on her PDA from consulting with scientists in the audience and asked what many wanted to know: "Are the Ancient Visitors our creators?"

Shaking his head from side to side, he answered, "No, but they have tried to influence us throughout our history. They are not responsible for all things, but they think all things belong to them to do with as they like. What they did to change the abducted captives like myself is what humans would have evolved to be anyway. They just sped up the process because they are pressed for time. They have throughout history manipulated our culture because they wanted to keep us aggressive, as they have done with other species throughout the universe. So they have been here since our beginning, and the discovery of the spacecraft only sped up their timetable a little bit."

"OK," she said. "What else do you know about this Ruler of the Realm?"

"My impression from Lango," he said, "is that the Ruler was in conflict with the Prince and his followers' belief of where their position in all of existence should be. I do know the entity started this universe to put the Prince and his followers in it. Lango also mentioned that the Ruler of the Realm has influenced man throughout history as well. He would counter their plan to develop human aggressiveness with more non-aggressive behavior. I was confused when he said that the Ruler of the Realm acquired life energies of humans. He did not elaborate any further during my time with him. Sorry."

An overburdened Matt looked at Jennifer and the audience as if to say he was sorry for the predicament the human race was in, but he couldn't do anything about it. He said, "I wish I could help more."

An appreciative Jennifer was quick to say, "You have really helped a lot, and we all appreciate your coming here to speak to us today, especially after all you have gone through. For the rest of us, we need to digest this information to understand the landscape and try to formulate options, if there are any. I hope and pray that we are able to do something where our people have a future not of servitude to another race but of hope. If not, then instead of being able to tell our children that the future is bright, we will be leaving each generation a little bleaker than the last. God help us all."

Then the broadcast came to an end, and the newscasters from every news organization on Earth immediately started to dissect everything Matt had said and what the implications were for mankind. One person watching the broadcast was sitting in his modest Scottsdale, Arizona home, and he turned it off as the newscasters came on to speak. He thought about the Revelation that Matt spoke about regarding the Ancient Visitors' plans and the ordeal the abducted had had to go through to survive. Then there was his friend Jennifer trying to make sense of it all. But most of all, he was thinking of how he could possibly help. Up until now he had not helped at all. On the contrary, he had been a hindrance to himself, his family, his friends, and the human race. His selfishness had caused much grief and despair for a wide range of people. He couldn't help but wonder what would have happened if instead of stepping to the left on that hill in the Kibish formation he had stepped to the right. Whether it would had have changed anything, he was not sure, but at least he wouldn't be responsible for people's lost faith or people's being abducted or the destruction perpetrated by the terrorists. It took time, but he had come to understand his responsibility, and he now had regrets.

He wondered what he should do now. Maybe he should approach Jennifer and offer to help. But what value could he bring that could help the world-renowned scientists and the intellectuals working to defend Earth? If he had anything to offer, his credibility, unfortunately, was low with them. The religious community's trust in him was even lower, but the problem the world was facing was not solely going to be remedied by just a scientific solution. After watching Matt's interview he believed the world would need a much broader approach, and maybe that was where he could help.

In the morning he would need to contact his mother and ask for her help to make introductions to people who wouldn't be too happy to talk to him. From there he would need to work hard in order to be helpful. Redemption, if it were possible, would take much longer.

Chapter 8

At Pastor Charles Robinson's house it was about four in the morning, and he could not sleep because his mind was running with ideas he had after hearing the broadcast of the interview with Matt Schaeffer. The interview really affected the pastor in a way that made him feel good. He even thought to himself, "I can't believe that impending doom has got me excited, but this is amazing, and I can't stop thinking about it". He had not been this excited since before the discovery of the spacecraft so many years ago. Sure, the outlook for the human race seemed bleak, but Reverend Charles Robinson could not believe his ears as Matt told his story because it was very familiar.

Hours later he heard his wife say, "You are up already? I usually have to threaten you with the wrath of God just to get you on time for breakfast."

Then she looked around the family study to see many of her husband's old books open on the tables and spread out on the floor. He was sitting there typing away at the virtual computer screen he seldom used. She could tell he was doing a lot of thinking, and she knew every time he came up with an idea because he would jiggle his index finger in the air. She just looked at him as he hopped up and quickly moved around the room, picking up the books to read a passage, and then grabbing another and then another.

The pastor's wife stood there mystified because she had not seen him run around this much in years. It was like going back in time to the days when he was a little younger, not now as a semi-retired pastor. He had handed the keys to the church to his son Charles Junior, and he was now a prominent member of the World Interfaith Council. He was now a church elder, and his son carried on the daily duties of running the First Congregation Church.

Though the church had been close to closing its doors for good, he had turned the tide with hard work and grit. The hard work paid off, and the congregation began to increase once again. It wasn't back to the levels he had seen when he first came to the church, but considering the reduction of congregations around the world, he had done an incredible job to get even a portion of the membership back. He now spent his time conferring with the council as they tried to bring faith back to a now-skeptical world. The council tried to understand how, with what was left of the different faiths, to recognize how they could deal with the changes in the world and each other. They hoped the work they did could help bring people back.

It had been a tough road, though, since the discovery of the spacecraft. Knowledge of alien interference in man's development had made people rethink what they believed in. It was tough to proclaim that the hand of God had influenced human development when the alien presence might have been pivotal in human growth. People just didn't know what to believe.

"You old fool," his wife yelled. "What in God's heaven are you doing? Did you finally lose your mind? I am going to call a doctor 'cause you are off your rocker. I knew this would happen someday. I only thought it would be later in life!"

"Will you cool your jets, old woman? I am as sane as I've ever been," he said.

"Well, that's not saying much," she quickly responded. "Now tell me, what on earth are you doing?"

After a deep, relaxing breath, he replied, "I am researching. Then I'm going to call for a council meeting. Then we will have much to discuss. So please let me be, and I'll be down for breakfast in a few minutes."

A few weeks later in Chicago, Pastor Charles entered with vigor in his step and determination in his mind. He walked through the doors of the Ambassador Hotel followed by his trusted assistant Sha'nay Barnwell, who was between semesters of her studies at the Wake Forest University school of divinity. As soon as he walked in the door, two familiar people acknowledged him. He put his arms around them and asked, "How are you two? It is good to see you."

One of them was a short Asian woman dressed very conservatively, and the other was a Caucasian man in business dress carrying a briefcase. They smiled at the pastor and responded happily.

Pastor Charles then grabbed Sha'nay by the shoulder and brought her over to meet his friends. "This is Reverend Sandy Chen," he said.

Sha'nay bowed and shook her hand while saying, "I am so happy to meet you. I've been a fan of yours. Your televised sermons are accessible where I live, and I enjoy watching your passionate, inspirational sermons. I hope someday to have a congregation of my own, and I'd be happy to have a fraction of your talent as a teacher of the faith."

A now-bashful Sandy said, "Oh, you are helping feed my prideful side," as they all laughed.

Pastor Charles put his hand on the man's shoulder and said, "Sha'nay, this is Cardinal Dan Polanski."

Anticipating that she might be confused, Dan offered, "Due to my other career as a business analyst, I seldom wear my priest clothing."

Sha'nay recognized him. "I have seen you as contributing guest on CNBC. You give great insight!"

"Ah yes," he said. "By God's good grace I have been able to forge a career and obtain enough extra money after my personal needs are taken care of to finance my charities. Since the finding of the spacecraft and the decline in church attendance, we priests have had to find employment to be able to get by. I'm afraid that the old days of living on the generous giving from the church collections at mass are long gone. The biggest shame is that our charities and the people they help have suffered."

"Well then, maybe we can turn the tide and bring people back to the faith," Pastor Charles said.

Sha'nay, Sandy, and Dan yelled out, "Halleluiah! Praise be to God."

"Now, let this old man get some rest, and we will see you at the conference in the morning. We have much to talk about," said a suddenly tired Pastor Charles as they headed to their rooms.

"Good morning, all my friends, and God be with you," said a man with a long gray beard, black clothes, and a black turban. He was also the reigning president of the council and friends with all in the room.

"May Allah be with you, Imam Mohammad Rashoni," was heard in the room at the end of the table.

"Thank you, Charles. Now, can you enlighten us as to why you have requested this meeting? We were not supposed to meet for another four months. Your insistence was quite vigorous. It is quite expensive for all of us to be here today. We could have done this by teleconference, but you insisted on a face-to-face meeting. So please, enlighten us."

Pastor Charles looked over the other members of the council. He saw representatives from most of the religions on earth. Before the spacecraft discovery, many of these religions had been in conflict with each other. Throughout history there were wars and unspeakable crimes done between many of the religions now working together in this room today. If one looked at the cause of almost every war ever fought, one would find that religious conflict was part of, if not the entire reason for, the conflict. Yet today the representatives of the different faiths sat in the same room. There were no conflicts there, as everyone was friendly and on a first-name basis.

"Friends," Pastor Charles said to the room. "We have been through a lot over the years. We have worked hard to stay relevant when scientific discoveries have put our religious foundations in doubt in the minds of many of the people. Throughout history, disagreements between our faiths have made us distant and intolerant of one another. Death and pain reigned. But today we sit here working together. At first I did not think that any good for religious faiths would come out of the spacecraft discovery, but as I look around, I see a miracle. I see brothers in faith before me with respect for all. It took having our churches, mosques, temples, and gathering places lose a great deal of our worshippers before we would understand. Before the discovery over twenty-two years ago, I would not have thought that this could happen, but it did.

"Now we need to extend that tolerance to the scientific community. I know what you are thinking. They are our adversaries. Yes, science and religion have been at odds. But I say we need to cooperate with them to save the world. I believe it can be done. I know that some of you were thinking the same thing I was during the broadcast of Matt Schaeffer's testimonial of his experiences with the Ancient Visitors. You heard it when he talked about the end of time, which I would call Armageddon. When he spoke about how the four ships would break through the center of the universe to end time, it brought to mind the Four Horsemen of the Apocalypse. When he spoke about how the Ancient Visitors were expelled and put in this universe, I remembered how Satan and his followers were cast out of heaven. The Prince? I heard Prince of Darkness. When he spoke about how the Ancient Visitors and the Ruler of the Realm interfere with the minds of man, I heard the conflict between good and evil. And the Ruler of the Realm: I heard the Kingdom of God."

All those present nodded in agreement.

Pastor Charles looked over the group, thinking of their similar experiences, and said, "I believe the world needs faith more than ever before, and we need to help serve those needs. But I also believe to save the world we need to work together. Not just with the faithful. We need to work with the scientists who are trying to figure out how to avoid Armageddon. The situation we are all in will need both the scientific and religious communities. Throughout history, religious organizations have defamed or arrested critical thinkers of science who questioned religious beliefs. Critical thinking that conflicted with our foundation of beliefs was hidden away and called heresy. We have always been afraid of science when we should have embraced it. As the saying goes, 'The truth shall set you free.' Many scientists look to prove religion wrong because they view us as a way for ignorant man to misunderstand the unknown. To them our understanding of the world is not backed up with scientific fact. What we learned from Matt was that God is very much relevant to the human race's dilemma. I think that we need the scientists, and they need us. Together we can form a plan of action to attempt to save mankind."

"Charles," said an inquisitive Imam Rashoni. "There is no question in my mind that that entity Matt was speaking about was God, and our knowledge about what was written in our ancient texts about the end of days could only help the powers here on Earth in their efforts in the human race's survival. But our clout in world affairs is minimal at best. Many of the leaders of the world bunch us in with the Followers of Divinity. They look at us as fanatics and charlatans. So what makes you think they will want our help?"

Cardinal Polanski spoke up, "I think someone whom I invited to be here can help us with this." Then he acknowledged a woman whom they all recognized but hadn't seen enter the room. "I know you all know Dr. Ann Marie Connor."

She stood up and looked over the few people in this small conference room, thinking back to the conferences she had been to before the spacecraft discovery. If a meeting of the different faiths were to have had a gathering, there would have been a lot of people in attendance. The numbers would have been in the thousands and dignitaries like Cardinal Polanski, Imam Mohammad Rashoni, and Rabbi Wolmetz would have had an entourage with assistants and secretaries.

Maybe this crisis had not been all bad for the religious community. People like Rashoni and Wolmetz, who in the past would have fought vigorously to defend their interpretation of religion, were now good friends. For good or bad, the discovery of the spacecraft had changed the landscape of the religious community.

"Thank you for giving me the opportunity to speak to you," she said. "I think that Reverend Robinson's conclusions are correct, and this is a case where the scientific and religious communities can work together. I believe that as they continue their efforts to come up with a plan to help save the human race, they will need input from the religious community. Whether they like it or not, we may hold the key to helping us understand how to stop the Ancient Visitors. We are in a battle of good versus evil, and the future of the universe is at stake."

Sandy Chen cut her off. "I agree with you, Professor, but to the world we are obsolete. No more do governments ask our opinion on subjects, and as a matter of fact, they think we are fanatical. Even though their battle with the Followers of Divinity is at a standstill, they are still a feared terrorist group with control of 30% of the world. The rest of the world thinks we are associated with them or are just plain crazy. So how are we going to get them to listen to us?"

As Sandy finished speaking, in walked James Connor. Not only was his presence a surprise, the people in the room did not welcome it. Many of them thought he was the reason for the sorry state of religion, none more so than Sandy. She remembered one speech James had given a few years earlier to a nationally televised audience at the height of his fame, when he said, "I am here to tell you that our ancestors mistook aliens for God. Early man saw unimaginable technologies and believed it was the magic of the Gods. They saw an intelligent being and assumed he was an all-knowing deity. The evidence uncovered in the Kibish discovery is proof that a higher intelligence came to Earth, interacted with life here, and left an impression on our ancestors. Imagine if you lived only five thousand years ago, what would you have thought of the aliens as they came down from the sky? Would you have done as they ordered, worshipped them, and lived by their commandments? I would think you would because the aliens had the power to heal the injured, cure the sick, build runways for crafts, construct giant pyramids, part the seas, and so on."

These comments were a thorn in everyone's side, and James was not a welcome sight to Sandy or the others.

After a cautious and deep breath, James said, "Hello. For those who don't know me, I am James Connor, and I have come to assist you, if you will have me."

At that point the people in the room erupted into hysteria, and many started to let loose pent-up anger for him. James just stood there and took their abuse because he knew that he was in the center of their frustration, and he could not blame them. He also knew that if he hadn't stumbled into the hill covering the spacecraft and then used his fame to try to debunk the foundation of all religions on earth, then the world would be as it had been before for the people in the room, at least for a little while longer. Their churches, synagogues, mosques, temples and meeting places would be filled as they had been before. These teachers of faith would be in front of filled places of worship and doing the work of their faith. But that time had passed, and their frustration had boiled over.

"Brothers and sisters," Ann Marie tried to shout as loudly as she could over the crowd. "Please let him talk. He has something to say."

Imam Rashoni questioned Ann Marie, "Why would we want his help? Every day I have to answer questions from the few worshipers I have about many of his statements on God and his work to discredit us. The damage was deep and hard to repair."

"I know," Ann Marie said, trying to calm everyone. "But he is here to try to mend some fences. Please, I beg you, give him a chance to speak."

So Imam Rashoni rubbed his face with his hands and then looked around the room. Out of respect for Ann Marie, he waved his hand as if to say reluctantly to go ahead. The people in the room quieted down and sat back in their chairs to listen to what James had to say.

"Thank you," said James. "I would like to help you. My thoughts on the influence of God on mankind have changed."

These new thoughts did not come easily for James. While he was injured and recovering in the rehab center in Arizona, he picked up the Bible and began reading it. When he finished it, he reread it, and when he was done he looked for more material and spent months researching. The guilt of knowing that the attack by the terrorists that killed thousands of people was a response to his discovery had him reevaluate himself and his beliefs. As he did that he thought that maybe it was time to learn more about the religious beliefs of the people he had hurt and offended. So he read as much as he could and then inquired about more.

Cardinal Polanski acknowledged the crowd, "Friends, James here has embarked on a religious studies program in his mother's university. And as a matter of fact, this spring he will have earned a doctorate to add to his scientific doctorate. That much I know. Let's hear what is in his soul and give him a chance."

After looking around the room and getting gestures of cautious approvals from the other people, Imam Rashoni again waved the back of his hand.

"Thank you," James said. "I too, like Reverend Robinson, believe that the powers that be here on Earth need us to help them in their plans to save the human race. When Matt Schaeffer spoke, I heard talk about the Prince of Darkness, the Four Horsemen of the Apocalypse, the battle between good and evil, and the kingdom of heaven.

"Another connection I learned from Matt's interview was the name he heard on the ship with the Ancient Visitors, Belial. I remembered that

I had heard it before. After doing a little checking, I found it. There is a mention in one of the Dead Sea Scrolls about the war of the Sons of Light against the Sons of Darkness. It was written there that Belial was the leader of the Sons of Darkness and an angel of hostility. It is my belief that these connections to religious writings are not coincidences, and there is a reason that we can connect passages in our ancient religious texts to the Ancient Visitors and the entity the Ruler of the Realm. I think that it is intended to be a message. Maybe it is a warning, or maybe in there we can find guidance to help save mankind. It just can't be a coincidence."

After a quick look at his PDA, Rabbi Wolmetz informed them, "In one of the Dead Sea Scrolls, the War of the Sons of Light against the Sons of Darkness, Belial is described as the leader of the Sons of Darkness. It says, 'But for corruption thou hast made Belial, an angel of hostility. All his dominions are in darkness, and his purpose is to bring about wickedness and guilt. All the spirits that are associated with him are but angels of destruction.' The apocalyptic passage describes a military battle. It is believed that it was written by a small Jewish sect, the Essenes, in the first century."

James agreed, "This sect flourished between the second century BC and the first century AD. Some scholars believe that Jesus might have been one of them, and they may have been lost to history if not for a Bedouin man and his cousin who found the scrolls. These apocalyptic passages, like similar writings in many of your religions, have what I believe are clues to the battle between good and evil. Matt did say that the Ancient Visitors not only influenced our genetic development, but also helped mold our thoughts. They were angry with the Ruler of the Realm because he interfered with their molding of man's thinking. I think that clues were left with mankind about what we are about to face, the final battle for heaven. I have to admit it, I always thought that apocalyptic passages like Revelation were nonsense and were the musings of a crazy man. Now I think I may have been a little harsh."

Cardinal Polanski pointed out, "In the early church, there was much debate as to whether the Book of Revelation would be added to the Bible. I personally thought that it was a metaphor or symbols of some sort that describe the actual end of the world. Maybe James and Charles are right, and with our expertise in religious understanding we can be a help to the world's efforts in coming up with a plan to avoid mankind's end. Brothers and sisters, we can't sit on the sidelines while the battle for Heaven rages before us. Let's not sit here and dwell on what we have lost and whom to blame because this is the time the world needs us the most. If God instructed man in Scripture on how man is to defeat this evil, the world will need our knowledge."

After a short pause, as the councilmen and women took a second to think about what was said, Ann Marie asked her son, "James, can you tell us what is your motivation for coming here?"

He formed a half-smile. "I realized that I bore a great deal of responsibility for the death of thousands because of my discovery and my interpretation of what I thought it meant. It made me reevaluate my thinking. I destroyed people's strong belief in God for my own selfish motives. Now I look at the world after the spacecraft discovery, and I find a world without hope. It made me look deep into my beliefs and myself. When my mother left me a Bible to read during my rehab, I was interested in understanding its meaning. Over time I developed a passion for religious studies, and it has given me a whole other perspective on the religious views of man and his reason for being in God's universe. I guess I want to help reverse what I did. However, most of all, I want to ask forgiveness from anyone who will listen, and I know I may not find redemption for what I have done, but I want to try to help. So, please, can I be of assistance?"

Imam Rashoni looked around the room at the other council members then toward Pastor Charles for his approval. After Charles quietly nodded his head, Imam Rashoni said, "OK, Dr. Connor, you can join us in our quest. But just to let you know, the people here and the religions they represent don't quite have the clout we once had. Even though our numbers are improving, we have a fraction of the worshippers we had before. I doubt that they will let us come to the table. So why do you think that it is possible?"

James, relieved and thankful for the chance to help, offered, "I think I still have some pull. I know someone high up in authority."

A few weeks later, a delegation from the council included James, Charles, Imam Rashoni, Rabbi Wolmetz, Cardinal Polanski, and Charles' assistant Sha'nay Barnwell. They sat in a conference room at the United Nations waiting patiently for an important person to enter. After a few minutes, James' old friend Jennifer La Mont, who was now a science minister at the United Nations, entered the room.

She was quick to say as she sat down, "I don't have much time, James, so please begin. I hope this is good."

He jumped right in, "We appreciate your time, so let's get to the point. We believe that we can help as the world attempts to avoid the end of time and the destruction of mankind." James and the delegation explained to Jennifer their findings in scripture that were similar to what Matt had described.

After it was explained to her, the scientist in Jennifer looked at their findings as, at the most, coincidence. "James," she said. "People have been taking verses in the Bible and have applied the meaning to present-day events since before the time of Jesus. People like Nostradamus have made many predictions that, depending on what you believe, are accurate descriptions of actual events. In reality, however, these are wild predictions and, at best, are only partially right. So why do you think that we should be listening to the religious community? If you all can help, I'm all for this, but I need a compelling reason to include you all."

James looked at his old friend and said, "First of all, thank you for this opportunity. Now we believe that the battle between the Ruler of the Realm and the Ancient Visitors is the ultimate battle between good and evil. As Matt has said, the Ancient Visitors have not only influenced our genetics, but also, through interaction with man, tried to influence our thinking.

"Think about it, the Ancient Visitors have bred us to be warriors and slaves, so what would irk them the most? The answer is the introduction of ethical behavior. As Matt stated, the Ruler of the Realm has upset the Ancient Visitors as they try to influence man's behavior. Where we can help is that man has documented the battle between the Ruler and the Ancient Visitors in religious writing with their perspective of that influence. Books like the Bible, the Torah, and the Koran have episodes of people being spoken to by these two battling parties. There we may get clues as to how to protect the human race and defeat the Ancient Visitors."

Jennifer sat there for a few moments and then let out a large exhale as she said, "Maybe I'm crazy, but I will let you speak to the committee because, to tell you the truth, we could use any help we can get. We are looking at conflict between two sides that has lasted since the beginning of time and have technologies that dwarf ours by billions of years. To catch up by the time they return a thousand years from now to take mankind for their army will be impossible. What is worse is that we don't have a thousand years, and we need to have a plan to execute by the time the Ancient Visitors retrieve the abducted again in five years. We will have to figure out the best way to save man. You see, this conflict is bigger than the universe, and if we lose time, we'll be lost in time. I have to say that our scientists can use help in understanding the parties involved any way they can. They may find that your information is not relevant, but at least they will have the opportunity to rule it out. At this point, nothing is dispensable. So let's get you up to date as to what we know."

Two months later, the United Nations Subcommittee on Religious Writings' Possible Relevance to the Ancient Visitors and Ruler of the Realm Battle was in session.

"Dr. Weiss," said Rabbi Wolmetz to the ranking scientist. "I believe that there is a correlation between the end of time battle described by Matt Schaeffer and the end of time described by the prophet Isaiah, when he said, 'the stars of the heavens will be dissolved, and the sky rolled up like a scroll; all the starry host will fall.' We believe that that is just one of the examples of how religious writings are a picture of a possible future."

Rabbi Wolmetz continued, and as he was finishing up, Jennifer came by the marathon meeting to say, "Today we have a couple of guests to speak to you."

At that point in walked in Steven Moran, one of the abducted, followed by David Cho and two individuals that looked familiar only in history books: the Homo Kibishensis or Kibish Man. They were a male and a female. They were dressed in jeans and shirts. It was not exactly the view one would see in a museum with an exhibit of early man. As they stood before the subcommittee, it was hard not to notice the family tree before them, Homo Kibishensis, Homo sapiens, and Super Homo sapiens.

Amazingly, the male Kibish Man stepped forward to say in broken English, "Good afternoon. We are happy to meet you all."

With a look of wonder, Sha'nay spoke up first in a compassionate tone, "We are happy to make your acquaintance. My, my, what is your name?"

He looked over at David for support, and David nudged him a little bit. "My name is Shishal, and this is Libna," he said, pointing to the female. "We are from your past, and we have met what you call the

152

Ancient Visitors. They came here and told us that we should worship them. Before that we had worshipped things in nature, like the moon and the sun. But when the Ancient Visitors came they taught us to worship them as they taught us to fight and kill. We did not do that before. We lived in peace, but then they had us taking what we wanted from others and hurting them if they resisted. They lived with us for as long as I can remember. One day they said that I would be sleeping for a while. Then I woke up here with David looking down at me. That is all I know about them, but Libna knows something else."

The female hid behind Shishal, but he pushed her forward. She reluctantly told them, "They feel pain. I saw one of them get hurt and feel pain."

At that moment Steven offered, "Many of the races on the ship while abducted spoke how the Ancient Visitors were indestructible, god-like figures, and this information could make the races look at them in a different light."

Jennifer thanked them and addressed the subcommittee, "The Ancient Visitors may have passed themselves off as gods, but they are just as destructible as we are. Not only did they feel pain, but two of them died on Earth. Our friends here from our past confirmed your belief that the Ancient Visitors have tried to control us religiously. So it is important that you keep working because we have come up with a plan. So far, the plan we have is not great, but it is the best we think we can do. There are a lot of holes in it, and we need you all to help fill them before they come back."

She then thanked the committee and dismissed them for the night. Leaving the conference, she stopped to talk to James. "Do you really think this panel can help? You know what we're up against."

James stood there and felt contrite while saying, "First of all, I want to thank you for giving me this opportunity, and, Jennifer, I --"

She cut him off, "James, we have been friends for so long. I was happy to help. I like what you are doing here. This is an angle we were not working on, and you have the experience."

With a heavy heart he explained, "Don't you mean I have experience screwing up?"

She countered, "Your insight should be a help to that subcommittee."

"Well," he said, "again, thank you."

The two friends walked out together, catching up. The subcommittee had its work cut out.

Chapter 9

After morning services at his three hundred-year-old Italian church south of Naples, Monsignor Grazzani decided to take a stroll on this sunny day to see his good friend, Isaiah Goldman. He and Isaiah had grown up in this very town together. Even though they were from different faiths, the monsignor was Catholic, and Isaiah was Jewish, it had not mattered when they were kids. They became such good friends as little boys, when they would climb trees and dig holes together. It was an innocent time, when playing tag or with action figures would be at the forefront of their thoughts, not the differences in their religious beliefs. As they grew up in the south part of Naples, they stayed close and confided in each other every now and then. Today, Monsignor Grazzani had something on his mind, and he needed to talk to someone. So he walked all the way to Isaiah's small jewelry store in the busier part of town where tourists visited.

"Good morning," Monsignor Grazzani said to Isaiah, who was sitting behind the counter.

He was just finishing with a customer, who grabbed her new earrings and headed out the door. Isaiah acknowledged the monsignor. When the customer left, Isaiah used a towel behind the counter to clean his hands and then made his way over to hug his old friend.

"Anthony, how are you? I mean, Monsignor. I forget sometimes."

With a halfhearted response, he said, "I am OK, Isaiah. I was wondering if we could talk. Do you have time?"

Knowing that his friend came unannounced and looked like he had something heavy on his mind, he said, "Oh sure, we can walk over to the park. It is a nice day, and we can find a bench to relax on."

So the two friends headed out of the store and to the park. During the walk, they asked about each other's families and talked work just like always. Then they reminisced about playing together on these very same streets as boys. But as they got closer to the park, Isaiah could see that something was troubling his friend.

Sitting on a bench, Isaiah said bluntly, as he always did, "You look like crap, Anthony. What the heck is wrong with you? Do you have some bad news to tell me? Like you are sick or something?"

Shaking his head, he said, "No, physically I'm fine. I appreciate the worry. No, I feel that my soul has been injured, and I don't know what I should do."

Isaiah then offered, "Maybe if you get it off your chest, we can talk about it. That is what you always tell me when I am troubled. So, why don't you take your own advice?"

After taking a deep breath and looking up to the sky, Monsignor Grazzani explained, "I am having doubts. Not about God. I have doubts about the doings of man. To be exact, I'm having my doubts about the Followers of Divinity movement. I was, like many, very happy the movement brought God back into the forefront. Prior to that, the world began for the first time in history to lean towards the unthinkable, toward a world without God. I thought that that should not happen and joined the movement. Even though the movement had a violent element to it, I thought the ends justified the means because there were episodes in the Bible where God sent His people into battle against the unbelievers. I thought we were fighting for God. Now I am not so sure, and I don't know what I should do."

With that, Monsignor Grazzani pulled out his handkerchief from his jacket pocket and wiped his forehead.

Confused, Isaiah asked, "Why the change? I remember how you were a big supporter of the movement. As a matter of fact, you talked me into supporting it. You said that the movement turned the tide in the war against religion and the increase in nonbelievers. The fear was that science would usher in a world without God. They would come up with some formula that would prove God never existed, and the world would go on without Him. The discovery of the spacecraft, you said, clouded people's minds, and the conjecture of the existence of God by scientists was morally reprehensible. You viewed the scientists as minions of Satan out to do his work to deceive mankind. As a result, you joined the Followers of Divinity movement. As it gained strength, the movement took action so that God would not be irrelevant. The movement had an unprecedented cooperation between the different faiths of the world. Jews, Christians, Muslims, Hindus, and anyone else you can think of formed an alliance to combat the forces of evil. In this case, science is the evil monster they have come to battle. So, what has changed? You don't feel the same anymore?"

Monsignor Grazzani, eager to get it off his chest, answered without hesitation, "At first, I was all for it. The speeches and the blogs got my blood boiling. The way they communicated it to me was totally believable and hit the foundation of my soul. It seemed that they had an answer to everything that had been bothering me for so long. It seemed so clear as to the course of action we should take, that we should fight to save man's soul. They were so believable that I thought the UN exaggerated the acts the Followers of Divinity had done, but now I am not so sure. Over time, I guess, the charismatic speeches by Bishop Terapion and his close followers have started to be less convincing as to their true goal. I get the feeling it's more about power and control and not about the salvation of man's soul."

Now as Monsignor Grazzani got nearer to what was bothering him, he inched closer to Isaiah so that no one else could hear. "As you know, I can't divulge what is said in confidence in private or in the confessional booth, but I will tell you the gist of what they are saying."

Isaiah asked, "Who are saying?"

Monsignor Grazzani inched closer, "As you know, the Followers of Divinity have a paramilitary training center north of Naples, and I travel there to administer communion and confessions to the trainees. At first, I thought that it was normal training any country would have their military do to defend their country, but it seemed different. Some of the people came forward to me in private and mentioned to me that they are asked to do unspeakable acts in the name of God. They had a problem with their comfort level with what needed to be done. Things like sanctioned kidnappings, torture, murders, and suicide bombing, all in the name of God. They are told that true believers need to battle these foes with any means possible, or the scientists would turn our people into nonbelievers and our souls would be condemned to hell. They tell them about hideous acts the scientists have done on people and that the spacecraft was made by them to fool man in believing there is no God.

"They are told that in this army of God that if you do these acts upon the scientists, you will be rewarded in heaven, and if you die during the battle, you would be rewarded above all people and the riches of heaven will be yours. To infuriate the soldiers, they are told that throughout history, scientists have been the demons Satan has sent to destroy man. Everything from plagues, earthquake, and floods has been scientist's fault. They blame them for the Inquisition, the Holocaust, diseases, and oppression by leaders like Joseph Stalin, Napoleon, and even the Shah of Iran. They are told that all of the world's pain is because of the scientists and the nonbelievers, so they must be eliminated, all of them. But as unholy as that is, I am hearing even more disturbing information. It seems that the soldiers are not only fighting the enemy from outside, they are fighting the enemy from within as well."

Now very intrigued, Isaiah asked, "What do you mean within?"

Monsignor Grazzani inched closer. "I mean that people are disappearing. At first, I heard it here and there from people in my parish that doubters were brought in by the authorities to be schooled in the faith. From what I'm hearing now, many of those people don't return. It is not well known, but the Followers of Divinity have a police force that is made up of hard-line religious clergy and lay people who enforce religious doctrine. Rumor has it that they have been picking people up. I know it happens in some hard-line religious countries, but now here? I don't know, Isaiah. I am getting the feeling that this is not what I signed up for."

Isaiah asked, "Are you sure about this? I mean, what you are telling me is something that has happened throughout history. One group gains power and tries to expand that power. It is like a drug addiction that can't ever be satisfied. They gain power at any cost, and once they have it, they hold it at any cost. Average people are their pawns to be molded into what the power mongers want and need. They don't settle for battling for more conquests outside. They battle just as fiercely inside to control their people. Dissenters are eliminated and history is changed to make it easier to promote their doctrine.

"It has been said that those who control the past can control the future. I have to tell you, this sounds much too familiar. In the 1930s, a small group of people led by a charismatic leader fooled the population into thinking they had an answer to their ills. They blamed one group of people for all their problems and began to eliminate them. They believed that the whole world needed their leadership and started to force their ideals on the world. If there were dissenters, then they were brutally put down. Remember Hitler and the Nazis? They built a massive conquering army and employed a secret police to watch the people. They promised great things, but their sadistic ways became their ends, and in their wake they left destruction and misery.

"As you know, I was not as taken in as you were by the Followers of Divinity, but I was taken in at any rate. I have to admit they are a charismatic group with all sorts of remedies for our problems, but I always wondered, what is their real motivation for doing this? Sure, the saving of our religions is important, but what do they really want? Power is a funny thing that can change people with even the best motivations.

I'm starting to wonder what their intentions are. Maybe we should dig deeper into it to find out."

Monsignor Grazzani quickly said, "No, we shouldn't. I should. It was my concern, and I just came here to air my frustrations. I will ask some questions, and you should not get involved in case there is merit in my doubts. I would feel awful if you were tangled up in this."

Isaiah tried to relieve his concerns about him and offer his help. "Listen, I'll just make some inquiries with some of my friends and let you know what I find. Don't worry, I will be fine."

Then the two friends hugged, and Isaiah went back to his jewelry store, and Monsignor Grazzani walked all the way back to his parish, reflecting on what he needed to do.

When Monsignor Grazzani got back to the rectory, his virtual message board was flashing on his desk. It was Bishop Sarno with news. "Greetings, Monsignor. I hope you are well. The reason for my reaching out to you is that the leadership of the Followers of Divinity is making its rounds in southern Italy next week. Bishop Terapion will grace your church next Saturday night. Please make the arrangements with his subordinates. I have texted their contact information to you. Please give him your best welcome and…"

Monsignor Grazzani then turned off the message and prayed. "Oh Lord, when you test me, you really go all out. Then again, maybe this is what I need to trust the movement. Maybe Bishop Terapion will enlighten me so that I return to the path and stop this nonsense of my doubt. Or maybe my fears will be confirmed? Either way, Lord, like they say, you work in mysterious ways."

So then Monsignor Grazzani listened to the rest of his messages and contacted Bishop Terapion's handlers to make the arrangements for the visit. He would do it the way he did everything, thoughtfully.

Two mornings later, Monsignor Grazzani headed out to the base to administer to the military personnel as usual. Most of the day, he heard confessions that were much the same as he had throughout the time he had been coming here. As he was finishing up the long day, Monsignor Grazzani started to pack his things and just happened to look up. Standing there was a young soldier. She looked like she was fifteen. When he noticed she was nervous and anxious, he quickly called her over.

Since this was not a church and much of the training was outdoors, Monsignor Grazzani heard confessions near an olive tree alongside a makeshift barracks. He found that inside the buildings on the compound there was not sufficient space for the privacy he needed. So each day, rain or shine, he stood next to this tree and waited for people to come over to see him.

As the girl walked toward him, he gazed at her and got a feeling that this was not going to be an ordinary confession. He hoped that he could help her because she looked as though she would reveal something that pained her deeply.

"Hello, child," he said.

The girl didn't speak and just kept looking at the ground. A few moments went by and he tried to get her to talk. "Child, I can see you have something to say, and I am here for you. I will stay here as long as you need me to."

After hesitating, she said, "Is it true that what I say here to you cannot be repeated? I mean, that you can't tell anyone?"

Without hesitating, the monsignor replied, "That is absolutely true. I'm bound by a vow I took to not divulge what we talk about. What you tell me will not be repeated, I promise."

Now with tears coming down her face, she continued. "I joined the fight because I believed that God and everything He stood for was under attack. I swore that I would give my life for the Lord, and I would freely do so. I knew coming here that I might have to do some hard things, or maybe horrific things in battle, to help this world become a world of

God's rule. But now I don't know. I am confused, and I don't know what to do. I need guidance."

Very concerned, Monsignor Grazzani asked, "Are you being asked to do something that is bothering your conscience? Not to justify it, but in times of war, you are sometimes forced to do what otherwise you might think is against your judgment to do."

Cutting him off, she answered, "I understand the things that need to be done in war, and I accepted what I needed to do, but this is different. My unit has not been used in battle, exactly. It has been used as a hit squad. But not against the enemy: it is used against members of our movement. I'm confused. Why would they do that? Most of the people we hit are ordinary folks. What we are told is that they have been spreading lies about God's movement and are now enemies. One such target, when captured, swore that all he did was doubt our message. He was brought back to be executed without a trial."

Monsignor Grazzani asked, "Are you sure? Could you be mistaken? Many things in times of war are done in a confusing manner, and maybe you misread the situation."

She answered quickly, "I know what I heard and saw, Father. It happened like I said. But what bothers me the most is our next target. It's Cardinal Pesta of Turin. He is our next target. Plans have been made to extract him and bring him in."

Quickly he responded, "Child, you must be gravely mistaken. Cardinal Pesta is a respected man of the cloth and a member of the movement. This has got to be wrong."

Crying even harder she said, "I am not wrong, and what bothers me the most is that he is my uncle on my mother's side. I know this man. He is gentle and loving. He would give the shirt off his back and wouldn't mind giving a needy person the last coin he had left. But an order came down saying he is a threat to the movement, and his elimination is vital in our success over the forces of evil. I don't understand why, and I don't know what to do. I can't let this happen, and I want to warn him so he does not get hurt. Can you help me, Father? Can you help him?"

Gripped by his own doubts, Monsignor Grazzani was apprehensive and hesitant for a moment, but he then remembered that he took an oath to help others, and she needed him. This confession only helped confirm his suspicions, and he knew he must act.

"I will help you. What is your name?"

"Claudia. Thank you for helping me," she said.

He replied, "Don't thank me yet. I haven't helped you yet. First, we need to get you out of here. What we will do is take these two chairs back to my car, and then you get in and get under the robes I have in the back." From the tree they made their way, and she hopped in as planned.

Sliding into the driver's seat, the monsignor warned, "Keep low. We have to get by the checkpoint."

At the checkpoint the guard approached his car, "Oh, it is you, Monsignor. Did you have a nice day here?"

Nervous and afraid, he thought that in the last few years he might have driven too fast from time to time or snuck a cookie from the parish rectory kitchen before dinner. He had never done anything at this level before, though. Today he was smuggling out a soldier from her base with intentions of going AWOL. So he was tense as he said, "It was a wonderful day," and since he did not know what to do, he just looked forward.

The guard noticed a difference in the monsignor. "Are you OK, Monsignor Grazzani? You don't look so good."

This perked him up, and as coolly as he could he said, "No, I'm fine. I think I was in the sun too long today. The shade inside my car feels good, and the air conditioning on my face has made me feel better already. I'll be fine, son. Thank you for your concern."

The guard signaled the gate up, and Monsignor Grazzani waved good-bye to the guard and his companions.

On the road back, he said, "How are you doing back there? It will be about forty-five minutes for my car to navigate us back to the rectory where I can hide you for a while, so keep down so none of the street cameras get an image of you. When we get back to the rectory, you stay in the car until darkness, and I will let you in through the back door."

Claudia nervously asked, "Father, could you also help my mother and little brother? If they find out I am missing, they will surely be detained for information. I fear for them."

"Sure," said an unsure Monsignor Grazzani as he wondered how in God's name he was going to get her to safety, much less her mother and brother. Right now, the enormity of what he was about to do was making him feel his world was about to change.

Later that night, with Claudia safely hidden in Father Tonelli's bedroom while he was on holiday in Sicily, he heard a knock on his front door. When he opened it, his heart skipped as one of the officers of the movement's police force, God's Healers of the Faith, stood in front of him. He had seen him many times before, but seeing an officer at his door when he had a secret was nerve-racking. Standing there was a man no different from any other, yet he had left a lasting impression on Monsignor Grazzani.

Once the door was open, the man spoke. "Good evening, Monsignor. I am Salvatore DeRosa. I work for a branch of God's Military."

"Good evening, Mr. DeRosa," said Monsignor Grazzani. "Can I help you?"

"I understand that you were at the base today," said Salvatore.

"Yes, I was. Today I was there to administer confession, and I was there most of the day," Monsignor Grazzani said.

Salvatore came to the point, "One of our soldiers went missing, and we hoped you could help us. The last time she was seen was waiting in line for confession. Her name is Claudia Marino, and she was part of an important military unit that does special work. We are worried about her and hope she is OK."

"I remember the last person to ask for a confession was a young girl," said Monsignor Grazzani as he watched Salvatore look around the foyer of the rectory.

Salvatore asked, "Was there anything peculiar about the confession?"

Monsignor Grazzani was quick to reply, "I can't divulge what is said in the confessional."

"Of course. My apologies for asking," said Salvatore.

"It's all right, my son," Monsignor Grazzani said. "But I can tell you, if it helps, that there was nothing out of the ordinary. It was completely usual, and if you hadn't mentioned it, I would have forgotten all about her confession."

After peering around the room a few more times, Salvatore said, "Well then, Monsignor, I appreciate your help, and I will let you enjoy the rest of the evening. God bless you."

Monsignor Grazzani held the door for Salvatore and said, "Sorry I couldn't help you, and you enjoy your night as well. God bless you."

With that good-bye, Monsignor Grazzani closed the door. All he could hear was his own heavy breathing. He thought, thank God she didn't just walk down the stairs while he was here. Just as he finished that thought, another knock sounded at the door. Oh God, I must have looked guilty, he panicked. There was no stalling, however. Taking another deep breath, he opened the door.

Standing there was Isaiah. "Good evening, Anthony. Gee, you still look like crap."

"Get in here!" he said furtively.

Once in with the door closed, Monsignor Grazzani grabbed him and hugged him. "You scared the devil out of me," he said as he put his hands over his own face. "So why are you here?"

"You asked me to check on things, and I did so," Isaiah said. "I'm reporting what I found out. It turns out that you were right about your suspicions. My connections are telling me that people have been quietly taken, and no one knows where they went. Very few come back. All anyone knows is that they were taken for some sort of rehabilitation of their beliefs. It is all very secretive. I would have found out more, but my sources in the military have gone quiet due to an all-out search for some missing female soldier. Apparently she went AWOL."

Monsignor Grazzani repeated, "Some missing female soldier," with a very guilty look on a face that couldn't help but show his feelings.

A shocked Isaiah said, "Oh, no. You didn't. You couldn't help yourself, could you? Always leaping without regard for yourself."

A contrite Monsignor Grazzani said, "I couldn't help it. She just fell into my lap, and I thought it was God's will."

Isaiah asked while shaking his head back and forth, "So what are we going to do?"

Monsignor Grazzani asked, "Can you help me get her family to Rome so we can secure their passage away from Followers of Divinity territory? I need to contact Bishop Sarno. I know in private that he was not thrilled with the movement, and he can help me secure sanctuary for the girl with the Holy See's office there in Rome."

"It is too hot right now to get her out of here. Security is on alert," said Isaiah.

Monsignor Grazzani agreed, "That's good advice. I'll have to do it after Saturday night. The parish is getting a visit from Bishop Terapion as he makes his rounds through the local churches. I am worried that if that doesn't go as planned, they may get suspicious."

A surprised Isaiah remarked, "Terapion is coming here? That is just great. The security alone for his visits must be tight as a drum." Sarcastically he asked, "You sure it was God that dropped her in your lap?"

Despite their worries, the two planned for the extraction of the girl and her family. Isaiah left as soon as the streets around the rectory were clear.

When Saturday morning came and Bishop Sarno arrived, Monsignor Grazzani explained what he had done.

Bishop Sarno replied, "Let me get this straight. Anthony, you heard bits and pieces of activities that you believe the Followers of Divinity are secretly doing. This has caused you to doubt the movement, a movement that has helped promote the continued worship of God in these troubling times as the world tips toward nonbelievers. Are you sure you want to go down this path? Once word gets out, I am afraid that you will not be safe."

Monsignor Grazzani accepted his plight. "I am sure that I am doing what is right. It is not my welfare I am concerned about; it's the girl and her family."

Then Bishop Sarno looked at him and gave his blessing, "OK, I will do what I can to help. You know that I'm not thrilled with the Followers of Divinity. Killing scientists is not the path to spirituality, and killing your own people because they are not as enamored with the movement as the leaders like is murder. This was not what I pictured when I signed up. Of course, I'll work with the Holy See on this matter. As you know, these times have been hard on the Pope. He has balanced a movement that has kept the spirit of continued worship in God by partnering with an organization that he feels does not always go down a righteous path. It is hard because most of the believers are in territories controlled by the Followers of Divinity. He does what many popes before him have done to secure the survival of the church: walks a very fine line. But I know he will help us and make sure the girl is safe. Anyway, let's plan on getting her out of here the day after Terapion's visit, when it quiets down a little bit."

Monsignor Grazzani and Bishop Sarno then made arrangements.

Later on that day as Monsignor Grazzani was preparing for the official visit of Bishop Terapion, Salvatore DeRosa arrived once again. When he saw his opportunity, he approached Monsignor Grazzani.

"Monsignor, it is good to see you again."

Anticipating running into him, Monsignor Grazzani replied, "How nice it is to see you again, Salvatore. I hope you found that poor girl safe and sound."

He replied, "Not yet, Monsignor, but we are working hard." As he said that, he peered around the rectory as cleaning people were working on the rectory and the church. Salvatore said, "So I see you are cleaning the place on account of Bishop Terapion's visit, and it looks like the place is almost spotless. And, oh look. Your car has been through a thorough cleaning at the car wash as well. You really are cleaning up the place."

Knowing that Salvatore was going to do a DNA scan, Monsignor Grazzani made sure he employed ten times the people normally needed to clean the church premises for such an event. Using the event as an excuse, any evidence of Claudia was cleaned away.

Monsignor Grazzani said to Salvatore, "If there is anything I can do to assist you, please don't hesitate to ask me. But now you'll have to excuse me, for I must prepare for our esteemed leader, Bishop Terapion, who will grace us with his presence tonight. I look forward to his inspirational sermon. I hear that in person, it takes your breath away. So again, please excuse me. I have so much to do and so little time to do it."

As he stepped aside Salvatore said, "By all means, Monsignor. Please go about your business, and if you don't mind, I will stick around here tonight to hear the bishop speak to the flock."

Monsignor Grazzani bowed his head in approval and walked away. As he put distance between him and Salvatore, he took a little pride, though sinful, he felt, in how he successfully planned to wipe evidence away of Claudia and leverage the Bishop Terapion's arrival to his benefit. Having Salvatore around added to his apprehension about Claudia's fate. For now she was hidden away in a secret compartment behind Father Tonelli's closet with food and drink. It had been built during World War II to hide Jews during the Nazi occupation of Italy. These days it was used as an extra storage compartment and had been filled with old boxes.

That evening, the church filled with many from its congregation, as well as local and regional dignitaries who came to have their picture taken with Bishop Terapion. The church was filled to capacity in anticipation of the evening's event. As the crowd waited, a convoy of limos and security vehicles pulled up in front of the church. Quickly, the many security personnel secured the premises, and as they signaled all clear, Bishop Terapion exited the armored limo and quickly made his way inside the church. When the people waiting saw him enter, they applauded as he made his way to the church's altar. At the altar were seated Bishop Sarno and religious leaders from many different faiths. They stood up to applaud as well. When Bishop Terapion reached the altar, he greeted Bishop Sarno and the other leaders. Then he approached Monsignor Grazzani and said, "Monsignor, thank you so much for having me today at your beautiful church. I am blessed."

"Greetings Bishop Terapion, the pleasure is all ours. We are so happy you have come here today to fill our need for your beautiful insights into God's plans for true believers. For you are His esteemed messenger."

Bishop Terapion thanked him, then turned to the pulpit and started his usual charismatic sermon. Monsignor Grazzani could not concentrate much on the sermon because his mind was racing ahead to Claudia's travels and how to keep her safe. Many things needed to fall into place for this to work, and as he glanced toward Salvatore's face in the crowd, he knew things could go very badly.

While Monsignor Grazzani was locked in his thoughts, an accident happened. Bishop Terapion, moving around to the front of the altar while speaking, was struck on the arm when an altar girl accidentally knocked over a brass candleholder. Being close to him, and as it was in his nature to help someone in need, Monsignor Grazzani left his chair and pulled out some of his handkerchiefs to cover the wound. The monsignor found the bishop's reaction to this accident quite odd, for Bishop Terapion got up quickly and ordered his entourage to leave. He did not think it was that bad a wound. It could swiftly be bandaged, and then the service could continue. But in any event, Bishop Terapion must have thought otherwise and made his way out to the convoy while some of his entourage expressed regret for his early exit. Once inside the vehicles, the convoy left. Monsignor Grazzani then apologized to the crowd as the disappointed people slowly left the church and went home.

As the church emptied, Salvatore made his way to Monsignor Grazzani to say, "It is a shame the visit was cut short, Monsignor."

Monsignor Grazzani replied, "We should be grateful for his presence today."

Salvatore replied, "I believe you are right, Monsignor. He blessed us today, and we should thank God for that. Now I am asking you to take my leave."

With surprise on his face and secret pleasure inside, Monsignor Grazzani responded, "You are not leaving us so soon, are you?"

Salvatore replied, "My investigation takes me up to Turin, where the soldier's mother and brother have disappeared, and we are now looking for them."

Monsignor Grazzani, knowing that his friend Isaiah must have gotten there first, responded, "Well then, your presence has been appreciated in your efforts to find that poor girl, and I hope you find more success there in Turin. Good luck in your travels. God bless you, my son."

Salvatore thanked Monsignor Grazzani and left for Turin. This left

Monsignor Grazzani standing alone in the church, thankful that the plan had not gone astray.

The next morning, Monsignor Grazzani woke up early and gathered Claudia. He prepared for her journey, and then he woke up Bishop Sarno, who had stayed the night in the guest quarters.

Monsignor Grazzani said, "Bishop Sarno, your ride sent by the Vatican will be here in a few minutes, and we need to be ready to hide Claudia in the secret compartment."

Hurrying along, the bishop quickly finished his breakfast. When he passed Monsignor Grazzani, the monsignor noticed the bishop had some of his breakfast on the corner of his mouth, so he pulled out his handkerchief in his jacket to wipe it. Then he noticed something strange. Surprisingly, this was one of the handkerchiefs he had used to help Bishop Terapion with his wound. He thought he didn't have it in his possession anymore because Bishop Terapion had grabbed the handkerchiefs used to cover his wound and left with them, or so the monsignor thought.

What he found strange was that it was still wet, and the color of the blood was not what he expected it would be. He thought for sure that blood would be dried by now. Taking a long look at it, he felt its texture, and smelled it. He thought that he had seen blood many times in his life, like when he got hurt climbing a tree as a child with Isaiah, or when he cut his hand on a rose stem when he was doing gardening at the rectory, or when one of the children at Sunday school got hurt playing ball before class would begin, not to mention when he volunteered at the medical clinic in town.

Looking down at it again he tried to remember the circumstances. He remembered there had been an accident to Bishop Terapion, and he had tried to help with the wound. But there was something else that did not occur to him at the time -- Bishop Terapion had quickly covered up the wound, not to stop the bleeding, but to hide it. He wondered why. So

Monsignor Grazzani looked down at the handkerchief again and realized what he had.

He turned to Bishop Sarno and said, "You need to take me along with you, and I will tell you why when we get to Rome. We must leave quickly."

They left with Claudia hidden away in a vehicle transport registered by the Vatican that would safely make its way through the numerous checkpoints on their way to Rome.

A couple of days later, Salvatore returned to ask more questions and saw a priest setting the church up for the next day's mass. He approached him, "Excuse me, Father. Is Monsignor Grazzani around? I would like to speak to him."

Father Tonelli said, "He left for reassignment a few days ago. He was brought back to Rome and from there reassigned. It happened too quickly, and I will miss him. You may have to try there, if you want to contact him."

A very disappointed Salvatore thanked the priest and walked away, anguished by his lost opportunity.

Chapter 10

It was now almost five years after the return of the abducted and Matt Schaeffer's Revelation. Scientists had been working on improving man's chances. Today in a secret United Nations meeting in the outskirts of London, many of the free world's leaders were there to unveil a substance that, it was hoped, would level the field a little.

United Nations Chairman of the General Assembly Sergio Perez addressed the leaders. "Friends, you have just heard Dr. Sinclair and his international team speak about the success they have had in replicating this formula that will enable humans to change from modern Homo sapiens into Super Homo sapiens. The hope is that this serum may help our descendants a thousand years from now. If it can be reproduced in large quantities, it could increase the percentage of people the Ancient Visitors tag as suitable to be taken and reduce the amount of people to be used as a food supply. Secondly, and more importantly in my belief, the faster we can help our children and their children evolve to Super Homo sapiens, the better chance they will have to defeat the Ancient Visitors when they return a thousand years from now to take the population away. Maybe as their intellect becomes more evolved, they can advance in knowledge and technology enough to defend our people and avoid the inevitable defeat of the people of this world. Now, here to speak to us is Cynthia Moss."

The tall, dark-haired Super Homo sapiens stood up, and the physical changes in her were obvious to all. The changes in her body were not the source of her greatest pride, however.

Before the Ancient Visitors originally took her, she was happy as a dancer touring with the Philadelphia Dance Troop. It had been her love since she was a little girl. She would practice day and night. Her mom would take her to the dance studio every chance she could, and even on days she wasn't there, Cynthia would go down to the basement of the house, where she had cleared a place to practice until her mom would put her to bed. As she grew up, her talent increased until she was exceptional at dancing, and she went on to live her dream of touring with a dance company.

She had been happy with her life, but it all changed after the abduction. The biggest change was in her mind. At first her intellect would race ahead as she accumulated information. Instead of dancing, she would read and research any topic that came to mind at that minute. As her dancing faded from her life, the thirst for knowledge took its place. As she learned to control the many thoughts racing in her mind, she was able to concentrate, and when she did, her learning came fast and easy. She decided to go to college and get the degree she had skipped for her dance career. Her advanced intelligence and her thirst for knowledge propelled her through school all the way to a PhD. Today she was one of the leading experts in advanced biochemistry.

Cynthia thanked Sergio Perez with a nod of her head. Then she addressed the crowd, "The serum, if the tests go well, should be able to change human DNA to Super Homo sapiens DNA within three months of gestation, combined with some time in a blue liquid chamber. The downside is that we have only manufactured enough in almost five years for just three doses."

She continued as the crowd gave sounds of disappointment. "Well, we hope that after these doses are used successfully on volunteers, we can manufacture enough to cover the world population in the next thirty years. The Ancient Visitors could only succeed at about 66% of the abducted. Maybe they were happy with that success rate, or that was all they planned for and the rest were designed to be a food source anyway. We're not sure. I can tell you this: we believe that there will be at least a 90% success rate with our serum. By doing this, our hope is that man can evolve at a faster rate, and the improvement in man's intellect will help in the next thousand years. Maybe then we will have the ability to defend the planet, or the solar system, or even this section of the galaxy. We have already explored the planets at the far reaches of the solar system and advances in technology double every year. Will we advance our people's intelligence enough to catch up to a race that is billions of years ahead of us? Maybe not, but just maybe we will be able to give our children a fighting chance."

When Cynthia was done, the first question was asked by Franz Becker, the head of the European Union: "This is amazing, but we have yet to hear the details of the plan to stop the end of time and the paradox it will unleash."

"What do you mean we are leaving?" said a surprised James, who was a guest of Jennifer and David's at the secret meeting. Jennifer had gone to great lengths to get James cleared to be there, but Jennifer had been instructed to not let him hear about the plan to be put in place. Only a few were to be allowed to know at this point.

"Come on, James. Let's get going. This is all you are going to see," she said.

James sighed, "Ah, it was just getting good."

She grabbed him by the arm and told him, "Your clearance doesn't go up this high, and I want to bring you over to the lab on the other side of London to see the facility where the serum is being manufactured. There's a small party going on there to celebrate the completion of the first phase of the serum project, and many of the scientists here at this meeting are heading there now. This team has worked on the serum for almost five years. They put in a lot of work just to get three small vials. It is not much, but from this work we will be able to prepare the human race for a future that belongs to our brothers and sisters, not to the Ancient Visitors."

Then Jennifer, David, and James got in the transport, and it whisked them to the other side of London in Upper Edmonton. When they got to the lab, the three headed up to the third-floor rotunda where the celebration had already started. As they walked through the door, they could see the head of the team, Dr. Susan Allan, who was also on the Subcommittee to Understand Religious Writings' Possible Relevance to the Ancient Visitors and the Ruler of the Realm Battle, put her hand up to make the toast. Before Jennifer, David, and James could breathe the air in the room, there was a flash of light. The blast threw the three back out the door.

As they came to their senses, they heard people scream and cry. Then there was the sound of weapons fire. Jennifer turned to David and James. "The serum. We have to get the serum!" she cried out.

The three got to their feet and ran through the corridor around the rotunda. Many of the security personnel recognized Jennifer and rallied around her as she repeated, "We have to get the serum!" Then with weapons drawn they headed to the vault, where they heard another blast. Once there, the loyal security personnel engaged in a firefight with the attackers.

One of the men attacking the lab yelled out, "Die in the name of God!" Then he fired into the opened vault, hitting the glass encasements holding the lab samples before he was shot dead. Much of the inside of the vault was in disarray, and two of the three vials were destroyed.

Jennifer yelled to James, who was closest to the serum vial, "James, take it and let's go!"

He grabbed the vial, and they started out of the vault room heading for the transports. When they came around a corner, they were fired on, and in the confusion James was separated from the others as he took cover in another direction. He then ran down a hallway, trying to open doors. When one opened he slipped through it and found himself trapped in a closet filled with gauzes, bandages, and needles. As the weapons fire got close, James looked for options, and then he heard the door getting battered. He looked for a place to hide the vial, but he could not find any. With much hesitation, he chose what he felt was the only option. When the door came down, the terrorists found James lying on the floor convulsing. The vial had been emptied into a syringe.

Angry but still determined, they grabbed James to carry him out. Because the weight of James' body slowed them down, Jennifer and the loyal security personnel were able to overtake and shoot the attackers. One by one they fell until they were all down.

David was the first to get to James as his body shook with convulsions. "Oh, what did you do? Stay with us, James!" He then hit the communication receiver on his arm. "Send the medics to the south exit. Now!" he yelled.

Jennifer held James' hand as his body shook uncontrollably, and they waited for medical personnel to arrive. He was obviously in pain, and she tried to comfort him as David rushed out the door to find help. It was then that Jennifer noticed his arm had a recent injection mark, and she looked through his clothing for the vial of serum, but it was not there. She looked at him and said, "Oh no, James. You didn't."

She knew what he had done and felt terrible, as her friend, who was fine when he arrived, would now leave as a medical experiment. When David got back, Jennifer tried to detach herself as James' friend and think instead as science minister. "David, we need to shut down this section of the building, call in the hazmat and DDC units to avoid contamination, and quarantine the area. He's got to be put in a blue liquid chamber. We need to examine him while keeping it secret. So make sure security is as tight as possible."

As she did her job, James lay there in agony. In pain, he knew things would not be the same again. It was one impulsive moment, and now his life was changed forever.

Time had passed, and most likely this was the last time Steven

Moran would be home for a long time, if ever. He knew this would be the last time he would enjoy the holidays with his parents and friends. Even though he would see them before he went, his parents were doting over him. He noticed it and tried to help his mom, but she would hear nothing of it.

Even his dad tried. "Eva, will you sit down and enjoy dinner? You need to relax."

She ignored him and told him, "Shut up, Eddie. I will do what I want. This is Steven's day, and I want to make sure it is special."

Briefly, it did make him forget about the journey he would have to take. It was a great day and night at the home in which he had grown up. He saw all his friends and relatives come by to wish him good luck. Both Tommy and Johnny were there with their families, as well as Brenda with her grown children and many other family and friends.

Toward the end of the night, he thought about the first time he had been taken, when Tommy and Johnny where teenagers and Brenda was planning their marriage. Back then, he thought he would have a normal life, but it now seemed like so long ago. Now he had a mission, and the next morning he was to be picked up by the authorities to be prepared. It would take months. He needed to be ready to be taken by the Ancient Visitors in the next six months. Today was the fifth anniversary of the day he had returned from the last abduction. Matt estimated that they would be brought back to the ship in five years and six months. So it was almost time to go, and Steven savored the last moments at home with his family.

The next day, Steven arrived at the away facility built for Steven and the other Super Homo sapiens. There they would train for their mission and wait for the aliens to come back to abduct them again. The training would consist of running though scenarios in a massive complex that had sections built to resemble parts of the Ancient Visitors' ship. Finally there was an area of the compound where they would be housed as they waited to be taken again. Looking around, Steven saw Cynthia limping into the compound with a bandage still on her head. "How is your recovery?" he asked with concern. "It doesn't look so bad."

She raises her eyebrow as she said, "I believe I will be fine by the abduction. Hopefully, the Ancient Visitors will come to the same conclusion, and I won't end up as food for the rest of you. If that is the case, I hope you all get heartburn."

As they spoke to each other, more of their friends came in and greeted them. It was not an occasion for much happiness, because the mission would most likely end in failure with their lives being lost.

"I still can't believe I agreed to this shit, and as it gets closer to becoming a reality the crazier it sounds," vented an agitated D'Shawn.

"You know we all agreed," responded Steven.

"I know. I was on the taskforce to develop the plan of action, but going back on to the ship to take on an alien race billions of years older than the human race with technology so advanced that it makes the NASA super computer look like a caveman counting on his fingers…it is crazy. But I know time is running out, and a better plan is not in the cards."

Steven added, "What were our choices? I mean, look at the reality of the situation. If we do nothing, the odds are that we get abducted, and if we are lucky, we get to be one of the 66% who are returned and not the 34% who are to be food. Even those returned become overlords serving the Ancient Visitors to prepare the people of Earth to become savage warriors, and when the Ancient Visitors return in a thousand years, the two-thirds determined to be of good quality become warrior slaves and the other third become nutrition for the warriors. I don't know about you, but I want better for my descendants. I want to leave them with hope for a better future."

"I know I agreed, but smuggling nanotechnology past the Ancient Visitors may not work," argued D'Shawn.

Quickly Steven rebuked him: "On the last abduction, three of us had nanobots in our bodies repairing injuries, and they were either not detected or were not found to be a threat to the Ancient Visitors. Since then the nanotechnology has made incredible advances. We can program microscopic nanobots and nanomicrobes to perform tasks. In this case, the nanobots carried in our bodies will have multiple tasks. They will disarm and destroy the shoulder harnesses used to keep us and the other captured races subservient. The second batch will be transferred from our bodies to the Ancient Visitors through touch, and they will attack the inner workings of the Ancient Visitors' internal technologies. The third task is to enter their ship's electrical systems and eat away at the vital systems. Another piece of our plan is for each of us on the teams to carry a part of the ingredients for advanced plastic explosives. Each person will carry a different ingredient that by itself will be harmless and hopefully pass through any check the Ancient Visitors do on our arrival. The final piece will be nanomicrobes that will be harmless in our bodies but will be able to devour tissue in the Ancient Visitors. None of the nanotechnologies will be harmful to us, but to the Ancient Visitors it will mean the end of their battle plans, if all goes well."

He had just finished rehashing the plan to D'Shawn when an Ancient Visitors ship hovered into the large opening in the roof of the common area. Most felt their hearts sputter and sweat drip from their foreheads. Even though they knew and agreed with the plan, some tried to run because they knew the deadly challenges ahead of them.

As they nervously awaited the inevitable blackout and then waking on the main alien ship, the craft landed in the center of the common area. As it powered down, the door on the side of the craft slowly opened, and out came Matt and Marcus. The sight of them left an expression of relief on the others' faces. After exiting the ship, they headed over to a podium to address their fellow enhanced humans.

Matt started, "Today we start our training here in secret for a mission to save the future for the children of Earth. As you know, the plan is to defeat them before they return to take our people on to a battle to be fought for the Ancient Visitors. Our descendants would be warrior slaves for the aliens, and we can't let that happen. So today we start working on our strategy and training for our attempt to thwart the aliens' plans. We may fail, but if we only delay them then maybe it will give time to the people here to find a way to defend themselves. So on to the plan. We 283 will divide into ten teams."

At that point Cynthia corrected Matt, "There are only 282 of us. We lost Ali Mussef in the London attack."

Matt then advised, "We have another," as he gestured his head to his right where a changed and weak James stood. He was taller and his limbs were longer, but the most noticeable feature was that his head had expanded. The serum had done its job and transformed him on his way to being a Super Homo sapiens. He was now one of them and was there to help execute the plan, even if he did appear unsure.

Matt continued, "The ten teams will all have the same mission. Hopefully, the redundancy will help our cause. Now as for the ship that was flown in here, it is the ship found in the Ethiopian rock formation. Every single piece taken off to study the technology has been returned, and now it is fully operational. For the last five years, Marcus has been learning how to fly the alien craft, and thankfully he has mastered it. This, I hope, is a good thing for us because, if by some miracle we can defeat the Ancient Visitors, we will need a ride back here. We will each be trained on the ship, and hopefully that knowledge will help us operate the crafts docked on the main spacecraft."

Cynthia asked, "All we have are the two dead Ancient Visitors found with that ship. So how do we know if the nanomicrobes will work in their blood? This was just added to the plan, so it must have been tested somehow or are we taking a leap of faith."

"Up until now we have only speculated, but we have gotten a sample recently," he said to the shocked crowd.

Back in Washington at a council meeting, Jennifer had known about the Ancient Visitors' fresh blood for a few weeks. She gathered the religious leaders' United Nations subcommittee. The idea of having this blood made her scared for the first time. Up until now the enslaving of the people of Earth was a thousand years in the future, and she thought that was far enough away for people to figure out how to defeat them. But the fresh alien blood changed things in more ways than one.

Imam Rashoni started the meeting and quickly yielded the floor to Cardinal Polanski, who started by introducing Monsignor Grazzani. "The monsignor is from Followers of Divinity territory, and he recently snuck out to potentially great peril to himself a few weeks ago. He has been in hiding while the scientists have tested the sample of blood he has been able to collect. Monsignor, please explain."

A short man with southern Italian features stood up and told them with a heavy heart, "I joined the Followers of Divinity, as many in my congregation have done. At first, a very charismatic speaker sways you. He convinces you that you should fight for your beliefs, but the fighting you have in your mind is not what actually happens. You think that you are on the side of good, but further investigation leads you to the truth. For some time I was starting to have doubts in what I thought was a calling, but I kept them to myself.

"Then one day Bishop Terapion with his entourage arrived at our diocese to encourage the faithful. When he spoke, the people were hanging on every word coming out of his mouth as if it came from the lips of God. They were mesmerized from the moment he started. But toward the end of the service, one of the altar girls accidentally knocked over a large brass candleholder with sharp corners. It was innocently knocked over and struck Bishop Terapion on his left arm. Since I was one of the priests assisting in the service and closest to him, I pulled out my handkerchief from the outside of my jacket, and I pulled out the extra one I kept in my inside pocket. I quickly put them on Bishop Terapion's wound. I thought it was odd that he covered the wound with his hand and took the handkerchief and covered it up with his vestments. The service abruptly ended, and he left with his entourage in tow.

"I did not notice right away, but he only took one of the handkerchiefs with him, and I without thinking put the other one back into my jacket. The next day I reached into the jacket looking for something and found the other handkerchief that was still wet from the accident. I thought it was strange that it was still wet, and when I looked at it, it did not look like blood. I thought that maybe I had used it for something else, but I did not. The more I looked at it, the more I realized it was not blood. When it did not dry for a day, I thought that I had better get this checked, and that was when I contacted friends who directed me to Cardinal Polanski."

Cardinal Polanski added, "After hearing his story and determining that it might be significant information, we were able to smuggle him out and get the handkerchief tested. Sorry for keeping you all in the dark, but this was a very sensitive operation between the Vatican and the United Nations. If word had gotten out that the Vatican had helped us, it could have meant the Followers of Divinity directing their attention toward the Pope."

Jennifer then spoke up, "Our scientists worked on it and determined that it was of similar makeup to the two dead aliens found with the craft in Ethiopia. We believe that Bishop Terapion is, in fact, not human."

A confused Rabbi Wolmetz asked, "If that is the case, then why are you telling us? Is it because he is a preacher and we can give vital information on his thought process if there is an attempt to capture him? Otherwise, why do you need our input?"

After a deep breath, she explained, "Many tests were done but one of the results came back with an odd coincidence. The two dead aliens with the craft, though still intact and much less decayed than what you would think, had some decay. Our scientist could only determine that the aliens have between 600 to 700 chromosomes. The remains were too old to get a good reading. But the fresh blood had allowed for more exact testing, and it has been determined that Bishop Terapion has 666 chromosomes."

Many in the room recognized the number's significances as the mark of the antichrist as written in the Bible. Jennifer then looked around the room. "Now you know why we are looking for your perspective on this. This is another coincidence, but the coincidences are adding up. We need to work together as our two worlds collide."

The members of the subcommittee, religious leaders as well as the scientists, were shocked to hear this. Many of the religious leaders paused as they remembered their religion's apocalyptic writing, and Charles, who was not one to be empty of words, was wiping the sweat off his forehead in silence.

The room was quiet until Sha'nay read a passage from 2 Thessalonians 2: "The man of lawlessness (will be) revealed, the son of perdition. He will oppose and will exalt himself over everything that is called God or is worshipped, so that he sets himself up in God's temple, proclaiming himself to be God." She then continued, "The beast will wear the mark of 666."

Cardinal Polanski offered, "This could be a sign of the antichrist. As many of you know, the antichrist or false prophet will be charismatic and use that false charm to lead us to destruction. He will gain power through commerce, politics, and religion."

Charles was finally able to speak, "He must be stopped, or we are doomed!"

Rabbi Wolmetz added, "Jennifer, all the pieces are falling into place, and for mankind to survive the reign of Satan, we will need to be proactive. Whether Bishop Terapion's an alien or the antichrist, this false prophet will lead us down a path to destruction. It is a path where the aliens are letting us destroy our own future. They are playing us against each other. Think about it; they are using the long-running conflict between science and religion for their own use. By inflaming our fury toward scientists, the aliens have had the religious people do their dirty work. The members of the Followers of Divinity have been deceived into attacking and eliminating scientists. A world without technological advances in the future will be easier to conquer. They played upon our fears."

"Many believed the Book of Revelation was more about the time of Nero's persecution of early Christians," said Cardinal Polanski. "There was much debate when the Bible was being compiled during the Rule of Constantine and even to this day whether the Book of Revelation should be included." Cardinal Polanski contemplated stories about the end of time. "We as humans have a finite time for walking on this world and assume that time has a beginning as well as an end. Many religions speculate about the end of time. Is it set in stone, or is it a warning to man of things that can come to pass? I'm not sure, but God, I believe, is providing these signs for a purpose to us today, and we had better listen. Look at the signs: a false prophet bearing the mark of the beast and a final battle between good and evil that could mark the end of time. It may be that things to come are set in stone, but why would He be sending us these signs if not to warn us? Maybe we have a say in things to come because we have free will and the future is not predestined. I believe our actions going forward will determine what future there will be."

The weight of the situation could be seen on the faces of those in the room and with no one more so than Jennifer. "I agree with Rabbi Wolmetz. If Bishop Terapion is in fact an Ancient Visitor, then this charlatan pretending to take sides for the purpose of inflaming the conflict between science and religion has duped us all. I also agree with

Cardinal Polanski that there may be signs in your ancient writing that may hold clues. In any event, the religious implications need to be figured out by the religious and scientific members of this committee. We'll have to work together because this foe will be powerful and hard to defeat. The United Nations doesn't want you to hear this, but Bishop Terapion has control of over 30% of the world with another 30% friendly to him. We believe that he is stockpiling weapons. Some of the countries in his control were thought to have been secretly developing nuclear technology and other weapons of mass destruction.

"And that is just what is in play for earth-made weapons. If he is an Ancient Visitor like we believe, then he has technologies that make our weapons look like cap guns. These are an extraterrestrial people who have mastered the four forces of the universe. We believe they have much more knowledge of electromagnetism, strong interaction, weak interaction -- also known as 'strong' and 'weak nuclear force' -- and gravitation. We pale in comparison. It disturbs me to think about how we are going to handle this problem and the challenge our people are going to have on the main ship."

As Jennifer finished speaking, two people walked into the meeting, and she alerted the council: "Good, they are finally here. You all should recognize Matt, and you may not recognize him, but this is a new and improved James Connor. They are here to give insight into our dilemma."

Matt offered, "You'll have to be careful because the Ancient Visitors are very intelligent and are dangerous if you cross them. One of the guards told us they could pull electricity from the air and throw what we would describe as bolts of lightning. If you run into their weaponry it could be deadly. They will not hesitate to use it on you since they have such disregard for other life forms. That disregard, I believe, could be their weakness and your opportunity to defeat them. They think that they are superior to every intelligent life form in the universe and would not be expecting anyone to outsmart them. Also..."

As Matt spoke to the council, Jennifer took James to the side, "I haven't been able to talk to you for some time. You know, government business. But I wanted to see how you are doing, and I'm so worried about what is next for you. Maybe we can still hide you from being abducted."

James, now a little taller, looked down at her to say, "It's OK. Don't worry about me; I get to try to fix something I helped create. What happened to me was meant to be, and it is not so bad. I get to try to save the world."

This made Jennifer think. "You have changed."

"More like transformed, and with my treatments in the blue liquid chambers now complete, I am fully transformed into the next level of evolution," he said as she looked at his long arms.

"No," she said. "I think you have grown on the inside. When I met you, I am sorry to say, you were self-absorbed and didn't think about helping someone else unless you got something out of it. Now I see a change in you, for what I believe is for the better. But soon you will be gone and on your way with the others to take on the Ancient Visitors. It upsets me to think what is in store for you all."

He tried to calm her down. "Listen, I have to do this, and if it all works out, I will be back before you know it, with a wonderful story to tell. Besides, I think this was always my destiny, and there is a sense of relief that I have a purpose. Hey, look at the time. Matt and I better get going. We have calculated that they will be here in a few weeks to get us, so we will need to get back to make the final preparations, and we need to say good-bye to our families before we go."

Smiling nervously, Jennifer let him go with Matt to head back to where the Ancient Visitors' ship would collect them all.

Back at the away center on the night that the Ancient Visitors would return, those who were ready to be abducted again waited in the common area while their families viewed them by closed circuit 3D television.

Before being taken, each bid farewell to their families and friends via closed circuit conference viewing. James was glad that he said everything he wanted to say to his parents and friends. He thought that it might not have been enough for his parents. They, as expected, were fighting back tears as he said his good-bye. His dad spoke about how proud he was that his son would take on such an important undertaking, and his mother told him to be careful. James thought that it must have been the same for all of the other families watching their loved ones about to be taken. The thought that they might never see them again must be tearing them apart. So James sat there smiling on the outside to give his parents some relief to know he was ready for what was ahead of him, but he was scared as hell on the inside.

For now, he just passed the time and waited with the others for what seemed like an eternity as he clutched in his hand the one thing his mother had given him. Days before they were to be taken, James received a pocket-sized digital reader with various versions of the Bible along with religious texts from every religion on Earth. It was accompanied with a note: Wherever you shall walk, God will be with you.

James thought that he might not be on God's good side since James had denied Him and encouraged the world to do the same, but his mother's faith gave him strength, even as a large alien ship appeared over the common area. His first thought was that hopefully they wouldn't take him, but as quickly as he thought about not going, he remembered that going with them was what he had to do. He then covered his eyes and tried to see it, but the bright lights glared into his face until he lost consciousness.

Patrick and Ann Marie were holding each other while watching as their son and the others were taken by a tractor beam of some sort and pulled into the ship. All were aboard the ship within seconds. When the last body entered the ship, the bright lights turned off and the ship was gone was quickly as it had arrived.

Back in Kansas at Eva and Eddie's home, all of Steven's friends and relatives watched as the ship moved on and disappeared into the night. Tommy and Johnny were there with their families. Brenda was there with her children as well as many other family members, friends, coaches, and neighbors. As soon as the ship disappeared into the night, the live feed of the event switched to network news.

Not wanting to hear the newspersons and their panelists overanalyze the event, Eva calmly said, "TV off," then got up and started cleaning the house as everyone there sat quietly. Eva just continued to clean while every one of their guests quietly and slowly filed out of the house one by one, until there was no one left except for her and Eddie, who sat in his chair motionlessly staring as if he were looking into the distance.

Chapter 11

The spirited debate lasted all day and late into the night, as it had done for the last two weeks as the United Nation's Religious Faith and Science subcommittee argued about what to do with Bishop Terapion. His mere presence frightened each and every person in the room, yet they were tasked with delivering information so that the United Nations could help defeat this Ancient Visitor and false prophet.

Looking for a resolution in the debate, Sandy Chen posed the question again: "If we can get at Bishop Terapion, do we take his life?"

Dr. Harold Sven of the Copenhagen Science Institute suggested, "Maybe if we capture him, then we can study him and learn more about the aliens. This may be our only opportunity to study one up close. We could learn their weaknesses and maybe find some way to defeat them."

Dr. Weiss suggested after giving it much thought, "It could be dangerous for our people on the ground as they try to capture this being. Remember, he potentially has weapons with technology that far exceeds ours. The weapons we already know about from Matt Schaeffer can do a lot of damage. Imagine those that we don't even know about. Maybe he has a weapon that can render all around him paralyzed, or that can blow up the entire city in a blink of an eye. We don't know. In any case, it will be difficult."

Rabbi Wolmetz interjected, "I would think that the world would be in danger if he were to continue. If we don't do anything, he prepares the world for man's doom; if we kill him, he could end up being a martyr, and his followers would continue his mission. But if we capture him, we could show the world that he is a fake and let the scientists do their studying."

Cardinal Polanski then agreed, "I don't see how the world would be better off with him here, but as bad as he is, I can't advocate killing him.

So I vote for the capture solution."

At that moment, Pastor Charles called for their attention and added, "Have we forgotten that God defeats the antichrist and ushers in the Messianic Age of peace and brotherhood on the earth, an earth without crime, war, and poverty? Maybe we are supposed to do nothing and let the Lord take care of the antichrist, as it has been written. Maybe the Lord doesn't return and uses us as the right arm of God. Then we prevent Bishop Terapion from leading the world to its destruction, and in one thousand years we keep our descendants from being enslaved for the purpose of battling the armies of God. It is a daunting task, since writings about the end of time are filled with ambiguities and stories that can be taken in many different ways. It is written that the antichrist comes to power and pushes the world toward darkness, but the Lord comes back to defeat the antichrist and imprisons Satan. Then in a thousand years Satan escapes, and God finally once and for all defeats Satan. But when looking at the Book of Revelation, are we looking at the writing of an inspired Biblical writer, or are they merely the ravings of a lunatic? That is the challenge as we look for signs as to God's intent and - _"

Rabbi Wolmetz interrupted Pastor Charles, his face pale. "I just got a message on my PDA that Jerusalem fell to the Followers of Divinity minutes ago. God help us."

He put the device on a table in the middle of the room so that it could project a 3D hologram of the newscast. There, for all to see, was Bishop Terapion entering Jerusalem after a lightning strike by the armies of the Followers of Divinity during the early morning hours. Israel had been the lone holdout in that area, a region surrounded by fanatical religious nations. Though the Followers of Divinity held territories around the world, they had concentrated their efforts in the Middle East and had their capital in Damascus. The Israelis had fought off every advance, but now many in their ranks had been swayed by Bishop

Terapion and laid down their arms. Bishop Terapion and his army easily captured Jerusalem and were pushing through the rest of the country. They would have it by nightfall.

As Bishop Terapion came to the Temple Mount, the reporters on the spot rushed him after his security let them through. He gladly offered his perspective: "Now the true believers have a new capitol, and the Followers of Divinity will rule it. Brothers and sisters, we shall rule it until God returns to lead us from evil."

Bishop Terapion kept speaking to the reporters, but Pastor Charles and the rest of the council watched in disbelief as they watched the beast, the antichrist, the Masih ad-Dajjal take shape before them, capturing Jerusalem to make it his capital.

"The city of God now belongs to a demon," sighed Imam Rashoni while the others looked at him and grudgingly agreed.

Four months later, at the staging area near Hamburg, Germany, at an old United States military facility, the assembled team waited for the green light. With the orders to proceed coming within twenty-four hours, the team was assembled for their final briefing. Leading the briefing was the United Nations' Commander for the Europe-Middle East Strategic Command, Field Marshal Maureen Montgomery.

"All right, all the preparation and training for this mission is complete, and your job is to execute it. This is not going to be easy because there are a lot of variables. The biggest is that we don't know for sure the extent of the capabilities of this alien. So we are going to be cautious, but once we go in there is no turning back. It is imperative that we succeed because if the alien gets a hint as to what we are doing, it could retaliate in force."

That was when the commander of the mission on the ground, Colonel James M. John, jumped in respectfully and addressed the team,

"So the devil is in the details."

The irony did not get past Pastor Charles, Cardinal Polanski, and Sha'nay Barnwell, sitting in the back of the room as they looked at each other.

Colonel John continued, "At 20:30 Jerusalem time tomorrow evening, the United Nations will issue a statement identifying Bishop Terapion as an Ancient Visitor with the hope to create doubt and confusion within the Followers of Divinity's ranks. The broadcast will go out through every media outlet in the world. At that exact time, we will attack Bishop Terapion's compound and get to him before he can access any technology he could use to fend us off. The hope is that we capture him and prove to the world that he is a fraud. If any of you have an open shot to subdue him with a net gun, you have authorization to take it. Remember, they have not hesitated to kill our people in the past.

"An hour before the broadcast, we will be dropped by stealth transport on the outskirts of Jerusalem's old city. We will have help from individuals on the ground supplied from a local orthodox church friendly to our cause. They will help us get close enough to the target. Remember that we will be alone once we are in the city because the defenses are strong, and that leaves out any chance for an air strike. If all goes well and the target is captured or taken out, then the extraction point is the Mount of the Gold Dome or the Temple Mount. Any questions?"

No one asked, as they had so carefully studied the plan for weeks in secret and each person knew it verbatim. Field Marshal Montgomery drew the briefing quickly to a close, advising, "Get a good night's sleep tonight. You will need it."

As the military personnel left, Pastor Charles, Cardinal Polanski, and Sha'nay Barnwell stayed behind.

"Sha'nay," said Pastor Charles. "You don't take any risks out there tomorrow, OK? I don't want to have to look for a new assistant. Good help is hard to find." He tried to add humor, but the worry on his face summed up his concern for his longtime assistant and friend.

Without any concern on her face, she answered, "Don't worry. I will be safe and protected. Now I'm tired and will go to my room to rest for a while and contemplate what needs to be done. I'll see you before I leave." With that she left and headed away.

Pastor Charles then looked at Cardinal Polanski and said, "Dan, I wish I were going and you and Sha'nay staying back here to monitor the situation and welcome back the team when it is over. Even Imam Rashoni and Rabbi Wolmetz have snuck into Jerusalem."

A sympathetic Cardinal Polanski said, "I know, and we have been over this many times. Imam Rashoni and Rabbi Wolmetz blend in when they are in Jerusalem. I've been running ten miles a day for the last twenty years in and around Central Park. Sha'nay was an exceptional athlete in college and easily accomplished the physical testing done before it was OK for her to be on the team. You, my friend, are a casualty of your wife's good cooking.

"Besides, Charles, we are going along as observers and to help with any religious overtures during the mission. Don't worry; the military will have us so far back that I will need high-powered binoculars to see any fighting. The military personnel are an elite bunch, and I would not want to mess with them."

Pastor Charles shook his head. "I know that you're just saying that for my benefit, and I pray that you'll be OK, but can you do me a favor?"

"Sure, anything, Charles," answered Cardinal Polanski.

"Please take good care of Sha'nay. She is a very special woman. Ever since she was a child, she has been a great source of wisdom for me and to the people around her. Her professors and teachers at school were impressed with her as to how knowledgeable she is with religious texts. One even said that she is so knowledgeable that it seems that she knows the texts as well as the people who wrote them. Even as a teenager, when we were able to organize Bible reading among the regional churches, she would conjecture about the writings with the best of them. She was a great resource if I needed a quote from the good book for a Sunday sermon. "

Cardinal Polanski admitted, "You don't have to tell me. I've seen her in action at our council meetings. If you had a disagreement over a particular text, she was a formidable one to argue with."

Charles agreed, "Yeah, anyone could see she would be just as valuable here, but she talked her way onto the team anyway. She is bright; I have to give her that."

Then as he thought about her going on this mission, he thought about her qualities, "This child is innocent and good. She has no pride or wants and is happy just helping others. She is a rare find, and I hope a hard mission like this does not spoil such a good child." The two old friends then hugged and headed to their rooms early.

The next evening, the team embarked on the mission in some of the United Nations' newest vehicles, utilizing much of the technology learned from the Ancient Visitors' spacecraft. These vehicles could perform like a plane, a submarine, or anything in between. Invisible to all radar, the vehicles traveled at speeds that made them a blur to the human eye, but the passengers inside felt no jolts, even during sudden stops. There was a time that a flight from Hamburg to Jerusalem would have taken hours; now it took minutes. For the people on the team, there was not much time to over-think the mission or be nervous.

The vehicles reached their destination outside of the Lions' Gate of the old city of Jerusalem in an old Catholic cemetery. Once out of the vehicle, the squad leaders signaled without speaking to exit the vehicle and form a perimeter until the ships left. When the vehicles flew off, the team of forty, accompanied by Cardinal Polanski and Sha'nay Barnwell, entered the old city through the Lions' Gate, where they met four individuals who had subdued the armed Followers of Divinity military personnel, who now lay on the ground unconscious.

The team secured the gate entrance, and a squad leader brought the four over to Colonel John, who said, "Well done."

One of them said, "Thank you, and it is good to see you. We had an opportunity to get to them before they noticed your arrival. My name is Gabe, and the others are Mike, Ralph, and Uri. We do work at the Church of the Holy Sepulcher. Usually we do masonry work on the church grounds, and Father Ulrich asked us to help."

An appreciative Colonel John said, "Whoever you are, nice work. What can you tell us about Bishop Terapion and his security?"

Gabe told them, "The bishop is about to hold a news conference outside of the Church of the Holy Sepulcher. The security is tight with many military personnel surrounding him, and the streets have security on every corner. At the moment he's trying to gain the trust of the city's people, and the military only have small arms with no show of powerful weapons."

Colonel John reacted, "Good, then maybe this is a good time to get to him." Then he instructed Gabe and the others to fall back with Polanski and Sha'nay.

When they reached Cardinal Polanski, he asked them, "I noticed new construction on the Temple Mount. What is it?"

Gabe replied, "Rumor has it that Bishop Terapion is having the seat of their government moved there."

Cardinal Polanski then thought out loud, "Gee, it looks big enough to hold only one seat...hmm."

Colonel John then motioned that they head into the old city. As they moved down Lions' Gate Street and were about to get on to Via Dolorosa, there was a sudden and hard shake felt through the ground. Colonel John held the team from advancing and said into his communication link, "Was that manmade or natural?"

Back at the control center in Hamburg, Field Marshal Montgomery was monitoring the mission and watching every movement through the cameras mounted on each team member. She yelled, "What was that, people?"

A few moments later, a major said, "That was an earth tremor. They are frequent in that area. The World Earthquake Warning Center issued a warning. The seismologists say that earthquakes take place all the time in the Rift Valley, and a major earthquake is due in the next few months when the Jordanian Plate moves a few inches. It is estimated to be about a 4.0 on the Richter scale. Minor building damage and no life loss is expected. What they felt is a small initial jolt before the bigger one in a few months. They should be OK to continue."

Field Marshal Montgomery instructed, "Colonel, proceed with the mission."

Back in New York at the United Nations' building, the Secretary General and his staff listened in on the mission and watched it through a satellite video feed in a secure conference room. He turned to his Science Minister. "Jennifer, do you concur with the field marshal?"

After looking at her miniature computer screen on her eyeglasses and viewing the up-to-date information, she said, "I concur with the field marshal and will let you know if there is a change."

He said, "There are a million things that can go wrong with this mission, and even though we looked into each one, it's the one we didn't think of that will screw everything up. So please let me know if anything changes."

As Colonel John motioned his people to advance through the Muslim sector down to Via Dolorosa, Bishop Terapion began his news conference. "People of the world, I am here in Jerusalem, the city of God, to offer the world peace. I stand before you with an olive branch I want to offer to the Secretary General of the United Nations. It is time for peace, and we would like to negotiate a truce so that our two sides can put down their arms and live together in peace."

At that point the Secretary General spoke up to the people in the conference room and at the control center, "Do we scrub the mission and talk peace terms with him? We might be able to save lives, and it can give us more time to figure out how to deal with this alien imposter. What do you advise?"

While many on the staff leaned toward discussing peace, Cardinal Polanski was heard over the communication link: "Mr. Secretary General, I implore you to continue with the mission. Whether you believe in what is written about the end of days or not, the coincidences here are too much to ignore, and we must see this through and capture this alien being. We have seen him build where he wants to rule, on the temple of God."

Imam Rashoni and Rabbi Wolmetz were in the city and linked into the conversation. Imam Rashoni added, "We are at the Noble Sanctuary or, to some of you, the Temple Mount, and we can see the construction. We agree wholeheartedly with Cardinal Polanski. Bishop Terapion is definitely building himself a throne to rule on."

Cardinal Polanski then reentered the conversation: "The antichrist is a master deceiver who is one of Satan's angels of evil and will con his way to the leadership of the world. You should stay the course and show the world what he is and not talk peace with him."

The Secretary General paused to think for a minute and instructed, "Please proceed with the mission and issue the statement now!"

Bishop Terapion finished his declaration, and all the newscasters were given the response to Bishop Terapion's news conference. Each put it up on the virtual screen for all to read. It said: "Even though we welcome Bishop Terapion's offer for peace, we can't accept it from him until we can confirm his origin. We have information that Bishop Terapion is in fact an Ancient Visitor sent here to disrupt our

198

development, and he is not who he claims to be. Let us test him to put the question to bed, and then if he is who he says he is, we can go forward."

Seeing that on the virtual screen like everyone else in the world, Bishop Terapion went into a rage and accused, "This is why we are at war with the United Nations. Their treachery has no bounds, and they make up lies just to be deceitful in order to trick you all into staying in your sinful ways. I extend my hand in peace, and these evildoers throw it back at me. So you see, they don't have the capacity to know what is good."

Then the Secretary General came on live. "People of the world, don't listen to this fraud. He is not human and does not have your best interests at heart. He is using his charismatic way of speaking and manipulating people's personal religious faith for the purpose of dividing us. Together we are strong, but they don't want us to be strong. They want us to submit."

Bishop Terapion attacked back, "Maybe you're the alien, and we should not be listening to you."

An assured Secretary General countered, "No problem. I will agree to a blood test, but will you?" At that moment the evidence was put on the virtual screen along with a recording of Monsignor Grazzani's testimony.

There was silence as people and Bishop Terapion's security guards around him watched Monsignor Grazzani tell his story. When it was over some of the people around him were asking, "Can you please tell us this is not true?"

Without warning, the ground shook again, lightly but noticeably. The people in the crowd paused again as they were startled, but when it was over, they pestered him again about the Secretary General's accusations, and that was when Colonel John's team surrounded the news conference.

After seeing himself surrounded, Bishop Terapion fired back, "Look at the treachery right before you. They lurk in the darkness and sneak in among you. How can you trust such deceitfulness? You have not seen that from me! For I have led you and let your voices be heard in this sinful world. Go now and battle these forces of evil, and even if you fall, you will be rewarded in heaven with riches beyond your imagination."

That was when Colonel John spoke out, "We don't want anyone to get hurt, and only came here to test Bishop Terapion's blood. We have a doctor here who can do the test on the spot. If any of you have medical training and want to witness the testing, we would welcome it. Our only purpose is to make sure Bishop Terapion is of this planet, and if he is not, then to take him into custody. If he is human, then we will accept being kept as prisoners."

Cardinal Polanski spoke up, knowing the crowd as people of strong religious belief, "It is written that you should beware of a deceiver, or a false prophet that will seemingly provide for your needs and will proclaim himself the risen Messiah. Do not follow the beast, for he will bring on the reign of Satan."

Sensing that the crowd would accept their testing of him and with Colonel John's team getting closer, Bishop Terapion reacted as one who would not be taken. He threw straight up into the air what looked like a small ball. About fifteen feet into the air, it seemed to implode, and then exploded outward. There was no loud noise, only momentary disorientation of the crowd and Colonel John's team. As the team tried to gather their senses and aim their weapons toward Bishop Terapion, he took out a device in one hand, pointed it at those closest to him and fired heartlessly into the crowd, sending out a pulse that fanned out fifty feet, melting flesh and bone. Bishop Terapion's other hand was covered by a metallic glove that projected a type of force field in front of him, repelling shots fired from the team's weapons.

As the exchange went on between the team and Bishop Terapion,

Sha'nay ran over to Cardinal Polanski, who was now lying on the ground in pain, his lower leg melted away. As she pulled him from the killing zone, he thought about what Charles had asked him and he yelled to her, "Leave me, child, and find cover. Save yourself."

But she did not listen, and with the help of Gabe and Mike, she pulled Cardinal Polanski safely behind a building and placed his back to the wall as he sat there holding his leg.

Since the force field only covered one side of Bishop Terapion, the members that were left of the team spread out, firing on him from different sides. Forced to retreat, the bishop ran toward David Street with the six remaining team members in pursuit. As he started running, the ground began to tremble under their feet. It was stronger than the previous jolts. People ran for cover away from shattering window glass and small pieces of the old building as they started to crumble off the sides. Colonel John, though he still led his team, had been injured and had lost vision in one of his eyes.

While still next to Cardinal Polanski, Mike peered around the building and turned to Sha'nay as if he were reporting. "He is on the move and most likely heading toward Jaffa Gate. If we go down this road, we can outflank him at David Street."

As they were leaving, Cardinal Polanski yelled, "Where are you going? It's too dangerous! Stay here!" Unhearing, Sha'nay ran down the narrow street with Gabe, Mike, Ralph, and Uri in tow. As Imam Rashoni and Rabbi Wolmetz finally reached the team, Cardinal Polanski called them over to help carry him.

When Bishop Terapion reached David Street, he headed toward Jaffe Gate, but Colonel John and his people had run down an adjacent street to block the bishop from the exit. As the bishop aimed his weapon toward them, the ground shook again even stronger, and part of a building standing between Bishop Terapion and Colonel John's team collapsed, forming a barrier between them. Bishop Terapion turned to head the other way when Sha'nay, leading Gabe, Mike, Ralph, and Uri, ran toward him as he pulled up his weapon.

Back at the control center, Field Marshal Montgomery shouted over the communication link, "Colonel John, what is your status?" as a cloud of debris blocked her vision.

Colonel John replied, "We had part of a building fall in front of us, and we are now attempting to climb over it."

On the other side, Bishop Terapion aimed his weapon toward Sha'nay and the four behind her, but it did not fire. She ran right up to him, and he looked at her for a moment. Then he screamed with surprise and fright, "It's you!"

Then a split-second later, more of the building collapsed on Bishop Terapion, killing him. Sha'nay went down on one knee beside him and said, "Rest now," with her hand on him.

Colonel John's team climbed over the rubble and held their weapons at the ready, pausing at the sight of the body of Bishop Terapion with his dark green blood pooling in the street. Coming up behind Sha'nay were Cardinal Polanski, Imam Rashoni, and Rabbi Wolmetz. When Cardinal Polanski arrived, he was thrilled Sha'nay was OK and relieved that the false prophet was no more.

The Secretary General anxiously asked, "What's going on? We can't see anything through the cloud of dust. Field Marshal Montgomery, Colonel John, or anyone, please tell us what is happening! Can anyone tell us?"

Colonel John answered, "The target is eliminated, and from what I could see, our fears were correct, and he was not who he said he was. He is right now lying on the ground in a pool of green blood."

Montgomery asked, "Colonel John, how did he meet his demise?"

Cardinal Polanski cut off Colonel John and said, "God got him. I mean, it was an act of God. The earthquake caused the building to come down on him."

While Colonel John asked for medical assistance for all the wounded, people walked up to view the blood and the alien the lying on the ground. Within seconds, they used their personal communication devices to broadcast images of the alien around the world.

Back at the control center, Montgomery ordered, "Send in the help they need, and let's get our wounded people back here."

The UN Secretary General added, "Please make sure our people are taken care of, and let's get our condolences out to the people we lost. Field Marshal, please contact the military leaders of the Followers of Divinity to show them the truth of their former leader. Let them know Bishop Terapion deceived them, and as a matter of fact, he deceived us all. Then advise them that we want to talk about ending this conflict and living together in peace."

The Secretary General asked all media outlets to give him airtime, and within seconds he was addressing the globe. "People of the world, all people of the world, we have seen how, when we don't respect the belief of others, it leads to conflict. Since the beginning of time, people have looked at others, and if they were different then they were in conflict. Whether it was politics, religion, or race, we seem to look at any other who is different as the enemy. Today we learned that an Ancient Visitor made himself out as one of us as a way to deceive us and cause havoc. He made us fight brother against brother. What he really did was take our fear of others who are different and add to those fears so that action would be taken. Action that he justified as needed, but in reality, it hurt others unnecessarily and many lost their lives.

"However, this Ancient Visitor did nothing we have not done ourselves. Our history is filled with examples of one group taking advantage of another. We have enslaved, raped, stolen, lied, and killed for our selfish gains. This should not be the reality for our descendants. We need to say today that from this moment forward we are one people, and respect for others should be the number one aspiration for us all. The energy we used in conflict with each other would be best served working together. Man has a future, and I believe it is a bright one. We can accomplish anything together. Thank you, my brothers and sisters, for listening to me today, and please go live in peace."

Later, back in Hamburg, Pastor Charles visited Cardinal Polanski at the hospital to see how he was doing.

"Hey, Charles, it is good to see you," the cardinal said.

"How are you, Dan?"

"I'm fine. Losing part of my leg was a small price to pay. The alternative would have been much worse if the beast had grabbed control of the world and put us all into slavery. Besides, with technology today, I will have a new leg in a few weeks, toes and all. But Charles, you didn't come here to talk about my leg, did you? So, what's on your mind?"

Charles was relieved that his old friend could see right through him. When he was confused, Dan was always someone he could talk to. Charles said, "I don't know, I was kind of expecting more. God was supposed to come down to earth and defeat the antichrist. Instead, He had a stone drop on his head."

Cardinal Polanski put his hand on his shoulder and said, "So you were expecting the heavens to open up and Jesus and his army of angels to come through riding white horses? Then when the antichrist is defeated we hear the trumpets of the angels and doves fly down from heaven?"

Charles started to laugh as Cardinal Polanski continued, "We believe as Christians that before Jesus walked on this world, people were expecting a savior more like a military general leading an army into battle. Instead he was a poor carpenter, and he spoke of peace and love. What I'm trying to say, Charles, is that God is not tied to our imagination, and we should trust Him."

Pastor Charles sighed. "I knew you were going to say that, but maybe I just needed to hear it. Anyway, I also wanted to ask you about the workers from the Church of the Holy Sepulcher who helped the team. We are looking for them so that they can be recognized for their help, but we can't find them. They never returned to work the next day, and the church said that they just turned up one day a few months ago to volunteer to do maintenance work around the church. They don't have any record of them because they were not paid. The strange thing is that we did not get a clear view of them on any of the cameras on any of the team's headgear or even the street security cameras. They were always turned away from the cameras, and everyone we asked to describe them all had a different description. It is as if they just walked away and disappeared. It's strange."

Then Cardinal Polanski said with a smirk, "Gabe, Mike, Ralph, and Uri -- maybe they were the archangels Gabriel, Michael, Raphael, and Uriel, and they came here to help us defeat the beast? Ah, it couldn't be! I'm sure they'll turn up someday. I wanted to ask you how Sha'nay is doing. She is one brave girl."

Pastor Charles was happy to say, "Oh, she is doing fine, and she is already looking forward to starting her own ministry. Even though she could use her notoriety with this incident to gain a pastoral position in a well-off diocese or teach at a well-known university, she will hear nothing of it. Instead, she picked some godforsaken place in the middle of nowhere to start from scratch in a small village church in some out-of-the-way African country. Like I told you, she is a special child."

Cardinal Polanski agreed, "Not only did she charge into harm's way at Bishop Terapion down at David Street, she comforted the dying demon in its last moments as if saying good-bye to an old lost friend who had gone down the wrong path. She is very compassionate and giving, even to those you would think don't deserve it. You are right about her, and I hope she never changes."

After approving Cardinal Polanski's description of Sha'nay, Pastor

Charles changed the tone of the conversation. "Do you think there will be more false prophets? Scripture mentions possibly more."

"Maybe so, but for now let's enjoy this victory and help bring peace to the world."

The two old friends just sat there reflecting on what had happened and where they would go from there.

After all the reports and meetings were completed, Jennifer and David finally got time to bring their family for some much-needed rest. They brought their kids out to Montauk, Long Island to the Ocean Beach Hotel. As the kids went back to their rooms, Jennifer and David stayed by the fire pit they had made on the beach. It was not the only fire; there were fire pits up and down the beach as far as they could see, like stars in the sky. Jennifer and David just lay back on their chairs and enjoyed the August night. After sitting quietly for a while, Jennifer asked, "What do you think James will find up there?" as she pointed toward the star-filled night. "I get chills thinking about what is in store for him there and hope he's up to the challenge."

David threw another piece of wood onto the fire and said, "I can't imagine what he's going to find there. I only know that he didn't go there to find any alien technology or discover all the knowledge in the universe. The purpose of going was to save the future of mankind, but that was not why he went. He went there to discover himself. He had wealth and fame, but when it came crashing down, he questioned his existence. So his journey to the stars is essentially a trip into his soul. I personally hope he finds himself and is happy with his personal discovery."

Jennifer asked, "What did we discover in all of this?"

He thought about it for a moment and said, "We learned more about ourselves as a people on this world. We learned about where we came from, and that is important if we are going to learn where we are headed as a species. The journey of our beginning as a speck in the primeval soup millions of years ago to what man will ultimately achieve is a long road. But it is a road filled with wonder and amazing adventures. I think that man has only scratched the surface of what he will become. What do you think, science minister?"

Jennifer advised the upper echelons of the world government and had to make decisions important to the safety of the planet, but for now, she just held her husband tightly as they sat by the fire. She said, "I think our future is still to be made, and we have to work hard to get there. With that said, I hope that James and the others succeed, or at least show that we want our future and will fight for it. I don't know, I look up at the stars and wonder where they are."

David just looked up and said, "We believe that they are in eastern part of the sky, just above where Jupiter is now. It is believed that they won't reach it for another year and a half."

Chapter 12

His eyes opened, and the blurriness started to fade. He sat up his stiff body and noticed the artificial light illuminating the familiar and unwanted room he was in again. D'Shawn mumbled to himself, "Oh great. We're back here, and look; here they already put our chains on."

D'Shawn was referring to the shoulder harnesses that the Ancient Visitors used to subdue their minions. People uncomfortably sat up and felt the harnesses around their necks. No one was more uncomfortable than James Connor. He was feeling trapped in the holding area of an alien ship deep in space, and the harness used to control him made him wonder why he volunteered for this. He thought that Jennifer had hoped his DNA could be changed back, or that he could have been hidden in a deep mine where the Ancient Visitor's scans would not pick him up. If he could have been hidden well enough, maybe he could have been very useful as the people of the Earth planned their defense of the planet. His thoughts of staying behind slowly faded, however, as he realized that he had made his decision, and there was no turning back now. Besides, this was where he wanted to be, even though he was scared out of his mind and feared for his life. It had not been easy for him to decide to go, especially since for most of his life he had thought about his own well-being before the well-being of others. The hard part was letting go of that notion so he could start to believe that he was part of a wonderful universe and not the center of it.

"Doctor Connor, the dizziness and the blurred vision will go away in a few minutes. It is best if you get up and hold on to the wall until you get your balance. At first you may get a little motion sickness due to the movement of the vessel in space. When we first arrived here, we thought the motion was due to being on water. Fortunately, the motion sickness fades and so will the uneasiness you will feel walking around in the artificial gravity that is keeping us from floating around the room. It is slightly different from Earth's. Now, let me help you up," said an experienced Steven.

James got up with Steven's help and immediately started to feel dizzy. "I've got you, Dr. Connor," said Steven as he held James' arm. "The air in here is a little different from the air on Earth. You'll feel disoriented for a while until your body acclimates to the different composition of nitrogen and oxygen. Don't worry, it does not take long, and you will be fine in a couple of minutes."

Marcus, after surveying the surroundings, reported back to Matt, "All 283 people are accounted for, but this time we woke up with the harnesses on. It looks like we are all fine, and the new guy is still getting adjusted."

Matt looked at him and said, "Thank you."

To keep their intentions secret, no one mentioned any part of what they were going to do. Since they could understand the Ancient Visitors' language, it would make sense that the advanced Ancient Visitors could understand them. Matt knew that if the Ancient Visitors learned what they were doing, they could quickly stamp out their feeble attempt. Surprise was their best weapon if they were to have any luck in disabling this ship and saving the people of Earth.

The waiting for the right time to make their attack was nerve-wracking. A nervous Steven looked to D'Shawn for comfort and to get his mind off of what they are about to do.

"So, you miss your family?"

D'Shawn, looking for his own comfort, said, "I sure do. My wife and I have fourteen children. Each one of them is smart and strong. Of course, they have many of the traits of a Super Homo sapiens. Some of my oldest kids have kids of their own. My wife and I are truly lucky. They are the reason I came back here. What about you Steven? How many kids do you have?"

He just looked back at D'Shawn and smiled. So D'Shawn asked again, "So tell me, how many kids?"

Steven deadpanned, "None."

D'Shawn said, "I don't get it. The people back home wanted us to procreate so that the superior species would have a better chance to defend Earth. So you did nothing?"

Steven was a little uncomfortable and hesitant to tell him, but blurted it out anyway, "Not exactly."

D'Shawn looked at him.

Steven continued, "I left over a thousand samples behind, 1,145 to be exact."

D'Shawn asked, "What do you mean 'samples'?" then suddenly understood as he started to laugh, "You filled up 1,145 cups?"

Embarrassed, Steven explained, "I figured that the most bang for my buck, so to speak, would be quantity. This way, there is a better chance that the Super Homo sapiens DNA could spread through the population."

Still laughing D'Shawn said, "So you are trying to spread the advanced DNA all by yourself? This is a riot. Well, at least you answered one question I always wondered: what do Kansas farm boys do in their off time?"

This made them both laugh. D'Shawn then asked a still-dizzy James, "What about you? How many did you leave behind?"

Still wobbly, he looked and said, "I left one sample behind. A friend of mine, Lauren Ritter, and her husband were good enough to volunteer to bring up my child. I didn't have as much time on my hands as Steven. No pun intended. So I have just one."

"So that is how you plan on populating the earth with the superior DNA? One."

Their idle chat did not last long because the door along the wall of the large room started to open, and the plan to save the earth was about to begin.

James was just getting acclimated to the surroundings and getting his balance as the door opened and out walked an Ancient Visitor. He had only seen the remains of the two he found in Kibish in a museum. Now he was before a live Ancient Visitor as it entered the room followed by creatures he couldn't ever imagine he would see, their shoulder harnesses the same as his.

Then the Ancient Visitor spoke. James' language training helped him understand the alien language. James thought that if he weren't so terrified, he would think this was the coolest thing anyone could ever do. He could communicate with an alien and stand on its ship deep in space. He briefly forgot the task at hand, and remembered all those conventions he went to and the crazy UFO enthusiasts wearing all those costumes, and then thought how they would be crapping in their pants if they were here now. They weren't here though. He was, and he needed to clear his mind and concentrate on what he was tasked to do. He thought back to the briefing Matt gave the night before they were taken…

"Listen up, everyone. We have compiled information from the experiences of those of us who walked through the ship. For us to understand how we are able to defeat them, we will need to know where they are vulnerable. So from what we gather, many of the Ancient Visitors have circuitry embedded in their bodies. It was put in them to enhance and stretch their life spans. These are beings that don't reproduce and must keep their bodies alive until they burst through to the other realm. So the circuitry could be a target for the nanobots.

"Also, they travel around the ship via a liquid tube transportation system, and if we could get the nanomicrobes in there, we might be able to neutralize their movement as they die in the tubes. The best place we believe to place nanobots will be the core of the ship's computer system. It is on the level right next to their control center. This technology is very advanced, and it is in liquid form in the center of the room. A drop of the liquid can hold more information than all of the computers on Earth. We believe that if we can get nanobots into that, they can disrupt and destroy vital systems.

"Now remember, the nanobots are not like a virus that attacks the software. These nanobots are programmed to find systems within the ship and cause havoc. The problem is that the pool is toxic to our bodies, so we will need to cut our arms to let the blood out instead of transferring nanobots through touch.

"The plan is, when the Ancient Visitors transport us from the holding room and bring us to the training facility, we will act. Prior to getting there we will use the nanobots to disarm the control harnesses on the guards and on us. We will initiate the attack the moment we are brought to the training facility because it is near the center of the ship where we can dispatch the assault teams. Some will attack the control room, the computer system, the power storage system, and the transportation tubes, while others secure transport ships so we can return to Earth. We will need to secure weapons with the help of the guards and hope the explosives we smuggle on the ship are enough to disable parts of the ship. There are a lot of variables we can't control, but if we work together we can get it done by using our imagination and believing in ourselves."

James thought of how that plan had sounded so good millions of miles away back on Earth. Now that it was about to unfold, he wished the plan were more thought out as they were brought out of the holding room. The guards took James and the others to the transports to ferry them to the training facility. As they headed to the facility, James peered out the doors to see the amazing technology and sights inside the enormous ship. James guessed that it was about the size of a small moon, and it was filled with races from all over the universe. Each one of them wore a shoulder harness and walked submissively behind an Ancient Visitor. It looked like a master and his slave. It made him wonder what was in store for mankind.

Are our descendants to be slaves to this race, and is that all they have to look forward to in their future?

Then as they were carried through the ship, an astonished James peered out the transport at the interior of this amazingly engineered ship and conferred with Matt, "I can't believe what I am seeing, and I am trying to comprehend what it is."

Still with the mission on his mind, Matt took a second to distance himself from the task they all were about to assume and asked James, "See those tubes filled with a clear liquid over there?"

James looked over as Matt continued, "When the Ancient Visitors enter the opening, the liquid carries them to anywhere on the ship in seconds by just projecting their destination in their minds."

Pointing toward another part of the ship, Matt said, "The guards told me behind those walls are chambers where the Ancient Visitors go to rest, although I haven't actually seen it myself. I was told they do not regenerate like any being we know of. They take turns sitting in the blue liquid, like what we found in the stasis chambers on Earth, and they encase themselves for what we would consider hundreds of thousands of years. In their time in the stasis chamber, their bodies are regenerated and improved with technologies they learn from around the universe. Because they are out here deep in space far from any gravitational pull and traveling at a high rate of speed, their relative time in the chambers is not hundreds of thousands of years, but a few thousand years. It would seem Einstein was right with his Theory of Relativity. Anyway, the reason for this is so they can live long enough to fulfill their plan to reenter the Realm."

As the transport moved along its path and passed an area where Ancient Visitors congregated, Matt pointed out, "Then over there the

Ancient Visitors can sit in what looks like lounge chairs and interface with their massive computer to communicate with other Ancient Visitors through what was described as a virtual reality social network. It also links them to a database that holds billions of years of knowledge they have accumulated from throughout the universe. It is sort of like a much more advanced Internet.

"See that? That ring around the entire inner part of the open interior of this ship. It is very long and very thick. It is a giant particle accelerator that makes the one on Earth at CERN look like a nine-volt battery. They are able to simulate the power of ten thousand stars. I am not talking a small one like ours, but stars that can fit thousands of our sun inside. The amount of power that device can make is mind-boggling," said Matt to James, who was listening to every word with amazement as he gazed out the transport.

Matt then pulled himself away from looking out the transport as he remembered the mission they must do. But he finished one last thought: "To tell you the truth, the thing that amazes me the most is seeing the art circulated throughout the ship and hearing the music that captivates you like eating the best piece of fine chocolate; it just soothes your soul. I could not believe the dreary-looking Ancient Visitors created such beauty. As it turns out, they don't have an artistic bone in their bodies and have been taking these artistic treasures from cultures throughout the universe."

All of a sudden, the transports stopped before reaching the training facility. Then the guards pulled them out of the transports into a big rotunda in the center of the ship. Marcus looked toward Matt to signal, what is this?

Matt then signaled back that he did not know, and they should wait and not panic. Then other transports pulled up and dropped off other races and their guards. When the transports stopped, there were hundreds of races with their harnesses on gathered in the rotunda. While they stood and wondered why they had been brought there, Ancient Visitors appeared on balconies and stood over the many races below. Some Ancient Visitors walked among the gathered races.

Standing near Matt was Lango, and the tall alien spoke to him, "This will be remembered for all of existence as the moment the Prince became the most powerful being of all time. Now when we battle for the Realm, we will win and take all from the Ruler of the Realm. This will help us all be rewarded with untold riches for eternity."

Matt tried to ask Lango to clarify, "I am not sure I follow. Can you tell me what exactly is happening?"

Lango showed contempt for the lower species but grudgingly told him, "We have gathered the power of this universe to transform the Prince into a being more powerful than he was before we left the Realm. We harnessed the power of the stars so that the Prince can defeat him. We transformed him from the physical being to one on a higher plane, and now he will be able to have power much like the Ruler of the Realm. Then once we harness the power of this ship combined with the other three, we will be back in the Realm with our army.

"You see, Matt. This is not so much a ship as it is a tremendous particle accelerator. It is creating the power to end this universe, and that power is stored in the belly of this ship. When we unleash it, time will cease, light will cease, and this existence will cease. Then we will arrive into the Realm and force the Ruler and his army to be submissive to us. Then the Prince shall rule all, and we will take our rightful place at his side. You were brought here to witness the Prince in all his glory. He will be the ruler of all and your God. When he appears, bow down and worship him, and he will reward you with the riches of all existence."

When Lango finished speaking, he turned from Matt and gazed toward the center of the giant rotunda where a large red mist started to take shape hundreds of feet in the air. That mist formed a large swirling cloud with violent electric discharges shooting out in all directions. It was tremendous; the size of a tall building -- when they looked into it, there was a darkness that accompanied it, a loneliness that made them feel cold inside.

Matt looked at it and felt anger, anguish, and despair. This was another obstacle and something they were going to have to contend with if they were going to have any chance of succeeding. He was not the only one with a little more doubt than he had possessed a few minutes before. As he looked at the others, he noticed that that the same feelings were written on their faces as they looked up at this thing they were trying to comprehend.

Then it formed into a large cloud and spoke! "My children, I am your God and creator. Without me you would have nothing, for I breathed life into your bodies and gave you the reason to live. For that alone you must worship and obey me. For your obedience I will give you ultimate riches and power once I ascend to the throne of the Realm and take my logical place at the center of all. I am the one, and there should be no other."

As the dark entity continued to spew accolades onto itself, Matt thought that this might be the right time to strike because there were many captive races and guards assembled, as well as interior ship transports they could use to move along this giant ship to vital systems. So Matt leaned over to Marcus, as the entity spoke, and said, "Start releasing the nanobots."

With that, Marcus used his mind, activating the microscopic machines to start up and launch their purpose. It triggered their computer brains to perform the program they were designed to do. Inside Marcus's body, hundreds and hundreds of the little machines headed to his fingertips through his blood vessels. Once there, Marcus just needed to touch a machine, and some of the nanobots flew out and attacked it. Within seconds, Marcus's shoulder harness deactivated and fell off. Soon the others did so as well, freeing themselves from their bondage. Marcus went to Uloog and freed him.

A confused Uloog asked, "What do you do? I don't understand."

Marcus replied, "We are fighting back. I know you are not happy being their slave, and you want freedom for your people. So you and all the guards now have the choice to either join us to fight for your freedom, or let your masters keep you and your people in bondage. It is up to you."

As he said that, Marcus grabbed the weapon Uloog was holding, while Matt and the others passed the nanobots to the guards and other races in the rotunda. More harnesses began falling off, and they took many of the guards' weapons and started firing at the Ancient Visitors. As the Ancient Visitors began to fall, it gave the other races confidence to fight back as the humans tried to overtake the Ancient Visitors. Marcus took aim and fired at Lango, who fell to the ground dead. With many races attacking them, the Ancient Visitors near the interior transports were overwhelmed, and the human teams headed for the transports. While the fighting went on, Matt and many from his team entered a nearby transport and headed for the control center to find the brain of this large ship.

James was one of fifteen of them, and as the transport flew up toward the control center, he saw many of the other transports being taken by the other teams. The giant dark entity used electrostatic discharge to destroy some of the transports before they reached their destinations. Then it aimed its wrath toward many of the teams and races on the ground, killing scores of them. As they lay dying, more Ancient Visitors appeared and started firing weapons James had never seen before, accurate and deadly. The Ancient Visitors quickly moved through the crowds, firing at anything that moved.

Then James and the others heard the dark entity speak with anger, "You ungrateful little maggots, you have no idea what you are giving up. I was going to give you minions to rule over and riches beyond your

belief, and this is how you repay me. I will wipe you all from existence."
Then it killed scores and scores without regard. But not all: Marcus was
still down there fighting. As the fight became fruitless and the races
started to scatter, Marcus grabbed an injured Uloog, and they headed
toward the interstellar transport bay with some of the survivors from his
team.

Matt flew the interior transport to the level they believed held the
computing brain of the ship. It crashed there, far from the control center
as James and the others were thrown about. When they could open the
door, they were faced with many Ancient Visitors poised to attack them
with their array of weapons. As their door opened, the aliens fired on
them, and the team was trapped. Matt thought that they were finished
and fired the only weapon they could muster up. While doing so, he
hoped that one of the other teams could be more successful in reaching
the control center.

But then there was an explosion that rocked the whole ship and
scared the Ancient Visitors. Some left the fight to get to their stations on
the ship. Matt surmised that at least one of the other teams had been
successful in causing an explosion with the plastic explosives they had
smuggled on board.

They hit the power storage area and caused systems to go down and
additional explosions to go off within the main ship. In the confusion,
Matt was able to hit some of the Ancient Visitors, and the team was able
to exit the transport and find cover. Once out, Matt started to direct the
team to advance to the Control Center when an Ancient Visitor came
around a corner and fired on Matt. It killed him instantly, and D'Shawn
quickly picked up Matt's weapon and fired back, killing the Ancient
Visitor.

The death of someone who had been their leader and friend for so
long made them feel lost, and they doubted themselves for a moment. As
they looked around trying to figure out how to find the control center,

Steven saw someone in the distance he had met on the first trip to this ship. It looked like Gabriel Peters. They thought he had been killed, but now he was waving them to come his way. So D'Shawn covered them as they ran toward Gabriel.

There was another explosion, and plumes of smoke filled the corridor. When they arrived, Gabriel was not there, but they could see what they believed was the control center in the distance and Ancient Visitors heavily guarding it.

D'Shawn said, "I'll fire and rush them. Maybe some of you can get through." But then he saw Gabriel again signaling to come toward him at the opposite corner of the control room level. Without hesitating, the remaining team headed toward Gabriel.

Cynthia was the first to get there to see Gabriel, but as before he was not there, only a hallway that took them around to the back of the control center where fewer of the Ancient Visitors stood guard. Along the way, some of the team picked up weapons of Ancient Visitors who had been struck down. Even with those weapons, they were badly outnumbered.

At the back of the control center, D'Shawn took up the mantle of leader even though he had thought that the plan was fruitless from the start. Unsure of the course of action to take as he frantically went over the options in his head, he briefly saw Gabriel again standing by the ship's computerized brain in the form of a liquid pool. When he blinked Gabriel was gone.

He quickly organized the remaining team and planned an attack. "We with the weapons will cover the others as they try to get the nanobots into the pool. Cut your hands and let the blood with nanobots flow into the pool. We need to get as much as we can into the pool to disrupt the ship. Get ready…go!"

The Ancient Visitors saw them coming and quickly fired on them. The barrage was intense as the Ancient Visitors were quite accurate, and it repelled them. As they went back, more of the team dropped from being hit with the weapons fire. The Ancient Visitors were deadly proficient and hit all but D'Shawn, Cynthia, Steven, and James. As they retreated, D'Shawn covered them as Cynthia, Steven, and James found cover.

Suddenly, D'Shawn was hit by a shot that ricocheted off a wall and struck D'Shawn in the back as he tried to get behind a doorway. It was not lethal, but it rendered him unconscious with his body shaking from the hit. Steven and Cynthia reached out and pulled D'Shawn back behind the wall. Then they picked up weapons and started firing back, but the return fire was heavy and increasing as the Ancient Visitors closed in to finish them off.

Terrified, James thought that it was hopeless, and they had come all this way only to fail as he looked at Steven and Cynthia frantically firing back at the approaching aliens. As he continued to look at Steven and Cynthia fire away, time slowed down in his mind to almost a complete stop as he thought about the life he was about to lose as the Ancient Visitors closed in. The things he reflected on most were his friends and family.

He remembered Jennifer asking him something their first year at the university. "You should know what you want to do after you graduate. Me, I want to do something that makes a difference and is bigger than I am. But all you can think of is sliding through classes and getting a job after graduation. James, you have to have a purpose in life. So what is your purpose, and how are you going to make a difference?"

David once told him as he spoke about the stars in the sky: "Those lights are thousands, millions, or billions of light years away from us and thousands, millions, or billions from each other. You would think that it would make you feel small and unimportant being part of something so

220

big. For me, though, it makes me feel that I am part of something grand and that I matter, because for me to be born a host of things needed to be done. The universe needed to be created, this sun needed to form, the Earth needed to be the right distance from the sun so life could grow, life had to fight to live on this planet, humans needed to evolve, and my parents needed to meet and fall in love. When you look at it, it is a miracle I am here, and I believe that makes me unique. That makes you, James, unique as well, and you matter in this universe."

His mother told him after he was injured in the terrorist attack and was feeling responsible: "I see that you are depressed. Don't be. I believe everything happens for a reason, whether we know it or not. Each experience is a building block as we learn who we are to become during life's long journey. It is these building blocks that help us develop and form the person we become in life. The person you are now is not the person you will end up being. If you take that difficult experience and learn from it, you will grow as a person."

His father told him when he had decided to go with the other abducted Super Homo sapiens: "I am scared to death for you, and I wish I could talk you out of it. With that said, James, I'm proud of you. You have come a long way, and I don't mean physically. You have evolved from someone who thought of himself first to someone who thinks of others and appreciates life. Now, I know you may have some difficult challenges ahead of you, and you may be confused as to what to do, but do what you think is the right thing to do."

He thought about what he had said to Matt and the others when he asked to go with them: "Many of you probably look at me as the cause of your anguish. You were taken from your families and changed, and now you are told you are needed to sacrifice yourselves for the future of the people of the Earth. I am really sorry. I wish I had never fallen in that hole in Kibish, Ethiopia. Maybe if I hadn't, the Ancient Visitors might have left us alone or forgotten about us. Or maybe I was destined to do it. I don't know. Either way, I am sorry for many things I did and said. I wish I could take it all back because many were hurt or died because of me. I can't take it back, but I would like to help. All I will tell you is that I will give it my all. So I beg you to let me go with you and let me help. I beg you. Please."

James' mind was racing, and the last thing he thought about was something his mother brought up to him when he was trying to disprove religious beliefs. She asked, "Don't you remember, when you were a child you used to speak to God?"

Well, he thought. I don't know if you are listening. Please help me do what I am going to do. I don't know if I am strong enough or brave enough. Please give me the strength.

At that moment his mind was back in real time with Steven and Cynthia firing at the Ancient Visitors and looking as if they believed the fight was hopeless. Their weapons were blazing at the Ancient Visitors, who were firing back and closing in. It was down to James, Steven, Cynthia, and injured D'Shawn lying next to them.

Without hesitation, James ran toward the pool in the center of the room past Steven and Cynthia, even as they tried to stop him. He ran through the weapons fire, and when he got to the pool, he jumped right in. He squirmed for a few seconds and died in the pool that had the knowledge of the universe and managed this enormous ship. Out of James' body came hundreds and hundreds of nanobots that looked for ship systems to disrupt. As the nanobots spread throughout the internal mechanisms of the ship, disturbances occurred in many parts of the craft.

Right before James' body completely went into the liquid, Steven and Cynthia watched as the Ancient Visitors dropped their weapons and frantically tried to fix the massive liquid computer. As Steven and Cynthia put their weapons down, Sintdon looked at them and yelled, "You ruined everything. Our ship is going to be destroyed because you inferior life forms did not understand our great purpose. Now the ship's systems that controlled the energy from the particle accelerator will not be contained. Your primitive explosives damaged its holding chamber. All is lost, and you will die here with us."

Not waiting to hear any more from Sintdon, Steven and Cynthia ran out of the control center, while carrying D'Shawn. They ran back to the interior transport on which they had arrived. Steven got to the controls and tried to dislodge the trapped craft, but he couldn't. He yelled to Cynthia, "We will need to find another way because the transport is jammed in too tightly."

Cynthia said, "I guess we will just wait for the next bus," and they sat back waiting for the aliens' ship to explode. As they sat there, glad that they had accomplished their mission and nervously awaiting the coming doom, another ship flew up to the control center level. It was Marcus flying the much larger interstellar transport. He turned the transport so they could hop into the opening at the door.

Marcus asked as they came in, "Is there anyone else? Matt?"

Steven just shook his head no.

At that, Marcus flew by the dark entity, which still taking weapons fire from some of the other worlds' races. Marcus then landed the transport and collected the survivors of the other teams to head back to Earth. He waited as long as he could and then turned the transport toward the docking bay. As he flew toward it, he saw Uloog, who after helping Marcus get to the transport bay was trying to save his people from being caught in the destruction of the massive ship. Uloog was in one of the transports Marcus had secured for the other races, some of whom were still fighting the Prince or dark entity.

The ride was not smooth because the transport was not made to fly inside the massive ship and because explosions were going on around them as the huge ship started to break up. He could not find a direct path to get out. Marcus banged it along the giant corridors, and as the giant ship started to break up, he flew it toward a crack in the bulkhead and out into space. In the rear of the transport, Steven turned on the viewer to see the massive ship. As they watched the cataclysmic event, they also noticed many other transports. Marcus and the human survivors watched as transports filled with survivors who had fought the Ancient Visitors escaped the massive ship. After small explosions, a massive one strewed debris in all directions.

Marcus yelled, "Hold on to something!" as debris hit the side of the transport. But as they pulled away from the debris field, the outward debris field then imploded back on to itself, creating a black hole that sucked in everything in its reach.

Steven yelled to Marcus, "Get us out of here before we are sucked in as well! Oh wow, the scientist back on Earth would love to see this. The theory the scientists believed was that the particle accelerator they built at CERN could create miniature black holes. The Ancient Visitors' particle accelerator created a very large one. And look at that."

They watched as all the debris from the ship began falling into the void, including the dark entity called the Prince. It fought furiously as it was dragged into the event horizon of the black hole, fighting a losing battle as it was sucked out of sight.

Cynthia said, "I guess he can use his superiority to help himself get out of there."

Marcus asked, trying to get the survivors organized on this transport that was now their lifeboat, "Steven, can you please get a head count? Let's see how many we got out of there."

A few minutes later, Steven returned and told Marcus, "The bad news is that we only have twenty-nine people coming back, and some of them are badly hurt. I suppose that is better than none of us making it out. Also, there is more bad news: there is no food at all on this transport."

Marcus asked, "What's the good news?"

Steven replied, "There are plenty of stasis chambers to go around. So we can sleep off the hunger pains."

After looking around at the survivors, Marcus spoke to comfort them, "We are alive, and the Ancient Visitors can't enslave our descendants. In the process we lost many good people. I can tell you this, though: they would be happy that we got away and can attempt to go home. Honestly, I have to admit it. Matt and I figured that we only had one chance in a hundred of escaping. So we did better than expected, I suppose.

"Now for some more bad news, part of the engine system on this transport got damaged escaping the explosion and the debris. We won't be able to cut through the fabric of space like we did to get here and get home in a few years. So by my calculation by our present speed, we are going to have a very long sleep in the stasis chambers, some 950 years or so. I guess the good news is that we are alive, and our loved ones would have wanted us that way."

With that said, they slowly put the injured in the chambers, and the rest of them followed until Marcus, Cynthia, and Steven were left.

As the three prepared for the long sleep, Marcus told them both, "You two did an amazing job. You survived a battle in the control center of the Ancient Visitors' ship, accomplished your mission, and carried D'Shawn back to safety. That's unbelievable in my book."

Cynthia added, "It doesn't feel so amazing when you consider how many people we lost. Two hundred and fifty four people didn't make it out. I find it hard to balance what we achieved with what we lost."

Consoling her, Marcus said, "It is a great loss when you lose so many good friends, and I think we should honor them by having long, productive lives. And we should never forget what they sacrificed."

A few moments later, Cynthia and Steven looked at each other as they struggled to bring up something weird on the mission. Steven then mentioned, "Something else happened as we went to the control center. We both saw something strange. I think we saw Gabriel Peters. He was abducted with us the first time we were taken, but I thought he perished with the others who did not return to Earth. When I saw him, I thought he was here on the ship the whole time, and when the fighting started where the guards were releasing many of the captured races, I thought he might have been freed then. It was strange -- not that you can't call anything on this ship strange -- but not a word was spoken, and he directed us from a distance to where we needed to go. When we got to each point, he was gone. I can't explain it."

Cynthia agreed, "I can't explain it either. There was Gabriel, calling us to come. It led us to the safe place to go, but he was nowhere to be found."

Marcus thought about it and said, "In times of war or great stress, many people have seen things they can't explain. You see visions so real they seem as though they are really happening right in front of you. Maybe it is your mind playing tricks on you, or maybe we got a little help from our friend, and or maybe someone else. I don't know. Maybe the entity the Ancient Visitors were going to battle with for the Realm thought we needed a little help. I don't know, and maybe we will never know."

With nothing else left to do, Marcus set the course for home. Then Marcus, Cynthia, and Steven got into the stasis chambers for the long journey home to the world and to the people they had helped save. For now, the twenty-nine souls would sleep for a long time.

Epilogue

On a grassy knoll in the hills north of Charlotte, North Carolina, three young girls were on a picnic breathing the fresh June air. They were just running on the grass and doing as little girls did, without a care in the world. There was a slight wind blowing in their long hair as the girls picked through the dandelions and white clover. Today was a nice day with the sky clear and blue and the sun warming the morning air.

This time of the morning, it was not the sun that made them have to shield their eyes. It was the shiny panels on the tremendous space station moving in the lower atmosphere and the traffic of titanium-plated transports traveling back and forth between the space station and the colonies on the moon and Mars. It was more than a space station; it was a city floating in the air, a city called New Jerusalem. It was one of six space stations floating in the atmosphere while orbiting around Earth and housing 25,000 people. There, scientific discoveries shared the space with commerce and travel for both business and leisure. But to the girls, the glare was a minor nuisance as they ordered their eye protectors to adjust before they were back to playing on this grassy hill.

The oldest of them, Millie, said, "Jackie and Krissy, the rescue vessel will be there sometime in the next few minutes, and the transmission will be seen by all."

Jackie, the little girl holding the dandelions, displayed a mixture of Super Homo sapiens features like the other girls. She said, "They have been traveling for almost a thousand years, and the space agency has been tracking and scanning the vehicle for the last five years until it came close enough for a retrieval. I'm sure we can wait a few more minutes. So let's play some more."

"Oh, Jackie," said Krissy. "Aren't you the least bit interested to find out who is on that Ancient Visitors' craft? It might be an ancestor of yours. Me, I am hoping it is Matt Schaeffer. I have 23.2% DNA match with him and 19.2% with Marcus."

Jackie replied, "If you should know, I have been tested for 17.5% Sheik Ali Mohammed. What about you, Millie? Who is your biggest percentage?"

She was quick to answer, "I, like most of the population, have Steven on both my mother's and father's side. I was tested 39.2% for Steven, but I have traces of James Connor in my DNA.

"Can you imagine, when the abducted left, the population of the world was all Homo sapiens?" asked Jackie. "I am most happy we have evolved because the Homo sapiens were slow and not too intelligent. When I look through the historic database, I find their world full of conflict, selfishness, jealousy, and corruption. Their tendency to force their will on others led to slavery, oppression, or war. The planet they lived on was almost destroyed by pollution, neglect, and weapons of mass destruction. We should consider ourselves lucky that this species is all but extinct."

Krissy added, "I agree with Jackie. The Homo sapiens were capable of that and more. They could hurt or kill for lust or greed and torture fellow Homo sapiens if they were a threat to their power. Their whole history is filled with stories of pain and despair."

Millie thought about it and said, "I can't argue with you. The Homo sapiens certainly had the capacity for evil, but they also had the capacity for good. They were the first species in man's evolutionary line to develop a culture, create languages, develop writing, build cities, and explore the world. As the species developed, it learned science, mathematics, engineering, physics, and astronomy. They made innovations in technology while also making advancements in literature and the arts. You are right; they were capable of conflict, selfishness, jealousy, oppression, slavery, neglect, corruption, and war, but they were also capable of compassion, kindness, humility, helping others, being charitable, and love.

"Let's not forget why Super Homo sapiens populate the world today. A thousand years ago, the Homo sapiens decided that to protect future generations from the return of the Ancient Visitors they needed to evolve to a higher level. For future generations, they made an effort to spread the seed of the abducted throughout the world. To speed the process, they engineered a serum to change the Homo sapiens of that day to Super.

"The science minister and future Secretary-General of the United Nations, Jennifer La Mont, initiated a worldwide program to spread the Super Homo sapiens' DNA throughout the population in just one century. But it was not easy. Many feared what dangers might come, and some refused to take the serum or let family members be pregnant with Super Homo sapiens' seed. There were demonstrations and threats of conflict. Their reasons were religion, purity of their race, or lost cultural heritage, but those were just excuses. The main reason was that they were afraid of change."

Jackie asked, "Afraid? How could they have been afraid of being improved? Didn't they want to better themselves?"

Millie replied, "First of all, the people taking the serum had to endure months of pain and discomfort as they spent time in and out of the blue liquid chambers. There was a fear of taking a serum barely tested for long-term side effects. Also, there was apprehension even spreading the genes. Many feared how far the Ancient Visitor's designed DNA would advance man. Would man evolve to be in an advance state, with wonderful abilities to make our world better, or would the evolution of the DNA eventually make man into drones who would obey their master, the Ancient Visitors? They had no idea where it would lead. In the end, they took a leap of faith."

Krissy asked, "Didn't the world need them to change? The more advanced DNA made them smarter, faster, and stronger. They needed to be in order to have a chance to defeat the Ancient Visitors."

"Yes," responded Millie. "The leaders of that day understood that to be able to give the people of this planet a fighting chance, they needed to utilize any advantage they could get. So, they started by educating the masses about the new DNA with classes, demonstrations, and scientific research papers. The worldwide effort resulted with an enormous response from the population. Soon, with the future on their minds, first hundreds, then thousands, then millions, volunteered to take the serum. They got in lines everywhere, from clinics in small towns to prestigious hospitals in major cities. It didn't go smoothly. For a while, they could not build an adequate amount of blue liquid chambers and manufacture serum fast enough to keep up with demand. In time, however, they became more efficient with serum and chamber production.

"While the physical transition was difficult, the cultural transition was a challenge as well. Soon the many languages melded into one, human knowledge expanded, and regional social structures became global. Not only languages melded, so did races as they traveled the world and movement became free-flowing. Society changed as they set new goals, values, attitudes, and practices for mankind. Everything from sports, literature, the arts, sciences, mathematics, and social interaction changed in how they looked at and performed it. One day there was an uneducated worker employed as a ditch digger, and after months of transition, he was smarter than the most intelligent Homo sapiens physicist and a better athlete than their most prized sports star. At the very least, their whole cultural structure underwent upheaval, but over time it settled down and society accepted it.

"So girls, you may want to show a little more respect for our ancestors and appreciate the sacrifices they made for us."

"One more thing," added Jackie. "I think they looked weird with their short bodies and their small limbs and heads. If one walked around today, I think they would be captured and put on display. It would be like looking at a dinosaur or a wooly mammoth."

Before anyone could respond, the girls received the signal that the event was about to begin.

"The transmission is starting."

The three little girls closed their eyes and instantly received a transmission directly into their minds. What they, the people on other world colonies throughout the solar system, the space stations inhabitants, and the people on Earth received was what the commander of the rescue ship said, heard, and saw as she entered the alien transport captured in the bay of the tremendous Earth vessel deep in space.

In a commanding voice, the leader of the Earth vessel announced, "I am Commander Christine Carroll, and today we are going to open this craft that has been floating in space for almost a thousand years. Our initial scans show that there are life forms in stasis chambers. What we know is that our people were taken, and they were supposed to have been brought back to Earth in about six years. As you know, however, they had a mission to do. They were to disable the Ancient Visitors' ship by any means possible so that the aliens could not come back as they had planned for the people of Earth, or at the very least, disable the aliens' ship enough so that it delayed their arrival on Earth, giving mankind more time to defend the planet. The last part of their mission was to try to find a way back home. That was the part of the mission no one at the time thought would succeed.

"Remember, we believe that they succeeded because, about ninety-nine years after they were taken, our telescopes registered a bright explosion in the area where we thought the giant alien ship was that took ninety-four years at light speed to reach us. During those ninety-four years, we waited for something to happen. The people of Earth worked together as never before in history. We had one purpose: the survival of the human race. We built a defensive shield that would make the security of this planet almost impenetrable.

"When we saw the light of the deep space explosion, there were celebrations, but when they were over, the cooperation among the people of this planet did not stop. Together, we have eliminated disease and famine. The life expectancy of every man and woman has quadrupled. Then instead of building a defensive shield, we built things that improved our lives and the planet we live on. We used our innovative spirit to create spacecraft that explore the solar system, and we now reach out to the stars. But the best thing is the peace and brotherhood that reign over the world."

The commander then viewed the exterior of the transport and surmised, "As you can see, this transport has damage, and that might explain the slow trip back to Earth. If we do find them inside, it will be a miracle they made it back at all, considering what they had to do."

This commander was the most decorated and experienced in the fleet. Space Agency Command chose her for this historic event because she was about to retire and the agency thought this would cap her distinguished career. This by-the-book commander mentally ordered the crew to secure the alien transport and inspect the vehicle for unwelcome microscopic life forms. At her command, robotic security clamps unleashed themselves from the bay walls and levitated to the transport, securing it to the bay floor. What looked like robotic aerosol cans then flew out from a panel in the bay and encircled the transport, covering it with a fine mist. When this task was done, the robots returned to their places.

With the bay now ready for entry, the commander entered with her crew, who prepared the transport for entry. She said, "I am standing back as my crew opens the door."

The crew members managed to open the door, and compressed gas was expelled before the security people went in. The commander continued, "Now, let me walk into the craft and see what is inside. It looks like no one is walking around. As you know, we scanned this transport long before we captured it to see whose life forms are inside this craft, and we were happy to find out that the scan showed the occupants to be human. Now I see about forty stasis chambers, and about three quarters are turned on. Most importantly, I don't see any Ancient Visitors staring back at us. Let us open the first one and see who we'll find."

The crew unlatched the lid, and the security people reached into the blue liquid and pulled out a Super Homo sapiens individual.

They got the individual up, and he slowly became conscious.

The commander asked the security personnel, "Can we identify this individual?"

One of the officers sent the image of the individual from his mind to the ship's computer, and the computer instantly matched his image. Then a DNA test was done to confirm that the image matched the individual. He said, "This is Steven. It's Steven Moran."

The commander said in relief, "Thank God, some of our people have come home. Today is a good day, and we celebrate the return of these long-lost souls." With that, the commander ordered all the stasis chambers to be opened. "Get the medical teams in here now, and let's help our people." As the medical personnel came to assist, the people inside the opened stasis chambers slowly began to move.

Steven, the first one up, said, "Where are we, and who are you?" But he was not alarmed because he was looking at people with many of the same features he and the abducted possessed.

They were all brought out of the alien transport on floating beds and seen to by the medical personnel alongside each bed. To the medical personnel and all the people aboard this ship, Steven and the others were royalty, and everyone took care of their every need. The technology of this time helped the injured recover in minutes as the devices that scanned the injured also repaired everything from tissue damage to broken legs. Recovery was immediate and went as expected as humans at this time had advances in healthcare that had only been a dream in the time before they were abducted.

Steven sat there in his room on the ship, happy to be alive but also missing the family he had left behind. The last time he saw them, they were sad he was leaving, but they were very much alive. From his perspective, he had only been gone for a few days, but in Earth time he had been gone for almost a thousand years. Now everyone he had ever known and loved was long dead. It just started to hit him that he was alone. His mom and dad, his brothers and their families, and all his friends were no more. Feeling their loss, he started to wonder why he even bothered going in the first place. Maybe he should have tried to find a way to stay and continue to enjoy their company.

One of the nurses came by and said to him, "You seem a little sad." He noticed that her language was combination of most of the languages on Earth when he had left.

She continued, "Maybe you want to see some of your messages from your family and friends?"

He was confused, since he would soon get back to Earth, and he did not think anyone would still be around after about a thousand years. He asked to her, "What messages do you mean?"

The nurse with Super Homo sapiens features said, "I'm sorry. I should have told you before. You have messages from your loved ones, and you could listen to them if you would like. The families and friends of those taken realized that they might never see their loved ones in their lifetime, so they recorded messages for them when they returned."

Now a little perked up with the emotions running through his body, he said, "Sure I would. Can you please let me see them?"

The tall girl reached into her pocket and pulled out what looked like a quarter. When activated, it projected a virtual reality hologram into Steven's mind. Before he knew it, he was standing in a representation of his living room just outside of Topeka, Kansas, and sitting on the couch were his parents, Eva and Eddie. Both greeted him at the same time: "Hello, Son. We are happy you made it back."

With tears in her eyes, Eva continued, "Unfortunately, by the time you hear this message, we will be long gone. But we wanted to tell you that we have not stopped thinking about you all these years. We don't look it, but we are much older now. I am now 145 years old and still going strong. I need to be with all the grandchildren I have running around our house because of you."

Steven laughed along with the holograms of his parents as he walked around the representation of the living room he grew up in as a child. He was amazed at technology of this hologram because it had pictures and trinkets with which his mom decorated the room, and in his mind he could smell the aromas he remembered, such as the stews his mom would cook or the smell of his father's clothes after a day working the dairy farm.

She then continued to speak to her son. "Things have changed since you left. Sure, there was a lot of conflict at that time. But over time, people learned to live together. Soon after the conflict with the Followers of Divinity, there were peace movements that gained favor. One particular movement started in a small village church in some out-of-the-way African country, and it spread across the world. Happiness, peace, joy, and serenity now reign over the world, and we owe much to you and your friends who went into harm's way to help the people of this world against the likes of the Ancient Visitors and their leader, that Satan guy. He and his followers were going to come back to rule the people of Earth and the universe. I bet you and your friends put a stop to him, and he won't be coming here a thousand years from now, like Matt Schaeffer said. No, you and your friends will have stopped him, and we are so proud of you."

She started to cry, and Steven did too along with the hologram. "Are you crying again, old woman?" asked a playful Eddie as he tried to lighten the mood.

"Oh, shut up, you old coot," she said in an equally playful response.

After a deep breath, she said, "Now, as for us, we'll get by. For you, we hope you have a long and happy life filled with wonder and awe. Now, go and live that life. Oh, don't worry. You will still hear from us because of your many children, and we plan to make many of these messages for all those rainy nights in the future. Good-bye, we love you." Then the transmission ended.

Even though they were long gone, that message made him feel at home in this changed world. When the nurse came back, he thanked her, and she replied, "Think nothing of it. I was happy to do it for one of my ancestors. Yes, I am from the Steven line. I bet my great-great-great-great grandfather was running around that hologram as a child."

This made him now feel that he was home since he had family, however distant. The nurse continued, "There are many people looking to meet their ancestors. We are lucky that thirty of you made it back a thousand years later."

Alarmed, Steven cut her off: "You said *thirty*?"

About the Author

Jim Reilly is a new science fiction novelist. In 2009, he finished an MBA program during which his professors gave accolades to his writing prowess. Upon graduation, Jim was caught up in the economic recession, and was laid off from his corporate position. Jim's wife suggested that he should write the book he had long envisioned, and to the gratitude of sci-fi readers everywhere, he did.

Jim is a married father of four, born and raised in Long Island, New York. He has a Bachelor of Science degree from the State University of New York -Empire State College and a Master of Business Administration from the New York Institute of Technology.

From an early age, Jim always had a fascination with science, religion, and science fiction to a point that it became a passion of his. Now he enjoys putting that passion to paper. He has already penned his second sci-fi book and is working on his third.

Evolution
Jim Reilly, 2014

www.ingramcontent.com/pod-product-compliance
Lightning Source LLC
Chambersburg PA
CBHW072351190626
46811CB00019B/501